STAY HUNGRY

STAY HUNGRY

Charles Gaines

1972 DOUBLEDAY & COMPANY, INC., GARDEN CITY, NEW YORK

Grateful acknowledgment is given to the following for permission to reprint:

"Too Late," Words and music by Jimmy Wakely. © Copyright 1941 by MCA MUSIC a division of MCA Inc. Used by Permission. All Rights Reserved.

"Two Different Worlds." © Copyright 1956 by Princess Music Publishing Corp. Used by Permission. All Rights Reserved.

"Roll Me Over." Copyright 1954 and 1955 by Peter Maurice, Inc. Sole Selling Agent for U.S.A. and Canada Shapiro, Bernstein & Co. Inc., 666 Fifth Avenue, New York, New York, 10019. Used by Permission.

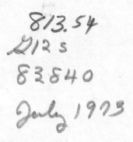
All of the characters in this book are fictitious, and any resemblance to actual persons, living or dead, is purely coincidental.

This book is for Patricia,
and for Latham, Greta, and Judge.

The wonder is always and always how there can be
a mean man or an infidel.

The friendly and flowing savage, who is he?

Song of Myself
WALT WHITMAN

STAY HUNGRY

1

HE IS NEARLY ten feet tall and he stands high above Second Avenue so that much of the traffic going across town has a view of him. You see him set in his looking-at-the-sun pose. It is his own and no one else has ever really brought it off. It's a dramatic pose, all circles and hard curves, its outside lines a clean upward sweep. The legs are almost in profile. The left one is ahead and bent to push forward the round muscle of the outer thigh, the

11

right one is turned behind him to show the calf, bulged like an upside down heart. His torso swoops back from the blue posing trunks in line with his forward leg: the pinched waist is turned toward you, upper body flaring from it like a giant funnel. His right arm shoots toward the roof of Newberry's in a straight line of curves—neck to shoulder to bicep to forearm; the left one is bent above his head, fingers spread against the glare, and his eyes look up, straight into the sun.

From a distance he looks absurd, posed nearly naked above chili dog stands and five and dime stores. Each day dozens of businessmen, on their way to the First National Bank of Birmingham, poke each other, chuckle and point him out. But from the sidewalk below him it is not the pose you notice, and looking up from there few people laugh. From there with good eyes you can make out the small letters to the side of his foot that tell you, JOE SANTO, MR. ALABAMA, TRAINS HERE. Beneath him, like a posing platform, is a much larger, glare-blue block of print that says:

ERICKSON OLYMPIC STUDIO AND SPA
REDUCING, GAINING, WEIGHT-TRAINING
SAUNA, MINERAL BATH, MASSAGE

The whole sign is bordered with little red bulbs.

Craig Blake had seen the sign often but never close up until one Friday when Hal Foss took him to lunch at the Ocean's Larder. It was a hot day in June. They ate a big lunch of fried shrimp, and coming out Craig felt bloated and sticky. He stood in front of the restaurant freeing his cord pants from the back of his legs and looked up at the sign across the street.

"Wait a minute," he said to Foss. "I want to see this guy."

They cut across traffic to the studio. It was in the middle of a seedy block of second-hand furniture stores and pawn shops—a tall, narrow two-story building with a brick front and one gleaming Doric column beside the door that supported nothing. A plateglass window ran the width of the building upstairs.

"Fantastic," said Foss, looking up.

The sun was fully on Joe Santo and from close up the proportions of his limbs, the great wads of muscle forced into their unnatural positions, did not seem at all funny: the figure was overwhelming, heroic. Despite its size it had the curiously real look of paintings made over photographs, but the artist had missed the color of skin by several shades and the immense flesh above them was dull red.

"The fuchsia Mr. Alabama," said Craig.

"The guy's a freak."

"I wonder if he really looks like that. Look at his face, Hal."

"He looks horny," said Foss.

"It's more like eager, or curious. If his tongue was out he'd look like a springer spaniel."

"A horny springer spaniel."

Craig tensed his stomach and rubbed his hand across it, feeling for muscle. "I think I'll go in."

"Don't you work?"

"I've got a half hour. I want to see what it's like."

"That's phony exercise that stuff, that lifting barbells."

"I don't know. I might try it out."

Foss grinned at him. "It'll screw up your tennis game but that's fine with me."

Craig hadn't really planned to go in but Foss's grin annoyed him. He reached for the door. "Thanks for the lunch," he said, and Foss waved and turned up the street.

The door opened into a small beige room that might have been a dentist's office. There were black plastic chairs scattered around and low tables with magazines on them. It was air-conditioned cold. A girl in a medical-looking white smock was chewing gum and reading behind a reception desk. Next to the desk was a glass case full of jars and bottles. Behind it a flight of carpeted stairs rose to a landing and at the other end of the office was a door with a fluting nymph outlined on it.

The girl at the desk looked up all at once with large chocolate eyes and smiled at Craig. Her hair was short, a piebald mixture of brown and yellow. She had a small nose and mouth and a wide straight jaw line that made her face seem broad and tilted back and delicately put on her thin neck. A lot of sun had been on her and she look tanned and competitive.

"Welcome to the Olympic," she said. "Are you interested for yourself?"

"What?"

"For yourself? Or for your wife?"

"Well, I just sort of wanted to look around."

She handed him a brochure and moved the gum to the back of her mouth.

"The men's section is upstairs. It's open five days a week from eight to eight. We have a complete gym, sauna, steam, whirlpool, sunlamp and a Vesuvian mineral bath. We also got a full-time masseur. An individual program will be drawn up for you by one of our competent instructors according to your requirements . . ."

"Is Joe Santo one of your instructors?" he asked.

She looked at him. "Yes. Are you familiar with Joe?"

"No," he said.

"Oh. Where was I? The programs are designed to aid you—did I say that part?"

"No."

"In reducing, gaining or simply improving the skin and muscle tone. They are continually updated to keep up with your rapid progress. A six-month membership is one hundred fifty dollars, a year is two-seventy-five and an Olympic lifetime is five hundred, massages and towels not included."

She paused for a minute and looked off into space, as if she had forgotten he was there. "Oh, and we got branches in Atlanta, Mobile, Galveston, Miami and New Orleans. The use of them is included in your membership. Would you like to hear about the women's?"

"Yes, I would. I would, but I'm on my lunch hour. Could I just see the men's part now and maybe get a membership later?"

"Sure, hon," she said and pushed a button on the phone. "Just take those stairs and somebody'll meet you at the top." She was chewing her gum again and eying him. "Are you a businessman?"

He couldn't tell whether she wanted him to be or not. "Yes."

"Oh," she said.

The door at the top of the landing had a satyr on it. Holding it open was a bulky, mean-faced boy. He had on a white smock also and it made him look like a ridiculously large male nurse. His head was wedge-shaped beneath a red flattop. What looked like a mustache from the bottom of the stairs turned out to be a thick line of freckles on his upper lip. His pants were tangerine-colored, pegged tight, slung low and creased.

Craig tried to look athletic coming up the steps. "Hi," he said at the top. "My name is Craig Blake."

"Franklin Coates. Did you want to gain, reduce or tone?"

"I just wanted to look around . . ."

"That's all we have: gain, reduce and tone."

"How about lifting weights?"

"I mean on the programs, man." He did a funny little shuffle with his feet and showed Craig a clipboard full of complicated-looking sheets of paper in three colors. The red ones said Gain at the top, the green said General Toning, and the blue were Reduce. "See we have to put you on a program."

"Could I look around first?"

"Uh, yeah," said the boy and let him in the door.

Inside was adazzle. Sun poured through the plate glass overlooking the street into a big rectangular room. Its two long sides were all mirrors from the floor to within two feet of the ceiling, and reflected in them was a gush of gleaming chrome and naugahyde. Padded, exotic machinery, elevated bicycles and racks of chrome barbells and dumbbells picked up and flung off light. Eight or nine men were scattered through the gym in various postures. Above them, all the way around the room in the pale-blue panel between mirror and ceiling, gamboled painted satyrs and nymphs.

"This in here is the studio." Franklin took in all the sparkle with a wave of his hand. "We'll start in the back."

He took Craig down an aisle between two partitions at the rear of the gym. Through a window in one Craig could see a big blond man behind a desk. Franklin opened the door of the other and showed him a little Negro giving a massage on a table in the middle of the room. On another table beneath a sunlamp lay a man with goggles on. "Massage and rays," Franklin said and shut the door.

The aisle opened at the other end into a large area with a tile floor and submarine, indirect lighting. Across from where they stood were four little rooms with glass doors, two on either side of a sunken, circular pool that bubbled and steamed and glowed. It was nestled into an oval niche between Sauna and Whirlpool on one side, and Steam and Cool on the other. Rising behind it was a fantastic plaster shell, its pink opalescent center illuminated by a spotlight.

Craig felt his senses go soft, the way they always did from the lights and movement of a fair.

"That's the spa—iss got everything you need. The showers and dressing room're through that door to the right."

"What's the thing in the middle?"

"Vesuvian mineral bath," Franklin said. "That's Thor's invention."

"Why is it all lit up?"

"It's got lights in it, man. Got *bulbs* in it." He shuffled. "That water's one hundred ten degrees and there's herbs in it." There were also two men in it—talking to each other, flushed and plump, their arms propped on the tile sides like little boys in a tub.

Back out in the dazzling gym Franklin showed him the equipment. In the center of the floor was a sprawl of bars, seats, benches and pulleys, all connected by cables to chrome weights that were numbered and stacked like bars of silver. "A Total-Tone," Franklin said. It looked capable of complicated work and Craig was not surprised to hear that it could stress eighty-two separate muscles. Stepping around and ignoring anyone who happened to be using them, Franklin demonstrated a squat rack, a leg-press machine, an incline bench and one of the wide canvas straps attached to a motor that jiggles the belly.

Across the room were a couple of long, popular naugahyde benches, each divided into two mechanical sections. On one a man lay on his back, still as stone from the chest up, watching his lower body being swung from side to side. "Good for the oblique muscles of the abdomen," said Franklin. The two sections of the other bench rose toward each other, curving the man on them into a crescent. Nearby was an old Western saddle mounted on a motorized rod. Astride it a pudgy man gripped the pommel and was gently bucked. Craig remembered renting him a warehouse and would have gone over to speak but for an absent, sexy look around the man's eyes.

"Well, what do you think?" asked Franklin.

"It's uh, not exactly like I thought it would be. What's the stuff over there for?"

In a big corner at the end of the room was a wooden platform. There were a few plain benches on it and some black, heavy-looking weights. Behind it was a wide chinning bar. Everything in the corner was dark and simple and so different from everything else in the gym that it looked sinister.

"That's the Olympic weight. Don't worry about that." Franklin took out a pen. "What's your name again?" He wrote it down. "Now here's the way we work, Craig. Let's say you need to reduce, right? Okay, you don't want to just lose weight, you want to replace those fat tissues with toned-up muscle. So we recommend a diet—and by the way my mama's the dietician at Phillips High School—and we put you on a program of exercises that gets you in shape while you're losing. We measure different parts of you and keep check on how you're doing."

Craig pictured Franklin measuring his parts.

"Well, that's fine, Franklin. Very sound. But I'm in good shape already and I don't need to reduce. I just came up here to see

17

about lifting weights once in a while. I don't need any program. Is Joe Santo on a program?"

Franklin laughed. "Joe Santo? Joe Santo is Mr. A."

"I know."

"You know Joe?"

"No."

"Well Joe don't need no program. You can bet your ass."

"Yeah. Well I don't either," he said. "But thanks for showing me around."

"Now wait a minute, buddy." Franklin was agitated. He shuffled his feet back and forth in a little dance and snapped his fingers. "Hold on just a minute. Look, just hold on a second." He backed off toward the office and disappeared into it. In a couple of minutes he came back out and motioned to Craig from the door.

"Thor'd like to meet you," he said, his eyes slitted and furious.

The man Craig had seen behind the desk met him at the door, shook his hand, took his arm and slammed the door on the ominous-looking Franklin. "I'm Thor Erickson, Mr. Blake. Have a seat."

Thor Erickson was scented. He smelled sweet and strong and was the biggest man Craig had ever seen. He was very tall and heavy, but all his bulk looked soft as stuffing under his white tunic. His blond hair was stiff with pomade and sculpted into high whorls, and his face was broad and tanned. Though he looked capable of huge leverage there was something wadded and ingratiating about him, like a department store Santa Claus.

He was grinning—a perfect, even grin. "Franklin messes things up. He doesn't understand principles. Of course you don't have to go on a program. You're obviously in first-rate shape. It's just that the men who come up this time of day—most of them aren't in any shape. And if you've got guys out there throwing around a lot of weight, well, it scares these other fellows. It makes them nervous, you understand that—to have strong guys like yourself out there throwing around weights while they're just breaking up a little tissue on a machine." His voice rose and fell soothingly. He smiled while he spoke. Clustered on the wall above his head were five framed photographs of the same big Thor—trimmer, bulging and younger, posed with a spear in a black jockstrap.

Craig wanted to get one clear answer before he left. "Does anybody come up here, at any time, just to lift weights—I mean without a program?"

Erickson smiled at him. "There's some builders and lifters come in from six to eight, that's their time. They're not your kind of people. But look, we're just talking a general principle. If you want to work out this time of day off a program, we can make an exception."

Craig stood up and put his hand on the door. "Listen, Mr. Erickson . . ."

"Thor. Make it Thor."

"Thor. If I joined, the best time for me to come up would be after six. Is that all right or not? Yes or no."

"At night?" Erickson rose and hulked over his desk. "Uh, Mr. Blake, you could come in then if you have to, yeah. But some of those boys are rough as a cob. Uneducated. That's another reason we give 'em their own time. Wait a minute, lemme show you something."

He opened a drawer in his desk, brought up a fistful of silver cloth and a Batman mask and shook it at Craig. "See this? One of them crazy bastads wears this while he's working out." His face struggled to comprehend it. He stared at Craig and leaned closer. "I'm telling you what's right. And there's another one we believe's got the crabs."

2

CRAIG WAS NEARLY two hours late getting back from lunch, but that was not unusual and no one even looked up when he came in. He doodled for the rest of the afternoon, skipped an appointment and waited for six o'clock.

He hadn't really meant to go in the studio and while there he had had no intentions of coming back, but in his wallet now was a tacky little gold card given him by the receptionist for one hundred and fifty dollars that made him a member of the Olympic Studio and Spa for six months. And he was excited about that without caring why. He had a strong private image of life being like a huge tent bazaar where the best experiences lay in among the used and cracked and old, undistinguishable from the rest until they were handled. The majority of people there were careful joyless shoppers who walked around with a hand to their chins checking out values and never making it down the first aisle. Craig tried to walk fast, not thinking, waiting for an impulse to grab something.

Mentally he had disliked Erickson and his glittering studio full of machines and heavy businessmen, but at the desk downstairs with the girl looking up at him, an impulse made him fumble for his checkbook. On the way back to the office another one sent him up to the third floor sports department of Loveman's to buy leather gym shoes, sweat socks, sweat suit, jockstrap and a wide black belt that the salesman told him weight lifters used to avoid hernias. He had reached his office feeling slick, ready, well equipped.

At about four Foss came across the hall and leaned on Craig's door, smiling. Foss wore only one kind of shirt to work—a Brooks Brothers buttondown with thin blue stripes. He owned forty of them. The sleeves of this one were rolled to his elbows. His tie was pulled away from the collar and Foss had a yellow pencil behind his ear. He looked like he was back at the University of Virginia, working on a physics problem.

"How'd it go? You busy?"

"How can you get busy around here?"

Foss shrugged. "It's not hard for me, but I'm not in the family. Did you meet that pink guy?"

"He wasn't around. Nothing but a bunch of fat clerks like you go in there in the daytime. Santo and I work out at night."

"You really going to do that?"

"Sure. I bought a membership."

"How are you going to work it in with sky diving, fishing, tennis, shooting manta rays with a bow and arrow . . ."

"Foss, you're dealing with a Renaissance man. Do you want to go tonight? I'll take you as a guest."

"Thanks a lot, buddy, but I've got a date."

Craig knew that. Foss always had a date in June. June was the debutante season and debutantes were Foss's passion. At thirty he still greeted that yearly crop of fluff with an appreciation as whole and fresh as milk. Every year he learned new dances and things to say but the charms that kept him on the lists were the same as they had been ten years ago. Foss was unswervingly safe, deferential, polite and witty—the first one at parties to find a guitar, or to organize mixed doubles.

"You going to pump her?" asked Craig, watching Foss wince.

"That place has already affected your conversation. You'll be grunting and picking lice on the tennis court tomorrow." He slid off the door. "See you there at nine," he said and left Craig to read his mail again.

At five he left Blake Realty Company with everyone else and drove to within a block of the gym. He sat in his parked car drumming on the steering wheel and reading a road map. At five-thirty he decided he probably should eat something for energy so he bought two packages of peanuts and walked around eating them and holding his bag of clothes.

It was a hot, damp evening like most summer evenings in Birmingham. The sky was low, the color of soiled cotton, and the light was flat and weak. Everything on the streets moved slowly under the soft push of the heat. Coming home—from prep schools, camps, colleges, cooler places—the first thing Craig always noticed, as he was driven home through the city, was the syrupy, wasteless downtown movement of people and machines: something evolved from years of motion in a concrete depression at the bottom of a valley, a place that might have been designed for holding heat.

At six o'clock he stood in front of the studio, his shirt soaked

23

through. The red bulbs around the sign were on but the door was locked. He tried the door, knocked, then knocked again louder and rattled the door. Finally Franklin opened it and said, "Yeah?"

"I've come to work out," Craig said, feeling ridiculous.

"When, now?" said Franklin. He looked surprised but not unfriendly. The smock was gone; he had on shorts and an armless sweat shirt.

"It's all right. Erickson said it was all right."

"He's gone to supper," said Franklin, but moved aside for Craig to enter. There were no lights on downstairs and the air conditioner had been turned off. It was stuffy inside but still cool. Franklin was smiling. "So you're gonna work out at night, huh? Djeetjet?"

"What?"

"Djeetjet? It's better if you don't have nothing on your stomach."

"I just had some peanuts."

"That's good. Good protein," said Franklin. "Listen, I'll take you through a routine if you want me to. Show you what you oughta do."

Climbing the stairs behind him, Craig noticed for the first time how oddly Franklin was shaped—like a series of globes set on stems. His waist and hips were wasp-slender and his calves were as thin and bony as an alcoholic woman's. All the rest of Franklin was puffed into orbs.

"You work this late everyday?" Craig asked him.

"Santo has it from two to eight. I just come up now to pump iron."

They went into the gym with Franklin still offering to help, his chatter sounding boyish and eager to play. The only light in the room came through the window from the blinking sign on the front of the building and what was left of daylight. The gym was a quiet gray. Down in the corner with the dark, serious-looking equipment were three heavy men in different stages of changing into bright-colored gym clothes. They stood around the platform

24

where another one lay on his back humming and beating out a
rhythm on his stomach. It was a strange, dim scene. Craig began
to warm to Franklin's new friendliness.

"Why don't they use the dressing room?"

"Cain't. Thor won't let us use nothing but the gym and showers
because of hygiene. You can though, I reckon. Since you bought
a membership."

"That's all right," Craig said. "I'll change here. Aren't those guys
members?"

"Them? Naw, they're not members." Franklin shuffled. "They're
from down at the Y. It gets too hot to use in the summer and
Thor lets 'em come up here free at night. You cain't turn on the
lights, though."

"What?"

"He don't let us turn on the lights."

"OK," Craig said, and dropped his pants.

The one on his back was Joe Santo. Franklin said he liked to lie
down before a workout and mess around with different songs. By
the time Craig had gotten into the stiff new clothes Santo was
sitting up watching him.

"These people are friends of mine," he said and nodded around
him. "Mr. Street, Mr. Johnson, Mr. Buell. I'm Joe Santo." He had
a timbrous voice with no southern accent. Craig said hello and
the other three stared back, slack-jawed but pleasant. "Do you
happen to work for Mr. Stewart? Douglas Stewart of Hattiesburg?
Don't be afraid to say."

"No."

"You sure?"

"Yes."

"Promise."

"I promise."

"It would be a lot like him to send a spy to filch my training
secrets."

"Stewart is Mr. Mississippi," Franklin told Craig. "This guy's just starting, Joe. He didn't want no program and didn't want to work out at noon."

"Couldn't blame you," said Santo and stood up. He had on baggy shorts and a tee shirt with a bucking mustang on the front. Except for the skin color he looked even less believable in the flesh than in the sign. The spread of shoulders, the depth of chest, the angles and curves and proportions of Joe Santo were not at all human: he looked inflated and carved. He had long black hair and a bent Mediterranean nose. His features were tough but his face as a whole looked playful and amused.

"Couldn't blame you at all. In fact I admire those decisions." He came over to Craig and walked around him, sniffing him out. Then he solemnly held out a big hand. "I like the way you look. You and I can be friends if you want to."

Behind him Misters Street, Johnson and Buell smiled. Craig took the hand, looked into the thin brown eyes, the least encumbered part of Joe Santo, and saw the same eagerness he had seen in the sign.

Franklin showed him some exercises and he spent the next hour struggling ignorantly with little chrome dumbbells and watching the others riotously heave around huge poundages of the black Olympic weights. It was like a circus of energy—they laughed, shouted, threw bars to each other, coaxed each other's lifts, grunted, sweated and grew. Craig could actually see, after each drop and thrust of iron, the swell of blood racing to tissue.

They did eight exercises, breaking each into four sets of ten repetitions. During short pauses between sets they gobbled handfuls of dun pills from a glass jar.

"Protein," Franklin told him, "raw protein," and pointed out the biggest of the four, a hairy sprawl of a man in yellow sweat pants. "Wall Street eats 'em all day. Eats the same as thirty steaks every day."

At about seven o'clock Erickson came back, accompanied by the little masseur. He went through the gym without looking at anyone, turned on the light in his office and shut the door. The

26

Negro sat on one of the mechanical benches, swung his legs under him and studied the workout.

"That's Newton," said Franklin. "He ain't right."

After a while Newton shot a bored look over at Craig. "What you call yourself doing—wukking out? Huh."

"Excuse me," Craig said.

"You call yourself wukking out with them little bitty weights, or what?"

"Go on, Newton," Franklin told him. He started to say something else but Santo cut him off.

"'The man is back, Franklin. Go get my suit."

Franklin went to the office and returned in a few minutes with the Batman cape and mask. "He don't like this wuff a shit, Joe," he said and handed them over to Santo.

The costume was made for a child. It made Santo look vaguely retarded. He fixed the mask. "Vroom," he said and whirled on his buddies. "In the flick of an eye from millionaire playboy Bruce whatshisname . . ."

Franklin walked over to Craig, shaking his head. "He does this when he's getting up for a contest—pretends like he's somebody like Tarzan or King Kong or Batman. He says it's to concentrate better."

"What's the contest?"

"The Mr. Southeast in August. He was second last year and it pissed Thor off, so he's got him bombing for it already. He's got to get his arms up and spread his delts some."

When Craig finished he stood with Franklin watching the others and feeling a surprising clean tautness throughout his body. He mentioned it to Franklin. "I know," the boy said. "Joe says it's like all your blood is new."

Santo and the three friends were seated, working their biceps —curling sixty-pound dumbbells from floor to shoulder ten times with each arm and then resting. The three heavies, guts spread in their laps, grimaced and bucked up their weights. Santo brought his up smoothly and slowly, counting the repetitions aloud behind the implacable bat-mask. Finished with a set, he whooped, laughed, punched at the others until they were laughing and whooping too, then reached for the iron again as though it were a goblet or a haunch of turkey.

The whole thing was loud, raw, jovial and self-contained—like some kind of feast or celebration. Watching it made you want to join.

When they had finished and were racking the weights, Erickson came out of his office and began turning on lights. He swept past Craig, looking impatient. "Enjoy your workout, Blake?" he asked. Then he turned to the platform and yelled, "Get your fat ass off there, Buell. Let's go, Santo."

Slowly Santo pulled off his tee shirt and stepped onto the platform. He stared at one spot on the ceiling and with deliberate movements like the ones in oriental dances, started flexing and curving his body into fantastic shapes.

"What the hell is he *doing?*" Craig asked Franklin.

"He's posin, man. That's some of the greatest posin you ever saw. Thor is checking him out."

Everyone moved in a hush around the platform except Newton, who stayed on his perch. Erickson stood, arms folded, about fifteen feet away giving weird little commands. "Abs . . . Lats . . . Tie-in . . . Now turn in. Quadricepts." And Santo, tongue between his teeth in concentration, made smooth reptilian shifts at each of them, throwing a leg out here, a shoulder there, to isolate a muscle, then pushed it forward for inspection.

"Beautiful," whispered Franklin. And after killing an initial impulse to laugh, Craig began to see that it was, it really was—like living sculpture.

"That left bicep needs more peak, Joe," Erickson said. "You gotta do more Scott curls; that motha's gotta have a *point* on it."

"He was cheatin on his left arm, Thor," Newton shrilled from the back. "I seen him."

Santo didn't seem to hear anything. His face was relaxed, impassive and remote. He looked as if he didn't have any idea where he was. He went through nine or ten more poses, ending up on the one from the sign, before Erickson waved him down.

"Buell, you keep your goddamn crabs out of my shower," Erickson said and walked off to his office. Newton followed him, annoyed-looking, snapping off lights.

They showered in the dark and came back to the gym to dress. Buell was gone. Santo was singing, *Send Me the Pillow That You Dream On.* He finished dressing before anybody else and stood with hands on hips waiting to direct, like a huge enthusiastic camp counselor.

"You want to eat with us, old buddy? We go down to Morrison's."

"Sure," Craig said. He folded his tie and suit coat in with the gym clothes and left them in the locker room. Franklin took back the costume and brought Santo a big red box of something called Tiger's Milk, and they banged down the steps through the dark reception room and onto the street.

It was cooler outside and the air felt lighter than before. They walked five abreast, bulging and laughing and clean feeling, to Morrison's, and as they swung past the greasy-smelling chili-dog stands, the shoe parlors and loan offices and cheap jewelry stores, Craig enjoyed this part of town for the first time in his life. He was dizzy and friendly on his first pump—a well-used, big, clear-headed feeling. He felt like they owned the sidewalk.

"Nice evenin," said Johnson.

"It's a hell of an evenin," Craig said.

3

ALL THEY ATE were vegetables. Each of them picked four or five from the cafeteria line of squash, corn, baby limas, turnip greens, black-eyed peas, carrots, spinach, okra and stewed tomatoes, poured them together on a plate and took the others in dishes. They each filled two trays with vegetables and glasses of water and it took three waiters to carry the garden of food to a table.

At the table Santo mixed Tiger's Milk into everybody's water, including Craig's. It was crowded stuff, he said: every thirty grams has nine vitamins, five minerals and eighteen amino acids. Craig watched his, waiting for it to fizz.

They ate and drank the way they lifted weight—loudly, greedily, ignoring everything else. Santo stopped them once to discourse on lima beans, studying one at nose level on the prongs of his fork. They were, he said, the most satisfying vegetable of all —full of carbohydrates; a fat, natural shape that was more interesting than a pea's, and a good green, a green you could trust. Franklin, Wall Street and Johnson (who was named Walter but called Hump for his curved, beefy back) stopped chewing and listened as though they had waited months for a lecture on lima beans. Their attentions never got far from Santo; they checked constantly on his reactions and their own seemed to be described and enlarged by his, as if he were a kind of lens that made everything look bigger and more important. Craig had never seen anyone as hungrily aware as Santo. His thin eyes sopped up whatever was around him and his face reflected everything he saw, heard or felt. He would stare at, smell, even touch a forkful of peas or corn or okra before swallowing it, and do it so naturally that doing it seemed normal.

They ate for over an hour, and then rode together in Wall Street's car to Five Points, to a bar near Santo's apartment that he said had good music and good pigs' feet. To avoid closing at midnight it was called a club—the Three O'Clock Club. But it was really just an upstairs, noisy room with a bandstand and dance floor in the center and weak-legged little tables ringing them. The band was on a break when they got there. A too-loud jukebox was playing and a few couples were dancing to it. The place disappointed Craig in Santo—it looked like a thousand other southern bars, heavy with bad air and a waiting on something violent to happen—and for the first time since he had left it he thought about getting back to his car.

A tall man met them at the door. He had one white eye and was thin and mean-looking as a knife blade. He nodded at Santo, who seemed pleased to see him. "Mary Tate's in the back," he said. "Y'all want a table?"

"Please, Hayes," Santo grabbed Craig's arm. "Hayes, this is a friend of mine—Mr. Blake." Hayes and Craig nodded. "You know the others."

"Uh huh. I know 'em. Franklin you stay offa people tonight, you hear." Franklin just stared at him.

Hayes gave them a table in the front of the room near the bar. Wall and Johnson each bought a pitcher of beer and a plate of pigs' feet and Franklin got a glass of muscatel. Santo ordered water for his Tiger's Milk and left the table. In a few minutes he was back with the receptionist from the studio and another girl. Craig had had a whiskey sour and was beginning to feel better about the place.

The receptionist's name was Mary Tate Farnsworth. She was from Opp, Alabama, was a champion water skier, and was Santo's woman—all this Craig got from Franklin in the first two minutes that she was at the table.

He didn't need Franklin to tell him she was mad at Santo, but Franklin told him anyway. She had been waiting an hour on Joe and had not expected him to be with all these people. She sat bent at the waist to him, her legs crossed and one little foot flicking up and down as she fussed. She was not exactly beautiful—her jaws were too square and her eyes too big for the rest of her face—but she was very exciting to look at. She was small with a straight back and lovely arms and legs. Her movements were clean and functional, as though they had developed on ice or roller skates, someplace where balance was important. But the thing that made you stare at her was a flickering vitality, an energy that throbbed like a pulse under her expressions. It was a very sexy thing. She almost seemed to glow.

The other girl's name was Terry and she looked like she had seen about anything the Three O'Clock Club had to offer. She gazed indifferently over the dance floor and popped her gum and

33

occasionally put her hands on the small of her back and threw out her chest.

In a little while the band came back and they were good in a loud, country way. The club was full. With the return of the band the noise got more cheerful.

Franklin sat next to Craig drinking muscatels as fast as he could order them and talking. He had gotten into weights, he said, after high school. He was working in a car wash as a back-seat man and doing a little bodybuilding when he heard Erickson had fired an instructor. He went up and told how his mama was a dietician and got the job. Erickson was a prick, he said, but he knew his stuff and Franklin owed him for taking him off back-seats. Craig asked him if he went in for the contests too and he shrugged and said naw, not too much. He finished his wine. The calves, he said; the goddamn calves had held him back. He had worked them so hard he thought they would pop off, but the mothers wouldn't grow. He got sullen after that and ordered another drink.

Gorging on platters of pigs' feet and pitchers of beer, Johnson and Street were in boisterous tempers and they wanted Santo to sing.

"Hayes *wawnts* you to, Joe. Cause all the pelts lak it so much." Hump grinned and the grin ran hundreds of laughter creases up his face.

"I don't want to sing," said Santo. "They got a singer up there." He grabbed Johnson by the shirt and pulled him closer to him. "But I'll tell you what, Hump old buddy, I'll tell you a story instead." Hump nodded. "It's a sad story about the failure of love. But you've got to *listen*." His eye glittered and Hump nodded again.

"Well, one day this guy was banging around in the woods, you dig, when he comes on a Rary. The Rary was just lying there curled up by a tree. So the guy takes it home and feeds it milk, and the Rary starts to grow. It was small at first like a ping-pong

34

ball, but it grew fast and pretty soon it was big as a basketball and still growing and the guy was giving it four gallons of milk a day. Then the Rary started getting tired of milk and wouldn't eat anything but calf liver—he'd eat maybe ten, twelve pounds of that a day. He got so big he was taking up most of the guy's living room, his hair was shedding all over everything and he was eating the guy out of house and home, so the guy, whose name was Walter like you, Hump, decided he had to get rid of it. He tried giving it to his friends but none of them wanted it, and the zoo didn't want it . . ."

"Why didn't he put him back where he got him at?" asked Wall. He looked thoughtful, like he was trying to decide whether to believe all this or not.

"Because man, he couldn't let the Rary starve. Whenever the Rary got hungry he made little screams and the guy couldn't handle that." Santo was hunched over the table, fingering his glass. His hands were very quick and active despite their size; they were always picking up things, twirling things. "So the guy decided to have a talk with the Rary. He went into what was left of his living room and said, 'Listen, Rary, you're taking up my whole room here, shedding hair all over the place and eating me out of house and home. Nobody else'll take you so I've got to get rid of you.'

"Well the Rary was upset, but he said, 'OK, Walt, just do it the quickest way you can.' So the guy pried the Rary out of his house and tried to shoot it but the bullets just bounced off, then he rolled it down to the lake and tried to drown it but the Rary just floated like a big cork. He tried some other things and they didn't work either so finally he rents a huge dump truck, see, puts the Rary on and drives out to the highest cliff he can find. He backs up to the edge of the cliff and yells back, 'Well, so long Rary. This is it,' and starts raising the bed of the truck."

Santo looked up to gather their attention. Mary Tate and Terry were talking to each other and listening to the band. "The guy raises it and raises it and raises it but the Rary won't fall off.

Finally the bed is vertical and the Rary is just stuck up there in one corner, so the guy gets out and walks around to the back and says, 'What the hell is this?'

" 'Let's go home, Walt,' says the Rary.

" 'Home, hell,' the guy says. 'Why don't you fall off?'

" 'Well, Walt,' says the Rary, '. . . it's a long, long way to tippa-Rary.' "

Santo looked around, his face holding in his own laughter, waiting for the others. But nobody was ready for him. There was an embarrassing minute of silence, then Mary Tate tore away from watching the band and jumped beautifully into the breach. Her face forgot everything but that Santo needed her. She shot a hand over to take his on the glass, said, "Oh Christ, baby, that's great," and roared laughing. Santo followed her and they rocked back and forth at each other, mouths wide, her laugh rising high and raunchy over his. Then all of them were laughing, looking refreshed as if they had just fallen into cold water.

It was the first time Craig saw them do that to people and the picture stayed the clearest he had of them: Mr. Alabama and his woman, joined at the hands around a glass of potent milk, laughing like hell, by themselves.

After four drinks the Three O'Clock Club looked much better to Craig. He felt like he had known the other people at the table all his life. There was a pool table near the bar. In graduate school he had killed a lot of Iowa nights fingering felt, developing an impatient, flashy game. He asked Franklin if he wanted to play. Franklin didn't, particularly, but played anyway and they shot a game of straight to fifty. Franklin played like a farmer, resting the cue on his knuckles and closing one eye as he shot, but he took a long time between balls and sank a few.

"You're pretty good," he told Craig after an easy combination bank.

"I'm pretty good at most things," Craig said and immediately regretted it. The whiskey had loosened up like a cough his feeling of having been absurdly outmatched and beaten earlier that evening. Franklin looked over at him and he covered up. "I used to play a lot in college."

"Uh huh," Franklin said. And after a while, "Joe went to college."

"Did he?"

"No shit. He invents things too . . . collects glasses."

"He's quite a guy," Craig said and bent over a shot.

"Joe? You goddamn right he is." Franklin's voice got louder. "Lemme tell you something, buddy, when he takes Mr. America, the big one, he'll have done it *all*. And he don't even care about it. Sheeat. If it wadn't for Thor he wouldn't even be messing with this crap. He don't *need* it, man; he's done it all. You know they ast him on the Edward Sullivan show to sing Indian songs? And that he was American white water champion in a one-man open canoe? And that he woulda made the U.S. Olympic team as a downhill skier except he broke his leg . . ."

Craig put down his cue and stared dumbly at Franklin, stunned at Santo's resourcefulness or sense of humor or at Franklin's gullibility, or at all three. Did he *really*, for God's sake, tell people . . .

Franklin was ending with a flourish. ". . . Mrs. Mamie Eisenhower wrote and ast him to make her one of his Indian necklaces."

"Oh."

That was all Craig could think of to say. He finished off the last five balls as quickly as he could.

There was a group of men between the bar and their table. As Craig walked past, following Franklin's broad back through the room, one of them stopped him.

"Hey buddy," the man said. "What are y'all?" He looked up curious and impressed like somebody asking for an autograph. "Y'all are the biggest bunch of men I ever saw. Y'all play football or what?"

"Yeah. We play for Auburn," Craig said. The man squinted over at their table. "Those big ones are defensive linemen and the redheaded one, that's Franklin Coates, the all-Conference end."

"What are you?"

"I'm a scatback."

"Oh. Yeah," the man said. "I figured y'all was something like that. Thanks buddy—hey, what's your name?"

"Blake. Buck Blake."

"Yeah. Well thanks, Blake. War Eagle." He waved and gave Craig that diminished little smile that people use on athletes.

Craig walked like a scatback back to the table.

Somebody had gotten him another drink. Wall and Terry were dancing and Santo was talking to Hump and Franklin, so he took the drink and sat down by Mary Tate.

"Hi," she said. "You know you look like a swamp."

"Like a what?"

"A swamp. With all that brown hair and eyes and stuff. I really like the way you look. I been wanting to tell you that."

Craig glanced over at Santo, then said, "Thanks. I like the way you look too."

They talked for the next hour, together at first, then as Craig kept drinking she only listened and he kept talking, getting louder, bragging. He told her about the trip he had made to the Keys in May for tarpon, the one in February to Acapulco for sailfish, the one in September to shoot dove in Texas. He explained to her, with a diagram, the principle of lead in wing shooting. She smiled him on and he talked until finally he ran down and just sat there, quiet and shamed.

"Do you want to dance?" she asked after a while and again he checked across the table. "Joe don't like to. He won't care."

He followed her out to the dance floor watching her walk, shoulders thrown back, moving so cleanly and economically she didn't seem to touch her clothes. She danced the same way—began and ended each movement at exactly the right place as he stumbled around following her.

38

After two dances he got dizzy and was guiding her messily back to the table when someone pushed him. He turned around into a furious little man in a striped tee shirt who said, "Watch where you're going feller."

When Craig turned back to Mary Tate the man stepped between them. "Hey. Djew tell my friend you play ball at Auburn?"

Craig said yes, politely. Then the man put both hands on Craig's chest and pushed him backward.

"Well, you're a lie," he said. He was trembling with anger and Craig wondered how in the hell he could have gotten so mad so fast. The man pushed again, gently as a gust of wind, and stepped after him. "You're a lie, eggsucker, cause I watch every game they play. They ain't *got* no Blake and they don't even *play* no scatback." Another push.

Craig had quit hoping he could walk out of this and was looking around wildly for a bottle or a chair when Franklin appeared like a genie next to him and shoved the man four feet back across the floor. Franklin crouched beside Craig, his rage blooming like a flower, up all at once with the other on a high complicated anger. Graceful and remote, they stared at each other across the dance floor, frozen right on the edge of moving to the real music of the Three O'Clock Club.

"You want to push, catfucker, push me." Franklin said. He did his little shuffle that was like putting out cigarettes with both feet.

"I'm gonna tell you *once*," the man said. "I gotta black belt in karate."

"I've got a black belt too, babe, and it ain't in no karate." Franklin told him this with relish.

Craig saw Hayes come flailing at them through the crowd and at the same instant saw the striped tee shirt charge and disappear as if it had been swallowed in the blur of Franklin's arms. Within the four or five seconds it took Hayes to reach them, Franklin shoved the man to the floor, pulled the tee shirt over his head and began hitting the place where his face was with full steady swings like chopping wood. Hayes and two of the man's friends got to

Franklin at the same time and started dragging him off what looked like a runover dog underneath. At that point Craig stepped mindlessly back in and was pelting the back of one of the friends with unnoticed little punches when he heard more than felt something go ca-thunk across his ear . . . and then nothing else but a loud buzz and the sound of himself throwing up.

"You got hit with a beer bottle," Santo said. Craig was sitting with Santo, Mary Tate and Terry at a quiet table in the back of the room. There was vomit on his shirt the color of whiskey sours, his ear felt sticky and hot and his right forearm and hand were bloody. People were still scrambling around on the dance floor.

"How you feel, old buddy?"

"Me? I feel fine, how's Franklin?"

"I sent Wall and Hump over there, he'll be all right. Franklin loves to fight. He'd rather fight than eat."

"Oh," Craig said.

"What do you like to do most?"

His head was buzzing and he was having a hard time concentrating. He tried to laugh but when he looked up he saw Santo really wanted to know. He sat there hulking and shadowy, ignoring all the wild commotion behind them, his tough face looking curious and eager and amused as a hunting dog's, waiting for Craig to tell him what he liked to do—as though they were two barebacked ten-year-olds, chewing straws and shooting the breeze on some sunny hillside. And all of a sudden Craig felt tremendously happy. It was a lightheaded, full sensation, like taking a deep breath of sunlight and cold air. Santo sat there looking like his downtown portrait wanting to know what he liked to *do*. Craig thought maybe he had grown up with that face . . . every line looked so familiar. It had been a long time since lunch and Foss— and for some reason he could barely remember Foss. He felt overwhelmingly content.

"I like best, maybe . . . to fish dry flies over big brown trout . . . with a bamboo rod." "Where?" "In rivers." His mind was smoky, drifting like a fog on water. Mary Tate was smiling. "What kind of rivers?" "Big clear . . . dark rivers."

"We'll do it!" he heard Santo say, and heard himself laughing. "We'll do it, then. You know Mary Tate here really likes you. We'll all go do it together."

"Look, were you really"—he wanted to know this—"a white water canoe champion?"

"We can talk about that," Santo said, bending over him. "Sure. We can talk about that too."

4

NESTLED IN THE red hills above Birmingham are three country clubs. The one called Woodstream is the most beautiful, the hardest to get into and the oldest. It is old enough to seem ageless. If you stand on the terrace behind the club on a late afternoon, everything around you—the caddy house, the wooden bridges crossing the stream, the big trees and shrubs—can seem to have been there forever just as they are now. Not even the club's members seem to change. They are still rich. They still hum *I Could Have Danced All Night* and stay at the Plaza when they go to New York. They still have their dinners served to them on silver by still-smiling blacks in high-ceilinged dining rooms. The Woodstream Country Club is theirs; its big, handsome rooms are full of their Elizabethan syllables and refined scents.

The clubhouse is an elegantly bright, columned building with the private look of a home. It is surrounded by thirty pastoral, tended acres that are absolutely free of annoyances: the land either sweeps broadly like a lawn or rises and falls gently between tender little hummocks. Lying around in here at pleasing intervals and in places where you can neither see nor hear them from the club, are a swimming pool, built so carefully into the landscape it looks like a lake, an easy eighteen-hole golf course, and six excellent Rubico tennis courts.

The tennis courts are fenced-in and staggered up a hillside like terraces. They are green with bright white stripes. In the early morning you park above them and walk down through the big pine trees that are all around and that make the courts seem like a gay, comfortable glade, hearing the comely thwock of tennis balls on gut, smelling the antique smell of boxwood and the courts themselves that have just been sprayed and rolled.

From his car Craig could see Foss, sparkling in his pressed white Lacostes, waiting in a lawn chair in front of the pro shop. On the number three court was a game of doubles, nobody else. It was nine o'clock and the sky was hard as blue enamel. As he walked down the needled path, the soft resinous air, with its formal quiet and almost palpable feel of healthful leisure and good spirits, touched and satisfied him as it always did. He felt bad, but at home.

Foss looked hearty and cheerful, like he had just eaten three bowls of Wheaties and brushed his teeth. "How was your date?" Craig asked him.

"Educational. Somebody hit you with a barbell?"

There was no missing the ear; it was swollen like a blood sausage.

"Beer bottle."

"No kidding? In that health place or what?" Foss looked interested.

"In a place called the Three O'Clock Club. In Five Points. Do you want to play tennis or not?"

"Nice company," said Foss.

They took the first court and started warming up. Foss had a pretty game, with the long backcourt strokes you get only from about a thousand dollars' worth of lessons. He hit the ball flat and hard and bounced around stylishly near the base line. Craig hurried him into playing before the heat got to his hangover. He enjoyed the first set—fresh gritty crunch of his shoes on the court and the soft, dry, early air. His serve was coming in and he won it, but Foss took the second and the third and by then Craig wasn't enjoying it any more.

They drank a Coke on the porch of the pro shop. There were people on all the courts now and it was seriously hot. Foss was chewing on a piece of ice and talking about his debutante for this season.

"She knows a lot but she doesn't enjoy anything. She's not interested in anything but talking." At a party the night before she had kept Foss in a back room away from everyone else talking about J. R. R. Tolkien for God's sake.

"She sounds fun."

"Yeah." Foss shook his head and chomped down on another piece of ice. "Well, it beats the hell out of Mr. Alabama and his friends."

"They enjoy themselves, Foss. You're really a snob, buddy, you know that?"

Foss snorted. "You are too, but a worse kind. This . . . *experience* thing of yours, digging into how different people live and all. That's a very selfish, snobbish thing. Turgenev calls it putting on a peasant's blouse. It's slumming is all it is."

45

Foss had a nasal tutorial sound in his voice and Craig suspected he had made up the stuff about Turgenev. "You're full of shit," he said and let it go at that.

They played one more set and a little after noon they walked down the hill to the club. In the basement of the clubhouse, along with the locker rooms and golf shop, was a big oval dining room called the grille. It was an airy, wood-paneled, comfortable place with heavy furniture and a tile floor. You could enter it directly from outside in tennis or golf clothes without going through the formal upstairs of the building. It was crowded and they waited for a table at the long bar and shot poker dice for the lunch. Craig took eight horses straight, then lost one and took two more—a week's worth of lunches.

"Them bullets is sho comin for you, Mr. Blake," Chub said and chuckled. He leaned on his counter, polishing a glass and wanting a game, probably the best poker dice roller in the state.

"They're not coming good enough to roll you, Chub."

He chuckled again. "Nawsir, I guess not."

Chub had been behind that bar forever, polishing glasses, chuckling, beating people at poker dice. On at least half the day of every summer between grammar school and college Craig had joked and shot dice with him at noon—between tennis in the morning and golf in the afternoon. Like everything else at Woodstream, that was a tradition.

They finally got a table and ordered club sandwiches and iced tea, the traditional lunch.

"Someday I'm going to order hash," Craig said.

Foss shook his head. "You can't; wouldn't work. They wouldn't even give it to you."

Two golfers came in, their cleats snapping on the old tiles. They stood at the bar talking to Chub, sweat towels dangling like tails from their belts.

"There's Halsey and Packman," said Foss.

"I see them. How about letting me finish my sandwich before you start your goddamn socializing." But Foss was already waving

46

and they came snapping over, bringing their beers and the dice cup.

"Yes *suh*, yes *suh*," said Halsey. For some reason that was how he greeted people. "Hello, my men."

He was a tall, freckled lawyer with a lot of inherited, blue-chip money, a big family and a whiney voice that sounded like wind in a louvred door. George Packman had been Craig's roommate for a year in prep school. He was sturdy, athletic and quiet.

Halsey looked at Craig. "Foss hit you with his rocket serve or what?"

"I ran into a door. How's the golf course?"

"It's *absud*. The grass on the greens is three inches high and you damn near have to putt with a wedge." He craned around the room. "I want to talk to somebody on the maintenance committee."

"Pete just means he's five strokes down," said Packman. "How was your trip to Mexico?" he asked Craig.

"It was all right. We saw a lot of sails and wahoo."

"Why don't you get a job, Blake?" said Halsey.

"I ask him that too from time to time," said Foss. "He's too busy chasing down weirdos."

Packman was smiling. "You all wouldn't know what to do with his time if you had it."

"Getting hard to say he spends it elegantly," said Foss.

Halsey ordered four beers and they rolled for the tab. "Are we going to play golf, or not?" Craig asked Foss. He was through with his lunch and was already tired of the sitting, the conversation and the steady drone from the roomful of perfumed, chattering ladies. Foss was in no hurry.

"In the heat of the day, my man?" said Halsey, and went into one of his bad imitations of W. C. Fields. "Why don't you forgooo. We'll have some gentlemanly conversation, an exchange of viewws, good lager and a roll of the diiice. Forgo today and we can play a foursome in the morning."

Packman was agreeable and so was Foss, who was always delighted by Halsey, and Craig felt the afternoon slip completely out from under him. Time did that often and usually pleasantly here, where built in as secretly and solidly as the plumbing was the comfortable sensation that any part of a day was as leisurely insignificant as any other. You might as well play gin as tennis, you thought. Might as *well* drink this bloody mary as drive back downtown to work. Usually limp enough to enjoy this, Craig was too restless for it today. He was in love again and that always made him antsy.

Since he was about seven years old he had been falling into complicated frequent love, less often with people than with ways of doing things, whole life styles, as they were suggested to him by little gestures and postures and sounds. When he was nine he had watched a man in a donut shop stretching and shaping dough and for years after was in love with being a baker. A big part of his long affection for salt-water fishing had to do with the way charter-boat mates, with a motion like turning a key, can wire shut a baitfish's mouth. At various times recently he had been in love with rodeoing (from having watched a man in a plaster cast from chin to waist being helped onto a bull), sky diving (a professional packer on his knees making precise pleats in a big orange chute), trapshooting (the gracefully mitered joint between man and gun and the sound of the shout to pull) and a score of women, because of the way they crossed their legs or fingered their hair or knitted their brows or held animals or threw footballs.

He had always gone around with his nose down like a truffle hound sniffing out fresh experiences to get excited about, to explore for their mysteries and ticks, and for their closeness to the heart of things. Yesterday he had stumbled into a whole grove of them—lifting, posing, vegetable feasts, bar fights. He was crazy about all that now, and about Santo and Franklin and Mary Tate (her straight back, her flicking foot as she scolded Santo, her rush to his story and her poise).

48

At two that morning in the living room of his house after they had brought him home, she sat in a spindly Chippendale armchair his grandmother had used, as quietly, with as elegant a purchase as that old lady herself, while Santo looked in the back for ice for Craig's ear and Franklin wandered around saying dazed things like, "sonofabich." She sat on the edge of the chair, hands in her lap, looking delighted and possessed by the room.

"God, y'all are great," he had mumbled to her, staring and still drunk. "I just think y'all are . . . great."

"Wudga pay for this goddamn place?" Franklin asked him, rubbing his hand over the crushed velvet arm of a couch.

"Not mine," Craig said, and Franklin looked at him like he thought he might have stolen it from a department store. "It's my parents' house."

"Where are they?"

"Dead."

"Oh. Then it's yours."

"No. It's theirs."

"Shut up, asshole," Mary Tate told Franklin.

Santo brought back the ice in a towel, holding in his other hand a bottle of crème de menthe and four small pressed glass goblets. "This is fabulous. It's fabulous," he said, his eyes jumping around the living room, handling everything in sight. He held up one of the goblets to a light and turned it on its stem.

"Teasel. There's some bellflower back there, and some twisted grape . . . Look at this, Mary," he said, squinting up at the tiny colored glass. "That's some of the best darned teasel I ever saw."

They drank a crème de menthe to that. Santo hummed *Your Cheatin' Heart*. The old house soughed around them out of its old unuse, and Craig had found himself wide-eyed in love again.

Halsey was talking about a party, his long freckled face cocked for sarcasm. "They're having everybody in the city as usual. A black tie dinner dance with quail . . . for the multitudes. It's ridiculous. The thing is, discrimination has gotten to be a dirty

49

word with all this Supreme Court crap and everything. I'll keep these four jacks in two."

"That's the thing all right," said Craig. "What are you talking about?"

"The Walterson's party in August. And they're having Guy Lombardo again in the ballroom for Christ's sake."

"Are you going, Craig?" Packman asked him.

"Nope. That's my vacation, I'll be in Montana."

"Why don't you get a job, Blake?" Halsey whined again. "Anyway she called me last week, Amy did, and wanted to know if I knew a singer. Said she wants her 'awthintic' this year to be a folk singer who can sing *Greensleeves*. Cause that's her favorite song."

"Did you know one?" asked Packman.

"How would I know somebody like that?"

"Craig's been hanging with some 'awthintics' lately," said Foss. They all looked up at Craig.

"Can you put her on a singer, Blake?" Halsey was grinning, dice cup in hand. Looking into his long soft, wolfish face, Craig suddenly had a beautiful idea, one he could see like a snapshot.

"Maybe so," he said and laughed at the thought. "Yeah, I might know somebody for her, Halsey."

5

HE LEFT THE club at three, just got up while Halsey was talking about the golf course at Ponte Vedra and walked out of the grille and up the hill to his car. Like a thirsty man going to water he drove out the quiet tree-shaded drive, down the long mountain fall of hot, noisy roads to town where the Saturday afternoon glare swirled like dust in the streets. He parked in a lot on Twentieth Street and walked four blocks through the cloying downtown air that smelled of bodies and the steel mill, in his tennis clothes, to the studio.

Thor Erickson opened the door, looking worn like he hadn't slept.

"Hi," Craig said. "Joe around?" He could hear country music upstairs.

"Yeah, he's here but he's bombing and he don't need to be bothered. He's getting ready for a contest."

"I know. I'm not going to bother him."

Erickson's broad, lamp-tanned face considered. "This is Satdy and we're not even open Satdy. I run a bidness here." He stared at Craig then shrugged and moved aside. "What the shit. Long as you don't bother him."

They climbed the stairs silently and Erickson went back into his office. Craig could see Newton in there, hunched over a checkerboard.

Santo was alone in the gym. He stood in the center of the floor with his back to Craig, in shorts and his Batman cape, singing with a little brown radio, "I wanna go-oo home. Oh, I wanna goo home . . ." Spread-legged he stood and held on his shoulders behind his neck an iron bar so heavily weighted at the ends that the center was bowed. Craig watched him bounce a little on his toes then drop into a full squat, his tail inches from the floor, and stand smoothly up. Ten times he did that, still singing, then he shelved the weight onto a shoulder-high rack.

"Can you sing *Greensleeves?*"

He spun around. "You snuk up on Batman?"

"How much is that?"

"That? Oh that's about four-seventy. Hiya doing, how was your game?" He turned down the radio.

"OK. I was a little . . ."

"Shaky."

"Yeah, shaky."

"Hah! Ought to stick to Tiger's Milk. You want to work out?"

"Thor thought it might bother you."

"Well, Thor's wrong. It helps. You get a rhythm going."

"I'd like to know something about it. I mean how the exercises work and all." Craig only half meant that but Santo got very excited.

"Yeah, that's good. That's *great*. Not enough people care about that. Look I've just started. We'll set up the weights and go through a whole workout, OK? And I can explain to you as we go along." He bounded through the gym picking up weights, placing them next to benches, on stools and racks, and talking in a steady gush.

"See you're tearing down tissue is what you're doing. You tear it all down, then when you rest it builds back up, but bigger. It's a joy. You've got six main muscle groups—legs, stomach, chest, back, shoulders and arms. Now we do a split routine, so on Mondays, Wednesdays and Fridays we work on the stomach and shoulders and arms, and do the legs and chest and back on Tuesdays, Thursdays and Saturdays."

"What do you do on Sunday?"

"Three hundred sit-ups. That's when you're boiling, on Sundays—amino acids are whipping down the blood stream and the cells are sucking 'em up like sponges and growing. You can *feel* those mothers growing. You don't want to do too much then."

He extended a leg and flexed the thigh and with his fingers explored it like a melon in a grocery store. "Come here," he said. "Now first you're going to do some squats, then hack squats and leg extensions." He poked different places on the thigh. It was divided cleanly into three huge oblong bulges that looked barely contained by the skin. "The squats and hacks get the rectus femoris here"—he poked the middle bulge—"and the vastus externus," the outside one. "The extensions get the internal vastus."

Craig wondered if he had them all.

"They look like almonds, don't they," Santo said quietly, studying his leg. "A nice thing is that a lot of muscles look like almonds."

They worked out. Craig followed Santo with lighter weights, in his rhythm, and unlike the night before or any of the other times when he had fooled with barbells he began to feel the physical logic of the stress, the peculiar pleasure of organized lifting, pushing and pulling.

After their legs they worked their chests, the wide twin muscles, pecs Santo called them, that were grapefruit-sized domes on him, curving out almost perpendicular to his body and connected to each other by fine tense striations.

Santo showed him the purplish stretch marks where the pectorals had pulled the skin away from his shoulders. "You hide those in a contest," he said. "You grease 'em over." He was on his back on a small bench. Perched above him on two slim metal arms were three hundred and fifty mean-looking pounds—the flanged, forty-five pound, black-iron plates, heavy and crude-looking as manhole covers; the Olympic bar, wider at each end than in the middle, long and impersonal as the axle of a truck.

"Now watch," he said, squeaking his back into the naugahyde. "This is the best one of all. This works about everything in your upper body. You gotta have the breathing right, and the rhythm. Watch the way the pecs spread as the bar comes down and peak as it goes up—it's beautiful."

He lined up his hands about two feet apart and equidistant from the ends of the bar, held it lightly for a moment, then rocked it off the rack and sucked in a long breath. As gently as if it were a woman he was letting onto his prone self, Santo lowered the vast weight. It touched his spread chest like a kiss, paused, and rose again solemnly as it had sunk. The lift was so smooth and quick it looked remote, as if Santo had just willed it to happen, and Craig had a brief, wild impulse to try the weight himself.

They did dozens of bench presses, prone dumbbell presses, inclines, declines and flyes—until Craig's chest flamed with torn tissue. Then they went to their backs, to the long latissimus dorsi muscles (Santo said it as three trochees, rolling the name in his mouth like hard candy) that run along the sides from the waist to just beneath the arms. They were Santo's most spectacular—as he hung from the chinning bar like a great pale bat, his hands wide, his legs crossed and gracefully curved, they flared into thick wedges ten inches wide of his rib cage.

"Look between the lats and the pecs," he said.

"OK."

"You see those little slanted muscles between 'em, tying 'em together?"

Craig saw them. They were thick and beveled like short hunks of rope. Santo smiled. "Proud of those. Those are serratus and they're a bitch to build. You get 'em with pullovers mostly." He did twenty chins as he talked, pulling up in front of the bar so that it touched the back of his neck. When Craig tried them he couldn't do one and Santo held his knees through the set, helping him up with light pushes.

"You're doing great," he said. "Nobody can do these right off."

It was peaceful in the gym. It was nearly dark outside and the room had grayed. The only sounds were the low raw music from the radio, their talk and the clink of weights. In the lighted office Thor and Newton were bent over the checkerboard, moving hardly at all.

"Why do they stay here on Saturdays, when the place is closed?" Craig asked.

"Because this is where they live. They live here."

"You mean both of them . . . *live* here?"

Santo looked at him. "Yeah. Newton sleeps on the massage table and Thor has a cot in the back. It's not bad. I stay here myself sometimes."

Somewhere in the way Santo answered was an insulted, defensive tone. It was the first time Craig had heard anything in his voice but excitement. He knew somehow he had hurt him and he was sorry, and being sorry made him realize all at once how close to Santo he had come to feel.

"It's fine," he said clumsily. "And you could take a workout before breakfast." Santo didn't answer. Craig looked around for something to say. "Look, after you win the Mr. Southeast, then what? I mean what do you go for then?"

Santo stood at the big window, staring down into the street. "I don't know," he said. "Depends on what Thor wants. There's Mr. East Coast, Mr. U.S.A., Olympia, Universe . . ."

"How about Mr. America?" Craig went over to the window and stood next to him.

"Yeah, there's that too." His voice was flat and quiet. "You see those people down there? In Gotham City." There were a dozen or so people on the streets and sidewalks, moving in quick shuffles out of the gathering dark. "Some big, some little, some dumb, some smart, right? But you know the biggest difference between 'em?" He held up a stubby forefinger.

"What?" asked Craig, and really wanted to know.

"Taste," said Santo. "Some of 'em have taste and some of 'em don't." He was quiet, watching the street, then he looked up at the sign of himself. The red bulbs popped on and off. From the window they could see only the outflung arm and leg and part of the face. "That's a terrible sign, isn't it?"

Craig didn't even have to think. He knew what to say and his voice was as steady and positive as it ever got.

"Nope. I like it."

Santo looked down and toed the carpet. He was beaming, his neck the color of the neck in the sign. And Craig felt them close again, closer than before.

"Aw shucks," he said for Santo and they both toed around, like two farmers buying insurance.

There was a point on the highway that brought him out of town from which he could look up through the car window and see his house, its rambling Victorian shape perfectly natural-looking among the pines and rocks right at the very top of the mountain. He supposed his father and grandfather when they had owned it had looked up at it from the same place—in the cars and buggies that brought them out the same road away from the city's work and heat—and had been reassured as he usually was by its cool height. As he glanced up at it tonight the house seemed just big and lonely and dark.

He turned left at the peak of the highway and climbed the mountain, up the narrow private road that wound between the banked lawns of his relatives and their pastures full of riding horses and Jersey cows, and then up the driveway that the road became, along the flank of the vegetable garden on one side and the fifteen-acre lawn on the other, to his house. His as his sharp nose was his, because someone had given it to him and he couldn't give it back. It was part of his father's estate, all of which had come to him for lack of anyone else eighteen months ago. And since then Craig had lived in just one of the fourteen rooms, the same one he had grown up in, as impersonally as a squirrel in one of the house's eaves, letting the garden go to weed, the grass grow, the furniture dust over and the silver tarnish.

He couldn't sell the place, despite the good advice of his relatives. Hard as he had tried to avoid it and well as he thought he had done that before his parents' death, he knew that for the time being he was tacked to the old house like a hide on the door.

He turned on the lights in the front five rooms, made himself a drink and a sandwich and called Dorothy Stephens to ask her to go skiing the next day. While he as talking to her he remembered and then decided to forget the golf game with Foss and Halsey and Packman. Then he changed out of his tennis clothes for the first time all day and took his sandwich and drink outside to the pavilion, a circular, semienclosed porch thirty yards from the house on the brow of the mountain.

With his feet on one of the wormy green railings, feeling healthy and powerful, he ate, listened to the tree frogs and looked over the scruffy yard to the distant lights of Birmingham in the valley. He found Twentieth Street, followed it up to Second Avenue and across to a blinking reddish smudge that might have been the sign in front of Erickson's Olympic Studio and Spa. He watched the smudge and wondered about what Santo had said in the shower after their workout.

Craig's arms had been so swollen and burned-out that he couldn't soap himself so he had just stood in the dark letting the warm water pour over him. "Some of us are going up to Guntersville tomorrow skiing, you want to get a date and come?" Santo asked him.

"Yeah, great. I'd like to."

"Mary Tate and I'll pick you up about eight then." He waited a minute. "You like her?"

"Who?"

"Mary. She likes you."

"Yeah, she's . . . well she's a great girl, Joe."

"Stacked ain't she?" Santo said.

Craig wondered what the hell to say to that. He couldn't see Santo's face but he figured it was smiling.

"She's a fine-looking girl."

"Uh huh. More woman than girl though—she's got a hundred ways to wind your clock." His water went off. "You two might be real good for each other," he said thoughtfully. And as he walked past, Craig saw he had been wrong, that Santo wasn't smiling.

Craig stared down into the hot swirl of lights at the center of the city and realized with a vague thrill that he didn't have any idea what went on down there, among the Santos and Franklins and Mary Tates, in the hotels and cafes and narrow bars. The twelve miles that separated this pavilion from the life down there might as well have been twelve hundred for all he knew about it. But he was always willing to learn. He stood up and yawned and leaned out over his railing.

"OK," he said to the reddish smudge, "OK, Mr. Alabama, let's go."

6

MR. ALABAMA of 1965, 1967 and 1968; Mr. Sun States; Mr. Gulf Coast since 1965 and Mr. Deep South, talked about himself for two and a half hours as they barreled through the morning toward Guntersville in his big red Pontiac. When they started off the sky was bunched with clouds but by the time Santo finished his childhood the hot sun had cleared them. He talked directly into the rearview mirror to a nervous Dorothy Stephens.

Dorothy was a Hollins graduate, an ex-debutante and a member of the Junior League. She had a pretty face with small distinct features and Craig had dated her on and off for years. She had come happily out to the car, cheerfully dressed and carrying her bathing suit in a monogrammed towel, and peered into the front seat expecting to see people she knew. Instead she found Mary Tate and Santo, ruddy and foreign, already *in* their bathing suits. And that scared her. For the first fifteen minutes of the drive she powdered her nose and chatted nervously to Craig. Finally, with a ladylike effort not to stare at his huge bare shoulders, she asked Joe Santo what he did. He said he lifted weights.

Dorothy wondered what the hell that meant. She said that must be interesting and asked how he got into that.

He said it was a long story but he would tell her because he thought people ought to know each other when they were going to be together all day. Later when Craig asked him why he had put all that on her, Santo smiled and said he figured it wouldn't hurt her any.

His father was French-Canadian and his mother was three-quarters Chippewa. He was born thirty-six years ago in Rugby, North Dakota, at the dead center of North America and during the depression. His father worked on a concrete elevator part time and market-hunted pheasants the rest of the time.

Market-hunted *pheasants?* wondered Dorothy Stephens. Did people really . . .

Joe said he remembered his father leaving the house early with a rope across his chest and a game sack draped behind him like a sail. He sometimes killed fifty pheasants a day. Baby Santo grew into boyhood on pheasant meat.

When Joe was nine his father moved to Hurley, Wisconsin, under the impression that he could get rich logging. Instead he handled a line loader and lost all his toenails, two fingers and the sight of one eye. After two years of that they moved down the state to Langlade. The first thing Joe's father did there was harvest a potato crop alongside some Menominee Indians who lived on a reservation nearby. Mr. Santo got very fond of the Menominees who were gentle and often misused by the farm owners, and they got fond of him. He helped to organize them into a harvesting union and when the union worked the Indians became convinced that Mr. Santo was not only nice but magical. At their invitation he moved his family onto the reservation and became a sort of adviser to the tribe. He was that for five years. During that time young Joe went to Indian schools and learned Indian things—that it was better to be strong than weak, how to sing Menominee songs and make their fantastic bead necklaces, to like sucker-head soup, and all about rapids on the Wolf River. And he learned how to ski, first on shaped animal skins and then on skis, well enough to win a midwestern junior championship in downhill (he never learned how to turn well, he said; he enjoyed gravity and liked to come straight down whatever he was on top of).

In the meantime Mr. Santo had become obsessed with Indian problems—with their education, their teeth, their housing. An Indian woman whose front porch he built made him a bead necklace showing a cross inside a circle. At the center of the cross was one white bead that stood for Mr. Santo. Mr. Santo began to think of himself, said Joe, as a sort of minister of a "church without walls." And that was fine with the Indians until he began showing dangerous signs of strain. In 1949 the Wisconsin Fish and Game Department hinted that it might restrict the numbers of deer and bear that Menominees could kill on their reservation. This incensed Mr. Santo. When he was called before the tribe's governing council for his usually sturdy advice, he said: "I have only wan recommendation. *War!* Let us take to our hills and valleys with zee bow and zee knife . . ."

So the Santos moved again. During one summer they drifted from Wisconsin to Indiana to Kentucky to Tennessee and finally to Ensley, Alabama, a mill-town suburb of Birmingham. His father, said Santo, had been digested south by this country; if he lived long enough he would probably be crapped out at Key West.

Dorothy Stephens made a strange little noise in her throat and Craig squeezed her hand abstractly. He was busy watching lovely, bare, graceful Mary Tate, who was relaxed and curved into the front seat, looking at the outside go by: liver-spotted dog, small hill, kudzu vines. God, thought Dorothy, why didn't he *tell* me. She looked at Craig who was looking at the cheap little thing in the front seat who was staring out the window . . . Joe Santo kept stabbing her with his eyes in the rearview mirror. His hair was long and black and matted like an animal's. And they were going so *fast*.

In Ensley Mr. Santo went to work for the steel mill and Joe went to high school for his senior year. He wore his hair long like a Menominee's and broke every athletic record the school had. He also met Thor Erickson that year. Thor was twenty and already owned a little gym.

As soon as he graduated from high school Santo was drafted, in June 1950 and in September he was sent to Korea. On the whole, he said, he liked it over there. The UN forces were made up of English, Australians, Canadians, New Zealanders, Indians, South Africans, French, Greek, Dutch, Filipinos, Thais, Turks, Belgians, Swedes and Ethiopians. He liked meeting all those folks and he liked the Koreans and he liked being a soldier. During the summer of 1951 his division was bunkered into the ridges above Suwon and Kimpo, often just feet from the also bunkered-in North Koreans. Much of the fighting was done crawling, at night and point blank, Indian style. Santo talked a major into arming all his reconnaissance patrols with Bear hunting bows. He also tried to unionize the Korean laborers who carried supplies up the hills on A-frame packs, but that never got off the ground because in September on Bloody Ridge he was shot through the stomach and the hip and had to leave Korea.

Santo stopped dramatically at that point and stared into the rearview mirror. After a while he said, "I hope this isn't boring you, honey. I haven't gotten to the best part yet."

"Me?" asked Dorothy. "Heavens no! It's really interesting." She went back to chewing on her lower lip with a regular bitter motion like sucking a cough drop.

They were in downtown Gadsden. It was bright and hot. A clock on a bank said nine-thirty and eighty-eight degrees. On the clefted swell of Joe Santo's back was a light film of wetness that Dorothy couldn't help noticing.

Santo was in an army hospital in Japan for eighteen months. To keep busy there he made Menominee bead necklaces and mailed them to the wives of men in the hospital. He also translated some Menominee songs and put them to guitar music and later when he was better he wheeled himself around the hospital singing and playing in the wards. He made the songs into long musical narrations with twenty or thirty stanzas and three or four characters and he would sing all the parts. There was one about a trapper who was caught in his own spring trap on the Wolf River in January and froze there. Joe sang the trapper and the trapper's wife and the trapper's mother and the little boy who found the trapper. It was a sad song, he told Dorothy, but there were plenty of happy ones. Listening to them was like a combination of hearing music and watching a movie and the wounded men loved it. Santo got so popular that as soon as he was released the Army assigned him over to the USO and for the next three and a half years he traveled to hospitals all over Japan and the Philippines singing to the wounded and making their wives bead necklaces. He got famous back in the States. *Time* called him a "military minstrel of mercy"; Mamie Eisenhower wrote to ask for a necklace and Ed Sullivan offered to fly him to New York to appear on his show.

When he finally came back to the States in 1956 he was a happy man. Korea had taught him how to enjoy things from minute to minute and how not to fasten on them. He was much too happy to want to work for more than enough to eat on, so at twenty-three he was, already, he said, semiretired. For the next six years he just traveled around America enjoying himself. He sang country in a nightclub in San Diego; he worked on a mango farm and picked Easter lilies in Hollywood, Florida; he worked on a mackerel boat out of Everglades City and for a while after that he was in the alligator-wrestling business with a Seminole girl and her father. Then he oiled a crane on a construction job in the Berry Islands. There was nobody out on their island but the twelve-man crew. They were building a yacht club. All their supplies had to be flown in once a week and the temperature was around one hundred degrees day after day. The only people the company could get to work out there, even for seven dollars an hour, were ex-convicts, and guys who couldn't get work anywhere else, and Joe Santo. He loved it; he went bonefishing at night and collected shells. He left only because he started saving money too fast.

Santo spent the next three years in Wyoming, working as a ski instructor in the Grand Tetons in the winter and as a guide on the Snake River in summer (in his second year out there he really did win a national white-water championship, in an open canoe that he made himself).

It was in Wyoming, he told Dorothy, that he learned the best things he knew. He got to know the country out there—by skiing mountains and floating rivers.

Santo stopped talking and just nodded into the mirror for a while.

Did she know Cézanne? he asked her finally. Well when you ski or shoot rapids you do to country what he did to it with paintings . . .

"You do?" whispered Dorothy.

Yes. You get beneath the surface to the thrusts and pulls and falls and stretches of a place. When you ski, Dorothy (his deep voice shaking with a celebrant's ardor), you discover with your whole body the breaks and rises of terrain: cornice, rill, coulee, bowl, ridge. You learn the intimate things about earth that a mole knows, say, or a snake. It's, well, it's almost like making love. And on a river, Dorothy, on a good river you find out how water *flows* . . . He paused, gave it weight. You feel through the skin of your boat that falling, shaping force, and *that* Dorothy is a joy, J-O-Y, joy.

Craig looked at Dorothy Stephens as Santo spelled the word for her. Her smooth, bored face had been transformed into passionate little furrows. Unabashed now she stared at Santo's glistening back, looking charmed and vulnerable as a child watching magic. There was something rapturous about the look that astounded Craig. He seemed to have missed some weird thing going on here —what was this girl *doing* looking like that? He had listened in and out of Santo's story, enjoying it and wondering how much of it was true. For Santo didn't really seem to him to have any past at all—he seemed to re-create himself minute by minute in ways that barely resembled a former Santo. Craig suspected he might have a history for every occasion. But here was cool, superior Dorothy Stephens, definitely affected . . . on her cheek was one pellucid, well-shaped tear.

"Why did you ever leave, Joe?" breathed Dorothy.

"I'd be there now, Dorothy. I'd be there now," Santo said in a gentle, faraway voice . . .

But his father, who had hacked himself dull against steel management at the mill, developed emphysema and Joe decided to go home and get him out of the city.

It was March 1962 when he came back to Alabama. His eyes were full of snowfields and alligators and white water and bonefish flats. He was black from the sun and he talked funny. He wore an elephant-tail bracelet, and a gold ring in his left earlobe and his hair down around his shoulders. No one in Birmingham would hire him but the mill, so he went on a night shift there and took college classes during the day. What he wanted was to get enough money to buy a hog farm for his father and mother and just about the time he figured out that he would never do that on a blower's salary he met up with Thor Erickson again. Erickson by now had four clubs and a corner on the physical culture business in the South. He liked Santo and he offered him a job instructing that paid about twice what he was making at the mill.

Santo didn't know anything about lifting weight, or muscle tone or amino acids or any of that, but he learned fast. And as soon as he started lifting himself he grew fast, fantastically fast. He found that he had a rare ability—he could control and shape his body as easily as a potter does clay; he could put on or take off inches anywhere he wanted in days.

As soon as Thor found all that out he called Santo into his office, his hands shaking with possibilities. You and I are going to the top, boy, he said. All the way. This whole country is watching bodies. With your metabolism and my know-how we can take it all. He told Santo to work only when he felt like it, to save his energy for eating and working out. He said he was going to get Santo any kind of car he wanted and replace it every year and he asked if there was anything else Santo wanted. Santo said yeah, he would like a hog farm for his parents. So Thor went out and bought the first one he found. It was in Guntersville on the lake. It had twenty acres, a good well, a sound house, four sound hog pens and twelve Duroc hogs. It cost fifteen thousand dollars and Thor just wrote the owner a check.

Into the mirror Santo said that Dorothy probably wondered what might tempt a sharp businessman into that kind of an investment. Well the answer was *endorsements*. He said he was, on the hoof, already worth nearly that much to Erickson and he wasn't even Mr. America yet. Besides he was paying Erickson back a little at a time and Erickson was a fair man.

"Shit," said Mary Tate. It was her first comment of the trip.

"Anyway, that's how it happened, Dorothy honey," Santo said. "One thing leading to another, you might say."

"How many contests have you won?" Dorothy asked, and Mary Tate jerked around to look at her. In Dorothy's voice was a new, soft, unmistakable thrill.

66

"About fifty. Mostly little ones," said Santo. "Thor doesn't want to try for the big ones yet. He says we're still priming the pump."

They were deep into real country now. Miles ago they had passed through Boaz and Albertville, the last towns, and were now only a few miles from the lake. The big Pontiac rushed past more and more thickened stretches of second growth pine and water oak. The houses had become shacks with pumps and hounds in the yards and corrugated metal roofs. Craig, who had traveled less in Alabama than at least a half-dozen other states, was surprised at how viney and primitive this Tennessee River delta was. It was a vivid morning. The rich, earth-smelling heat billowed through the car like dust. He began to feel active and to wonder what kind of day it was going to be.

By a small wooden church they turned off the paved road onto a dirt one. In the cracked clay churchyard a few old cars and trucks were parked around a seesaw. Behind the church was a cluster of tombstones, bare as teeth stuck in the ground.

"That's my daddy's church," said Santo. He stopped the car in the yard so they could look at it. It was a squat rectangular building, weather-bleached from blue to a faded denim color. A white cross hung over the door, bright in the sun. Through the open door they could hear people moving around and hear the scrape of furniture. As they looked, a white-haired little man appeared on the stoop and studied the car. "And that's my daddy. He's lay minister there."

All the man had on was a pair of tan shorts and an elaborate bead necklace. He was lean and brown as a squirrel and he stood in the door with his hands crossed in front of him looking oddly clerical and solemn despite his dress. Santo honked the horn and waved. Mary Tate waved too.

"He's about to start the service," Santo said.

"What, uh, kind of service?" asked Dorothy quietly.

Mr. Santo was making a series of gestures with his hands—he

might have been toying with a nut. Santo answered him with two quick jabs of his fingers.

"He wanted to know who you are," Santo said. "See what he's doing now?" The old man was making a soft downward arc, like the curve of a dome, with both hands. He was smiling. His face looked kind and dignified. "It means may the earth bless you. Old Menominee blessing. They believe in the earth."

The old man went back inside and Santo gunned the car on down the dirt road, chuckling. "He really shakes these rednecks up," he said.

After a few miles they turned onto an even smaller dirt road and stopped in front of a metal gate. On the face of the gate was a big sign lettered in a childlike scrawl. It said:

> shoot a deer
> mount a rack
> shoot a hog
> I shoot back
> signed Noel Santo

They drove through the gate down the slope of Mr. Santo's land, past a hog pen and the rusted-out bodies of a car and a truck, toward the lake. Topping a grassy rise they could see a long green curve of the far shore, intricate, distant and cool-looking against the bright water. Just then Dorothy Stephens started to cry quietly into her towel. Determined, liquid crying like released water.

"Oh for Christ's sake," said Mary Tate.

Santo stopped the car, turned around and put a hand to Dorothy's bent head. He asked her gently what was wrong.

"It's just so beautiful," she said.

"What, Dorothy?" asked Craig, beginning vaguely to worry.

"I don't *know* . . . Everything," she said. "Noel is such a beautiful name."

7

CRAIG SAT NEXT to Franklin out at the end of the dilapidated wooden dock. Franklin was fishing intently with a long bamboo pole, nylon string, a red bobber and worms. Three little bluegills flopped and gasped behind him on the boards. By his side was a half-gallon bottle of Thunderbird wine.

Though he pretended interest in the fishing, Craig was really out there for a better view. Far out on the lake, invisibly connected to a roaring old Chris-Craft, Mary Tate was carving out graceful S's on a slalom ski, throwing high combs of water from the surface of the lake. She had been skiing without stop since they arrived nearly an hour ago and she now seemed inscribed on the day, a part of the landscape: leaning backward, half lost in spray behind the quick red tip of her ski—distant, beautiful and angry.

There had been more trouble with Dorothy as soon as Santo pulled the Pontiac in to join two other cars and a panel truck at the edge of Mr. Santo's beach. Dorothy had looked out on ten or twelve strange bulky men and bikinied girls, heard raw blats of country music, and had balked. Still sobbing, refusing to move, she said she would be perfectly all right there and would everybody please go on and have a nice time. Santo, talking softly, told Mary Tate and Craig to go ahead, he and Dorothy would be along in a while. And Mary Tate had slammed out of the car without a word. Down on the beach she commandeered the boat and someone to tow her and took off from the dock (one foot in the ski, the other dangling gorgeously just above the water) without a look backward.

Santo did finally gentle Dorothy out of the car and down to the beach where he led her and Craig around, introducing them to his friends. Buell was there and Wall Street and Hump. It was a loud bunch. Radios played. People shouted and laughed and drank from cans of Busch Bavarian and bottles of wine. Santo walked among them with a dignified, proprietary air (Lara, I want you to meet two friends of mine, Miss Dorothy Stephens and Mr. Craig Blake. Hiyou says Lara. Lara, Miss Stephens here is with the Junior League). Like a bearish Gatsby, thought Craig watching him.

Whatever he had done to Dorothy in the car seemed to have worked. She had back her old poise as she picked her way around beach towels and coolers, her head tilted back, shaking hands and nodding. Only Wall Street seemed to throw her. Introduced, Wall

70

neglected to say hello and just stood hulking over her, his hairy belly spilling from the front of his trunks. Breathing heavily through his mouth he stared down, entranced. Dorothy had begun to back away when Santo took her arm, said, "Later, Wall," and led her off.

The last man they met was the only small one there. He was dark and intense-looking and had soft tiny hands. His name was Dr. Elijah Wright. Santo whispered as they approached him that he was Thor's partner and was fabulously wealthy from having invented green stamps. Dr. Wright was quiet and polite and appeared embarrassed by his date who lay on her stomach in a lizard-skin bikini and kept mentioning that she was being "burnt to a creasp." Dorothy seemed comfortable with the doctor so Craig left them talking and wandered first to the edge of the water, then to the end of the dock, watching Mary Tate.

"She can flat ski, cain't she," said Franklin and moved his worm.

"Yeah. Do you do it?" Craig asked him.

"Me? Naw. I'd rather fish."

"Do you all come out here often?"

"Just about every weekend. Joe's daddy don't care about us using his land and his boat. We buy the gasoline. And Hump tunes the motor for him. There's a bed right off the end of this dock."

"What?"

"There's a bream bed right off the end of this dock; that's why I'm doing so good. Look yonder, there's another one."

The red bobber moved slightly in the water, causing a ring, then it was still; there was another, sharper movement, a pause, and the bobber began to dance away in intent jerks. Franklin lifted the end of the pole, cleared the fish of water and swung it in. It had a bright orange belly and a blue lobe on its cheek. Franklin worked out the hook and there was dark gill blood on his hands when he finished and tossed the fish behind him with the others.

"What are you going to do with them?"

"Gonna eat em man. Gonna de-*vower* them little mothers. They're sweeter'n cunt." Franklin took a long pull on his wine.

The Chris-Craft had moved in closer to shore and Craig could see Mary Tate's face now.

"You want to catch one? I'll show you how to do it," said Franklin.

"No thanks. You're not catching anything but the little ones."

"You think you can catch big ones, hot shit?"

"Let me see your pole," Craig said.

He took off the bobber and moved the lead split shot two feet up from the hook. Then from the label of his shirt he pulled off about thirty inches of yellow thread. With small pieces of the string he fashioned hackles and a tail and with the rest he wrapped them onto either end of Franklin's hook. He wound the shank of the hook four times then pulled the end of the thread under and broke it off.

"Yellow Sally," he said, holding it up. "A classic pattern."

"What are you going to do with that goddamn thing?"

Craig pinched off a section of worm and fixed it to the barb. He threw the bait into the water where Franklin had been fishing, let it sink and began to jig it back. A bluegill hit it before it moved six inches and Craig swung the fish in—it was darker and much bigger than any of Franklin's. He threw the fly out again, and immediately caught another, even larger one.

"How come the big ones eat that?" Franklin looked annoyed. He took his pole back.

"Those are horny old males protecting the bed. They aren't careful when they're spawning and the fly makes them mad."

"Well I'll be goddamned." Franklin smiled and threw the bait back at the bed. "Pisses em off, huh?"

Craig got to his feet. The boat was coming in, following the shore line toward them, and Mary Tate was swinging back and forth across the wake, making her turns to the left only inches from the bank. The people on the beach watched her, their faces caught between the fun and danger of what she was doing. A hundred yards from the dock the boat turned out, ran at a steep angle with shore and then cut back in again, screw whining in the tight turn, and rushed for the beach.

At the turn Mary Tate swung out hard to her left behind the stern. She crouched to the end of the sweep, lifted her arms beautifully above her head as the boat took up slack and then strained against the water again, getting wide as they roared toward shore. Twenty yards out the boat flashed off. Mary Tate pulled the rope to her chest for extra speed, then flung it away. With her weight back, her left leg ahead and pointed like a dancer's, she rode the water like a skipped stone to the very edge of the beach; then she pushed down hard with her right foot, sending the ski tip around in a quick bright arc, and stepped dry onto shore. Craig felt like applauding.

Santo had walked down to meet her. Across fifty feet of water Craig watched him kiss her. His arms hung over her shoulders and she looked up at him, feet planted wide, hands on her hips. She had slight, nearly delicate limbs: like a child from the rear except for the swell of her tail. In a white, two-piece bathing suit, tapered naturally as grass, her skin earth-colored and catching light—she seemed almost to grow from that place on the beach. Craig felt himself swelling respectfully.

"Jesus Christ," he said.

"Yeah, I know how you mean," said Franklin. Franklin was cleaning a bluegill with a pocketknife. "But you can forget that piece of pelt." He pulled a slippery row of orange eggs from the fish and threw it in the water. "Who's that girl you come with?"

"Just a girl." Craig was stripping off his clothes, down to the bathing trunks under his pants, blood churning like warm water in his groin.

"Uh huh," said Franklin. "Well, she looks like she thinks her shit don't stank." He held up the yellow fly. "Can I keep this?"

"It's yours," he said and dove, awkward and tumescent, for the cold water and spawning fish.

Almost everybody roasted hot dogs over a scruffy little fire in the middle of the beach. Franklin cooked six fish spitted on a stick. And Craig and Dorothy, who had brought no lunch, sat on the end of the dock with Dr. Wright and his date sharing Santo's picnic. Santo had brought pâté and Ry-Krisps, breasts of capon on Canadian bacon, artichokes, spring onions, cheese, fruit and three bottles of Portuguese rosé. There was enough food for eight or nine people.

"Plain but filling," Santo said and bit off the tubers at the end of a spring onion.

Dorothy smiled at him with her mouth full. He was leaning back on one elbow, relaxed as the Dying Gaul. Perspiration gleamed on his skin and a gold St. Christopher disc and chain lay in a bright, loose V across the top of his chest. In repose his body was sleek, the muscles lay in quiet mounds against bone, just suggesting themselves when he moved. As he chewed his capon Craig studied one of Mr. Alabama's still and perfect legs. The workmanship was impressive—chisel-clean divisions in the thigh, flared calf and narrow ankle: it was a satyr's leg, a leg from the ceiling of the Sistine Chapel. It was not a leg you saw on the streets.

Santo reached for another onion, about his twelfth. He chewed up the hairlike roots first, taking his time, then the bulb and finally the stem.

"I could eat a thousand of these," he told Craig. "You want to know how I feel about spring onions?"

Craig nodded.

"There's a lake in Montana called Hebgen Lake, right outside of Yellowstone. Some days in the summer there's a hatch of black flies that covers whole parts of the lake, and those big brown trout you like so much come up for it. For about an hour they just swim

74

back and forth across the surface with their mouths open eating every fly in front of them until they can't swallow any more. They call them gulpers, those fish." He thought about it. "They say they die before most trout do, but I don't reckon they mind."

The girl in the lizard-skin bathing suit turned over onto her back. "All living thangs mind to die. I'dnt that right, hon?" she asked Dr. Wright and rubbed his knee.

Mary Tate laughed. She had eaten lazily like a cat, staring out at the lake while the others talked. "How the hell would you know, Rose Ella?" she said. Rose Ella grunted.

"In a sense. In a sense," said Dr. Wright, who sat with his skinny legs folded, eating a pear.

He interested Craig. Craig wanted to know how he had invented green stamps. "Joe says that you . . ." he began.

"Yes. Special sort of genius, I suppose," Dr. Wright nodded. "Convincing people they want something is all it amounts to— that they need, are due a particular thing. People don't mind paying if they feel they are *due* a product. Mathewson's law. Fortunate really. Of course health is the thing now—why we are so sanguine about our investments with Mr. Erickson . . . money to make money, really."

"Elijah here has money in the studios," said Santo.

"Had an assistant at Amherst," continued the doctor. "Political scientist with a sense of fun. He and I developed a foolproof method of having anyone we wanted elected to public office. Marketing research, really. Consumer manipulation. Simplest sort of thing in America. Find desirable hair styles, tones of voice, dictions, ethnic backgrounds, et cetera. Then effect subtle gestalt changes, negative advertising . . ." The doctor dwindled off, receded into thought.

"Tell him what happened, Elijah," Santo said.

"Yes . . . well we had this gibbon monkey seated on the Holyoke City Council. Depressing, really . . . most perfectly arboreal of the anthropoid apes. Couldn't stay of course."

75

Dorothy gave a little trill of laughter. She had had a lot of wine and her spirits had visibly improved. "What a charming story," she said. "What a marvelous story. By the way are y'all maaied?" she asked the doctor's date.

Mary Tate stood up. "I want to ski the course, Joe," she said.

"You ski very nicely, Mary Tate," Dorothy said, and Mary Tate glanced down at her as though she were something left of the lunch.

"Have to check it first," Santo answered. "Nobody's been back there for a while; we'll have to check it for logs."

"I want to ski it without checking," she said and walked off toward the boat waving for the boy who had towed her before. But Buell was already putting on the ski when she got there and Wall and his woman, wearing matching polka-dot hats and carrying their beers, were already climbing into the front seat of the boat. Mary Tate stopped by Buell, hesitated, then walked on off.

And Craig followed her. Dorothy was saying something to him but he didn't care about that. Right then he wouldn't have cared if Dorothy had disappeared in a puff of smoke. He wanted to talk to Mary Tate.

"What's the course?" he asked when he caught up to her.

"Slalom course."

"Buell probably won't ski long. He's too fat."

She shrugged. "Do you know how?"

"Uh huh."

"You want to ski double?"

"Sure, if we can get the boat."

"We'll get it, Swamp." She nodded out at the lake. "Look at him. He don't know what the hell he's doing." Buell was making ragged, heavy turns inside the wake, holding a beer can in one hand.

"How did you get so good?"

"Had to do something to get out of Opp." She threw a pebble in Buell's direction. Like every motion Craig had seen her make, the throw looked professional. They sat on a vine-covered rock where the beach met woods. It was hot and still and the air was musty with the smell of the lake.

"I skied at Cypress Gardens last year. That was the most fun thing I ever did." Her tense face relaxed remembering it. "They put us all up in a Howard Johnson's. We had color TV in the rooms and they had people to drive us around. You ever been there?"

"No."

They were silent for a minute.

"I thought you'd been everywhere."

"No. Listen, Mary Tate. I wanted to tell you about Dorothy."

"Don't worry about me, babe." She stood up and looked at him so directly it was like a blow. "I'm not going to mess with her."

"That's not what I meant." Big eyes narrowed, head tilted back, she looked at him and he looked away.

"That's a pretty house you live in," she said. Then she turned and walked off down the beach.

8

A CROWD HAD gathered on the beach near the dock. Craig walked over to where Dorothy and Santo stood with the others around Hump and a man named Ray who someone said was a stock car driver. Hump and Ray lay on their stomachs facing each other, shifting for purchase in the sand, staring each other in the eye. Their right forearms stood locked together, their thumbs twined and their fingers kneaded for grips on the back of the other's hand.

Pulling, Santo called it. He said Hump made part of his living pulling. Someone handed Craig a beer. He finished it and half another before the two men quit shifting and kneading. Dorothy was drinking too. She had polished off a bottle of Santo's wine almost singlehanded and now she was drinking warm Thunderbird from a paper cup. She stood jauntily by Santo looking sporty and amused.

"C'mon, Hump," she said throatily. Hump looked up and winked. Like the rest of him, Hump's right arm was beefy, shapeless and hairy. Ray's was sinewy and long. He had a thick wrist and long, dirty fingers and there was black grease under his nails. His was the more competent-looking arm. They stared at each other, perfectly still now, then someone dropped a hand to the ground.

Ray's head fell like a stone to his chest; he let loose a vicious, oriental sort of scream, flayed the sand with his legs and pulled at Hump's hand (veins popping into relief on his long, country arm). Amazed, Hump just stared back at the screaming Ray and let his arm be lowered four or five inches toward the earth.

"My God, why's he *doing* that?" said Dorothy and grabbed Santo's arm.

"That's from karate," he told her. "Yelling concentrates the energy. It's not a bad idea." Then in a casual tone he told Hump to get himself together.

Ray's body was twisted around his effort, his face was buried in his chest. He screamed, drew breath, screamed again. It chilled the blood. Still looking concerned, Hump brought the two arms back upright, checked Ray one last time, shrugged and put him down with one sweet, effortless pull toward his chest. "Yay!" said Dorothy. "Yay, Hump." She giggled and Hump grinned up at her.

Later in the afternoon they tried to get Dorothy up on skis. But she was tight from the wine and soft in the arm and she kept falling in a formless heap, skis splayed, before her hips cleared water. Craig handled the rope and spotted her from the back of the boat.

Santo drove. He was very patient with her and when after five attempts she bobbed by the boat, exhaustedly trying to smile, a thin thread of mucous hanging from her nose, he patted her head again and helped her into the boat.

"I used to be good. I really did," she panted.

"Oh, you can see that," Joe said. "You're just out of practice."

Then Craig skied double with Mary Tate for about five minutes, until she got bored and yelled over the engine at Santo that she wanted to go the slalom course; she was tired of screwing around.

The course was in a quiet piney cove about three miles from Mr. Santo's beach. It was made up of ten floating Clorox bottles anchored thirty yards from each other in a wavy line and arranged so that a skier being towed through them, with quick perfect turns, could round the outside of all the bottles. On the first run Santo drove slowly looking for logs and Mary Tate made all the turns easily. As they circled back she signaled Santo to shorten the rope. On the shorter rope she had to kick the tail of her ski faster around the bottle, and had to lean out closer to the water to make the ski's edge bite high—but she made all the buoys again. Craig, watching her quick, spare motions, was awed by the strength and concentration they required.

As soon as she had passed the last bottle Mary Tate signaled that she wanted the rope even shorter and Santo pulled another hitch in it. On her third run she missed two buoys. On the next one she missed four and as Santo circled for another try they could see her cursing behind a screen of spray.

But the next time she was perfect. By stretching her arms back toward the boat and heaving forward just before the bottles, she made them all. Santo whooped, and yelled over his shoulder to Craig and Dorothy that it was the best slalom he'd ever seen her make, that it was inspired, that America was built on slalom runs like that. He made an O with his fingers and shook it back at her and Mary Tate grinned and waved to him to take her through again.

Craig had sure instincts about chance. He knew as soon as Santo turned the boat that it was a mistake for Mary Tate to ski the course again. She had been through it five times—she had to be tired. He also knew there was nothing he could do about it. She nearly made it again; the tip of her ski caught the eighth bottle as she leaned toward it and she tumbled and gleamed into the air, graceful even in that, and plowed back into the water on her neck and shoulders.

Nobody in the boat doubted she was hurt. Santo's turn was like the loop of an L and it sprawled Dorothy against him. Dorothy made a coy, giggling noise and for the second or third time that day Craig could easily have hit her. Santo ran the boat full throttle to within a few feet of Mary Tate, then he swung it broadside to her and cut the engine. She was curled up in the water holding her knees. Craig dove to her off the stern, took her by the arms and sidestroked to the boat.

Dorothy was leaning over the gunwale, in their way. "Is she all right?" she shrieked. "Are you OK, for God's sake?"

"Baby?" said Mary Tate.

Santo reached down, took her beneath the arms and lifted her like a child into the boat. She came up curved, holding her legs. He stretched her out on the back seat and began feeling gently over her legs and back.

"I'm all right," she said. "Baby, did you see that run?"

"Why are you all scrunched up?" said Dorothy.

"Where does it hurt?" Santo asked her.

"The fall didn't hurt. It's my stomach. I've got this bitching pain in my stomach."

"She's so . . . *white*," said Dorothy, gone pale herself. "What if she . . . ? I mean my *father* . . ."

"She's all right," Santo said. He straightened up, gave Mary Tate a little slap on the tail and laughed.

"You strictly made a slalom run."

"Don't you think you ought to get her to a doctor?" Craig asked him and was surprised at the edge on his voice.

"Yep," said Santo. He turned on the motor. "You see if you can keep old Dick Pope, Jr., still on that seat."

On the way in Mary Tate's pain got worse and when they reached the dock she couldn't straighten her legs. Santo carried her from the boat to the car where Dr. Elijah Wright, who had followed them up from the beach, insisted on examining her.

"Abdominal muscles contracted. Uh huhh. Could be the spleen," said Doctor Wright, toying with Mary Tate's bare brown stomach. "Or a torn muscle . . ."

"What the shit do you know," Mary Tate said. She lay on the back seat, her face pale and strained, chewing on her lower lip.

"Of course the whole region is, uh, tender—could be something else. No medical experience myself. Appendix maybe?" He looked up at Craig, who was watching from the front. His eyes were small and dark like a furred animal's.

"I don't know. But do you suppose you could take your hands off her now?"

Craig sat beside her in the hot back seat. He covered her with a towel and made a pillow of clothes under her head. He squeezed her hand; he smiled at her . . . It was a new ball game.

"Hi, Swamp," she said.

Santo started the big Pontiac and the gunned motor roared lustily into the sunshine. They waved good-by to the people around the car and Santo slipped the car in gear . . .

But Dorothy! It was Mary Tate who finally noticed that Dorothy wasn't with them. Neither was she among the group outside. Where she was was out at the end of the dock, sitting between Hump and Franklin, swinging her legs, quaffing wine and laughing like hell as Franklin hauled up bluegill after bluegill. Santo went down to get her and brought her back after a brief argument with Hump. Hump had decided that he wanted to take her home.

The nearest town was Arab, Alabama, and Santo, driving like the wind, had them there in fifteen minutes. From a service station they got the address of a doctor. He was a baby doctor, the attendant said, but he was the only one he could think of.

The baby doctor lived in a little lime-green house in the middle of town. They came squealing into his driveway with the horn blowing and when the startled doctor opened his door, there was Santo trotting up the walk, huge and grim as Tarzan suddenly appeared in the middle of his Sunday afternoon. The doctor let himself be led skiddishly out to the car. He nodded through the window to Craig and Dorothy and helped Santo take Mary Tate into the house. Craig waited in the car with Dorothy who was clucking to herself and shaking her head.

"How do you feel?" Craig asked her, and realized that it was the first time he had spoken to, or even noticed, her in hours. She seemed to have gotten nasty drunk since then.

Dorothy shook her head. "Wouldn ever work. We come from two differnt worls." She sang the line. "Weee come from two differnt worls . . . No Craig, old frien. It wouldn ever work."

"What?" said Craig.

"Hump and me."

"You and Hump."

"Craig"—she gave her head a resigned, dramatic little toss and looked unsteadily out the window at the swingset in the baby doctor's yard—". . . he ast me to maayi him, Craig."

Now it was Craig who found himself patting Dorothy, patting her drunk head while she stared bravely out the window into the little green yard.

Nothing serious was wrong with Mary Tate. The doctor said that the fall and shock of the cold water had brought on the cramps of her period a few days early. He gave her an injection of morphine for the pain and told Santo to get her home and into bed as soon as he could. The doctor was very nice. He wrapped Mary Tate in a yellow blanket off one of his children's beds and he refused to take any money for the blanket or the morphine or the interruption to his Sunday. He told Santo that it had been his pleasure and that Santo, by the way, looked exactly like this anatomy chart he had had in medical school.

She lay against Craig all the way to Birmingham, moaning and jerking and whispering at first and then, as the drug quieted the uterine contractions and loosened her thoughts, she started humming to herself. It was nearly six o'clock. The lowering sun was in their eyes and the air through the car was ripe and cooling. His hands rested on her shoulders. Beneath the blanket, her vitality numbed, she felt spare, even frail. In the front seat Dorothy was asleep and Santo was silent, driving fast. He turned around three or four times to check Mary Tate and once he winked at Craig. It was a strange time. With the late sun in his eyes, in the broken quiet of the car, with Mary Tate reduced to a warm unfamiliar holding of wool and flesh beneath his hands Craig felt drugged himself and proprietary and anxious.

Halfway home Dorothy woke up and got sick. Santo stopped to clean out the car and to get her a Coca-Cola. "God, I've never been so embarrassed," she said while they waited for him, her head back on the seat and the monogrammed towel over her poised, pretty face. "You let this happen, Craig."

When Santo came back she was sitting up. She drank the Coke silently, fixed her face in the rearview mirror and hunched up stiff and ominous against the door. She didn't speak again until they were just outside of Birmingham.

Mary Tate was singing something softly on his leg. The words ran together, murmurous and uninflected. It was a strange sweet song, like a lullaby in a foreign language. "What's that song?" he asked, leaning over her.

"'Marezidotes andosidotes andlittlelambsidivy . . .'" she sang. "'Akkidllidivy too, woodenyou?'"

"*What's* she saying?" asked Dorothy scornfully.

"That's nice," Craig said.

"I love that song." Mary Tate crooned onto his leg. "My father would *sing* that and *sing* that to me . . ."

85

"Your friend Hump taught me a *lovely* song," Dorothy told Santo. "God what a song."

". . . Mare—zee-dotes. Say that," Mary Tate told him.

"You all want to hear it?" Dorothy asked and her voice was suddenly shrill and bitter. Nobody answered her.

"Now, *do—zee—dotes*. See? Does eat oats . . ."

"'Oh my numbers number one,'" Dorothy began, "'and the fun has just begun, roll me over lay me down and do it again. Roll me Oover in the clOover, roll me over . . .'"

"That's nice, Dorothy. That's a funny song," said Santo. It stopped her as cold as if he'd closed a box on her.

From the back Mary Tate's voice came up low and private, each word separate and soft, suspended in its own clear melody. "'A kid—will eat ivy too—wouldn't youuu' . . . You see, Swamp?" There was a long silence in the car.

"I really love that song," she whispered.

Craig bent over her, took her face in his hands as though he had been doing it for years and kissed her. He kissed her throat and mouth and open eyes and found after a minute with some surprise that she was kissing him back, mouth still murmuring, bringing him down against her.

When he looked up again they were inside the city limits and miles past the turn-off to Ensley where Mary Tate's apartment was. Santo drove on silently down Third Avenue, through the city and out of it again going south toward the mountain. Craig knew what he was doing before he told him.

"Listen," Santo said. "That guy said to get her to bed as soon as we could and your place is the closest. I'm going to let her off with you." Dorothy made a snuffing noise with her nose and cleaved closer to the door.

They passed through the dim, neat affluence of Woodstream Village, out to the Florida highway and up through the ugly cut in Shades Mountain from whose red, iron-rich soil most of the affluence had come (Would I mine for ore as the white man does? Santo told him Joseph, great chief of the Nez Percé, once mused;

86

Would I tear out my mother's ribs?) past the reservoir, its water calm and striped with moon, that houses on the mountain landscaped their views of to make seem a wild mountain lake, then up Blake Hill Road, the sky getting larger and excited with stars as they climbed, to the house—his house, that smelled quietly of boxwood.

The big Pontiac stopped and Santo turned off the motor. In the welling silence and dark, his hands full of drugged, murmuring stranger, it occurred to Craig that he had never, not even as a child, spent the night here in the same room with anyone.

Santo helped him ease her out of the car and his hands on her were polite and unpossessive. When she was standing, leaning on Craig, only half awake, Santo pecked her on the cheek. "Night, honey," he said. "Sleep tight. Don't worry about Dorothy," he told Craig. "I'll get her some eggs at the Dobbs House before I take her home."

"Uh, Joe . . ."

Santo tapped him on the shoulder. "Hang in there. You'll do fine."

"Good night, Dorothy," Craig said, bending to the window. There was not a sound from Dorothy.

Santo got back in the car and they were gone. Craig watched the tail lights as far as he could down the hill, a small gorge of panic in his throat, then he half carried Mary Tate up the wide stone steps and into the house. Still wrapped in the yellow blanket, formless, she was like some big present Santo had left him that he had no idea what to do with. He propped her against the door and she looked at him as he fumbled for a lamp chain.

"Don't turn it on," she said. "Come here." She took his hands and looked around the dark room. "What room is this? What did y'all used to do in here?"

All at once he went calm, placid as the moon-streaked reservoir below them. "It's a sort of parlor."

"Uhhh."

"Do you want something to eat?"

87

"No." She stood up straight, shrugged off the blanket and was suddenly unwrapped—unexpectedly lovely and vulnerable-looking in the pale swimsuit.

Her fingers glided up his back beneath the shirt, lambent and curious on the unfamiliar skin, to his shoulders. He held her bare waist with both hands as she kissed him, then slid them down her hips and peeled away the bottom of the swimsuit. It was mostly accidental and he half expected her to scream, but she flattened against him, moaning, working with his pants. "Oh babybaby-baby." She blew in his ear. The humps of her buttocks were tight and round as oranges and he kneaded them, sliding his fingers through the moist creases they made with her thighs.

On the Blake parlor floor was a huge Kashan carpet, a very old, brilliant oriental. "I've started," she said as he eased her down on it and covered her. "I'm all . . . slippery, baby." But she was taking off her bra as she said it and Craig didn't hear. Rocking wetly in her he pushed up from the waist, just off her spongy swell of breast, and looked at Mary Tate. Her head rolled back and forth, her eyes were closed, her mouth fluttered on fragments of moans and words and breath. Her face was remote and intent. Watching her thus he gave himself up inside her with relief so deep his bones seemed to shake. And as Mary Tate's rhythm mounted, as their liquids bled darkly into the vivid Persian design, whorled as a lake bed beneath them, Craig Blake felt himself totally possessor and possessed. He felt ten feet tall and stronger than life.

9

THE SUN GOT them up at nine. He brought her cereal and eggs and she ate sitting crosslegged on the bed, her eyes puffy, wearing an old blue shirt of his like a nightgown. From a chair Craig watched her and enjoyed her being in his room.

It was large and handsome, more like a study than a bedroom. He had paneled it himself with wide oak boards. The carpet was thick, the color of old moss. In each of three corners was a wing chair covered with black leather. A drake wood duck stared down from the writing desk; a pair of quail fed on the bookcase, and a smallmouth bass, its mouth wide, arched above the bed. At the far end of the room stood a tall glass-fronted cabinet, big as a telephone booth, with fishing rods hanging three deep from its roof. Above the cabinet two shotguns and a scoped rifle were cradled in an ornate rack.

All around her were exotically turned things—an Eskimo skinning knife, an old crossbow—but what fixed Mary Tate's attention as she munched her cereal were ten or twelve large framed photographs nearly covering one wall. The pictures were all in color and all of Craig: waving from the cockpit of a glider; shirtless on a dock by a hung tarpon nearly as tall as he; on his knees outside a log building lifting the antlers of a mule deer that bled quietly from the mouth; in waders and a red-checked shirt, snow-peaked mountains in the background, holding a huge trout with a crimson patch on its cheek . . .

"You like the way you look, huh?"

Her voice sounded tired and irritable. He saw that the pictures annoyed her and he wanted them not to.

"That's about all I've got to show for the last two years. I haven't been worth much of a shit lately." He saw her face soften as he hoped it would. He looked at the floor, made his voice very quiet. "Those were all new . . . experiences. Things I learned something from, Mary Tate. Now I own them. I hang up pictures to remember what getting them was like."

"Oh." She poked at an egg with her fork.

"You understand?"

"I think I can handle it."

After breakfast she went back to bed and he wandered through the house straightening furniture, dusting a table and opening the french doors to the bright morning air. He did some push-ups outside on the lawn and ran down to the stables and back. Then he took a cold shower and around ten-thirty he called Foss.

"It's ten-thirty," said Foss.

"I'm not coming in."

"You sick? Where the hell were you yesterday—we waited on you all morning. We had to pick up a fourth."

"I got tied up. Look, tell Uncle Henry I won't be in, all right? Maybe not tomorrow either."

"You know we're supposed to look at that property on the Cahaba. You *started* that deal. The guy can only get away on Tuesdays."

"Don't whine, Foss. Just get Fay to change the appointment to next Tuesday."

". . . Halsey was really pissed off about the golf."

"Uh huh. Look, Hal, get her to change the appointment and I'll see you on Wednesday."

After some wheat germ and coffee he put in an order on the phone with a gorcery store that delivered, and called a truck farmer from Newmerkle who used to mow grass for his father. Then everything was done that needed to be done and he got back in bed with Mary Tate, feeling very good. In a little while he heard the lawnmower down near the pasture—its pleasant drone blew through the screen like wind.

Mary Tate woke again around noon, fresh and rested this time, and went to the kitchen to call Thor. He waited for her outside on the pavilion. She was gone a long time and when she came out her hands were full of figs.

"I saw them out the window—I love these things. Jesus, what a *view*. Is that Birmingham?"

"That's it."

"Joe already told him."

"Told who?"

"Thor. Joe told him I was sick and maybe wouldn't be in all week. Do you believe it? Is that OK? I mean I feel all right. I could go home." She bit off a fig at the stem and looked at him, standing with her weight on one leg, her hip cocked out. She had tied the tails of his shirt around her waist.

"Why don't we call this home?"

"I'm sorry about your sheets, hon. I need to get some things."

"I already ordered them."

"Good." She smiled. "I'm sorry to be riding the rag for you, baby."

The crudeness of the phrase turned him on like a switch and he pulled her to him by the knot of the shirt. She dropped the figs and in a moment they were down among them on the warm pavilion boards where the sun lay thick as cream.

He took her through the house—into airless musty rooms upstairs that hadn't been opened for over a year. Pensively she looked at his grandmother's collection of prints and books and glass, his mother's Wedgwood. "What are you going to do with all this stuff?" she asked him, fooling with a china cream pitcher.

"Sell it. Give it away, keep it—I don't know," he told her truthfully.

They went outside through the high-ceilinged old kitchen with its rolling pins and meat grinder and butter churns and came out in back of the house. By the door of the porch was a thick clump of bamboo. Mary Tate broke off one of the tapered leaves and chewed it as they walked down the service driveway, gravel crunching under their feet, between two privet hedges. On their left were fig trees and the long shade of a scuppernong arbor, the vines curling delicately around the gray bark of the trellises. Below the arbor the ground fell off sharply in a jumble of rocks and woods down to the highway. A flock of mourning doves scattered loudly in front of them. The sun was warm and heavy and the building humidity brought out the green hedge odor and the nostalgic smell of honeysuckle.

Mary Tate looked around her as she walked and made a purring sound in her throat. "It's like a whole green world—like a story. Everything's so goddamn quiet."

At the end of the gravel road was the garage, and below that the crumbling stables and milking barn, the turkey pens and garden. They passed the moldy hill of ten-foot logs his grandfather had used in the living room fireplace, still banked neatly against the garage, split once and barked the way he wanted them. Craig took her inside the barn where the air was cool and stale and through the tack room with its long-unused English saddles and curry combs and halters and crops. The hard smells of leather and hay aroused him again and he considered the loft but Mary Tate thought the barn was gloomy and wanted to go back outside.

Through a rotting metal gate they entered the garden that was hot and aswarm with insects. A few day lilies and marigolds and larkspur pushed up through the weeds. He told her what it had been like when his mother and a gardener tended it—row after row of dahlias and calla lilies and roses and gladioli; below them a full acre of vegetables.

Mary Tate was delighted with the huge seedy garden. She knelt and deftly weeded a lily, her fingers moving like glints of sun, her face gay and empty as a child's. Then she stood, spread her arms and twirled around in front of him. "God, I love it. It's all *perfect*. Can't we just stay up here, Swamp? And have people bring us things?" She danced, cross-stepping perfectly over a row of weeds, and hummed. "We can eat hot dogs outside under them grapevines and drink Cokes . . . dadadada dadadada dadada*da* da da . . ."

Dragonflies buzzed around her like tiny helicopters and the sun clung to her like cloth. She danced to the end of the row, whirled and started back, the garden humming with her.

Watching her throb toward him down the aisle of weeds, dazzled by her, Craig, who loathed hot dogs, couldn't imagine a more perfect life. "Hell yes we can," he cried, groping toward her. "You bet your ass we can."

His pleasure in Mary Tate was perfect except for one thing and that tortured him. All that day and the night before he had tried to bury it under whatever they were doing, knowing they would eventually have to get to it. The thing was Santo.

93

He asked himself endless questions: What did Santo have going with her? Why the hell had he made all this so easy? And what if he decided he wanted her *back?* Wondering that made him frantic to enclose her, to dig a moat around her. He imagined her with Santo, saw them together, and wished his own arms bigger, his calves fuller. Twice that day when he stood up naked before her he stood quivering with every muscle tensed.

It finally came out that afternoon, nastily, on the way to Ensley where he insisted on driving her to "get her things." He wanted her formally moved in. On the way he stopped at a jewelry store in Woodstream Village with a craving to buy her something. "Anything you want," he told her and Mary Tate giggled and walked with mock seriousness among the sparkling counters, handling things, deciding against them with a wag of her head, putting them down. She finally settled on a tacky pair of sunglasses, its frame set in rhinestones. He laughed when she brought it over but she was serious. "They're the only cheap thing in here," she said.

"*I* don't have to get you cheap stuff," he said. She looked up at him and he hated himself.

After a long silence back in the car he finally asked her what Santo was going to do about her moving in.

"What's he going to *do?* What do you mean? He set it up."

Craig knew that was true but hearing it annoyed him. "I don't need him to set things up," he said peevishly.

After a minute she said, "You don't want me to then?" Her voice was dangerous.

"Of *course* I do. Hell yes I do. I just meant . . . well. I mean what's the deal between you and him?"

Mary Tate wouldn't answer. Wearing the sunglasses on the tip of her nose she stared out the window and did not speak except to direct him to the apartment.

She lived on a mean street in central Ensley, in one half of a duplex across from a restaurant called The Catfish King. She was out of the car before he turned off the motor, but he caught her just as she reached the door and held her by the shoulders. Her face was taut and furious; there were tears smeared below the glasses.

"Look, you don't have to talk about Joe. You don't have to say a goddamn thing. I'm sorry I brought it up. Now go get your stuff because if you don't come back with me I'm staying here."

She looked around in his eyes and her face calmed like a fist unclenching. She wrinkled her nose. Gratefully, he kissed her on the forehead.

But on the way back to the mountain she did talk about Santo: casually, while she chewed on a big apple from her apartment. She said that they had been, well, sort of into each other for about a year, ever since she arrived in Ensley from Opp without a job and met him at a party. He loved her, she reckoned—but he was strange. He had tried before to get her to date somebody else. He wanted her to have anything she wanted.

"Joe don't need people," she said, pursing her lips. "He hates to own anything. He's like a saint like that. That's what's screwing him up with that bastard Thor. He coulda *had* his own studio by now if he'd of wanted it. But he don't."

"Why not?" Craig decided he could quit worrying about Santo, who seemed to him now to have a definitely crazy streak.

"He says it would take up all his time. Put him in a niche, he says. That's why the Mr. Southeast is so important. If Joe can win that and maybe a couple more he can make enough money endorsing stuff in magazines and all to pay Thor back. If he wants to, that is." She dropped the subject with a shrug, propped both knees against the dash and fiddled with the radio. She had swapped the swimsuit for rope sandals and a short blue dress that clung to her like Saran Wrap and had put on perfume and pale pink lipstick. Craig could barely keep his hands on the wheel.

At a liquor store in English Village he stopped and hurriedly bought a fifth of scotch and three bottles of Mumm's. When he came out he could see heavy rain clouds building over the mountain to the south and he drove toward them happily, feeling snug.

95

Beside him Mary Tate hummed to the radio. Her white vinyl luggage made a pale mound on the seat behind them.

He was amorous. He was indolent. He could lie content for hours just looking at her. He seemed to develop a new layer of nerves, to be able to feel her when she was ten feet away. It rained all that night and the next day and most of that night, and the quiet rain mixed the day and nights together as they ate (oddly: out of cans, raw cabbage, figs), drank champagne, slept wherever they happened to be and made love.

At that Mary Tate was inventive and untiring—she made him try it standing and sitting, in the tub, on floors and couches and in the rain on the fresh cut grass. She was skillful and generous, quick with her hips and quick to come, which she did over and over, nibbling and clawing and rolling her feisty tongue inside his mouth.

Craig didn't care if he never left the mountain again. He found himself completely happy with a woman for the first time. He had had others, more than his share, he figured, but they had all been either easy pickups, bar waitresses and student nurses with carnivorous eyes, or girls like the ones he had grown up with, like Dorothy Stephens, whose element was conversation and to whom you usually had to lie to sleep with.

Mary Tate was a new experience for him. She was beautiful and gentle and simple. Everything pleased her; she seemed to want nothing more than what was at hand. And she loved to screw. Craig was amazed at her ardor. He wondered if maybe it had something to do with being from the country . . . if maybe everyone in Opp made this kind of urgent love all day. He began to imagine he could smell the earth about her; he grew fascinated with her strong feet and murmured to her rapturously about her peasant toes. She smiled and held him and said OK. She moved whenever he moved. She was adoring and tender as a child. The sharpness and independence he had seen in her at Guntersville were gone.

Sometime toward dawn on Wednesday he woke with a lump in

his throat at the wholeness and simplicity of her lying next to him in the dark bed, this healthy beautiful country girl. He imagined dusk in a trailer court, Mary Tate and he were in lawn chairs on a green patch of yard, sipping iced tea as the sun sank. There were barefoot children playing, a clothesline, a barbecue grill. And Craig, cooling off after a solid day on his crane, say, wondered idly what was for dinner, turned a page of his paper and didn't need a thing. The calm dignity of the scene touched him and he drew her to him, gently this time so not to wake her.

10

Santo hardly ever got out of bed in the morning before ten o'clock. He was awakened every day between nine-thirty and nine forty-five by his landlady's dishwasher upstairs, and he liked to lie in bed, his hands behind his head, and look down at the two blocks of Twentieth Street that he could see from his window where everything was going full tilt. He kept his bed next to the window even in winter for that purpose. His apartment was in an old brownstone, one of the oldest in Five Points. Across the street was a Medical Arts Center and often the first people Santo saw in the morning were bandaged or on crutches or in wheelchairs. There were only three other apartments in the building, two on the ground floor and one beside his on the second floor. The people who lived in those were all gone by nine-thirty and the building was always quiet except for the thrum of the dishwasher and the sounds that filtered in off the street.

Santo would lie in his bed watching the street and wake his body by tightening it one muscle at a time to see if there was any new soreness anywhere. After a while he would get up and make a milkshake for breakfast. The milkshakes were Thor's idea. Santo would put two glasses of Tiger's Milk, a banana, three raw eggs, honey, protein powder, peanut butter and wheat germ oil into a mixer and beat it all into a heavy yellow liquid. He drank the stuff slowly and thumbed through a few of the twelve magazines he subscribed to. Then he would wash out the mixer, shave and make the bed. The bed was old and the frame was made of brass. He had bought it in a junk store for three dollars. In addition to it Santo's furniture consisted of a table, three straight-back chairs, an old bookshelf that held his pieces of pressed glass, a refrigerator and a hot plate. But the apartment did not seem particularly bare. There was a nice oval rug on the floor that came with the place. And he had tacked up some posters. There was one of Julie Christie looking emotional, and a color print of Canada geese at dawn setting their wings over a field of corn stubble. The room got plenty of light and Santo liked everything about it except the wall paper, which was peeling and stained to the color of old mustard.

If it was not raining he would walk to the YMCA. It was a long walk that took him past office buildings and motels and banks and clothing stores. He had passed all these places maybe two hundred times before but he never got tired of noticing the different ways they dealt with the day. He talked to quite a few people on these walks and it was usually eleven-thirty before he trotted up the steps of the Y, waved to the girl at the desk and pushed through the big glass door and the turnstile into the locker room. The locker room was quiet and smelled strongly of disinfectant at this time of day, before the businessmen arrived. Santo would change quickly into a sweat suit and jock, three pair of socks and leather jogging shoes. Over the top of the sweat suit he pulled an old rubber rain jacket.

First he would run a mile around the track upstairs to loosen up, swinging his arms and breathing deeply. It was hot upstairs and he broke his sweat quickly and could sprint the last five laps cool and relaxed. Just off the track he did a hundred twists and sidebends and a hundred quick sit-ups, then he went down to the gym and shot baskets for a half hour, mostly jumpshots and lay-ups to keep his sweat. After that he would skip ten minutes of rope, up on his toes to stretch out the calf muscles, and beat the speed bag for fifteen minutes, raising and lowering his hands as different parts of his shoulders loosened.

At one o'clock he usually went down to the handball courts for a game with Calcagno, who jogged a thousand miles a year and was sixty pounds lighter than Santo, and who usually beat him. After the handball Santo would run another mile around the track, which was clogged by then with runners clicking off their laps on little plastic counters, and then cool off on a bench in the gym where he could watch a volleyball game as he waited for his body to calm to the right heartbeat and temperature, and for the stiffness to start to seep into his lower back.

He always took ten minutes of steam and there would be businessmen in the steam room talking about the stock market or management trainee programs or something. Santo loved the sound of those conversations and occasionally he joined them whether he knew anything about the subject or not, just to participate in the brass-tacks, good-humored sound of them.

After the steam he took a quick cold shower, a massage, and then a long warm shower. He would stand under the second shower for maybe ten minutes, with his whole body feeling new and his skin newly stretched, letting the water pour over his head.

This was his favorite moment of the day. His body was loose and relaxed and ready for the heavy work he would put it to that night. As the warm water ran over his head Joe Santo was his best and happiest self. Nothing bothered him then. Everything came together and looked wonderful on the yellow tiles before being swirled with his salts down the drain.

On the way to the studio he usually stopped at Al's Knife and Fork and had a minute steak with four eggs broiled on top of it and fried okra and sliced tomatoes.

For the next three weeks Craig and Mary Tate got together with Santo only a few times. Thor, he told them, had him working his tail off to get up for the Mr. Southeast, bombing for two or three grueling hours every night and stretching out all morning at the Y. Craig worked-out with him on Wednesday and Friday evenings and when they finished around nine o'clock they would walk down to Myoto's and meet Mary Tate for dinner. Then for an hour or two they would drink saki and eat egg rolls and pork strips, and Santo would talk with great verve about how various muscles were coming along as though they were children being educated.

Santo had made it impossible for the three of them to stop being friends or even to feel uncomfortable with each other, ever since the Wednesday night after Mary Tate had moved to the mountain. She and Craig had both gone back to work that day. Mary Tate had called Craig in the afternoon from the studio and said that Joe would like to see him around six if he was free. Listening to her say that, Craig had felt suddenly, unreasoningly terrified that maybe he had been set up, that maybe Mary Tate and Santo were out to get him. Did they want money? He gripped the phone, listening for violence in her breathing. Finally, with a trembling voice he said OK, by God, he'd be there.

By six o'clock his uncertainty about what Santo wanted with him had congealed and he was truculent and determined when he walked onto the floor of the studio. He carried his hands loosely at his side. Santo was lying down, doing tricep presses with a dumbbell. Craig walked around in front of him so he could watch the big fellow's navel as he had read pro football players do when trying to anticipate sudden moves.

"Well hey, buddy," said Santo. He dropped the dumbbell.

"OK. You wanted to see me and now I'm here," Craig said grimly, staring at his middle. "I've got friends in the car."

"I thought we could take a workout together if you and Mary aren't doing anything, and then maybe grab some Jap food." Santo stood up suddenly and stuck out his big hand. Craig froze. "Look I want to congratulate you, old buddy. I've never seen her in a better mood than today—she was grinning and singing all over the place."

At that Craig raised his eyes finally from Santo's stomach and found himself looking into the sweetest grin he had ever seen. He felt his own face go slack with surprise and admiration.

Since then whenever the three of them were together Santo had come on like a big brother—teasing them, asking if there was anything they needed. He treated Mary Tate with a tender sort of deference, as someone might treat his best friend's wife.

Occasionally at their suppers Craig would catch Mary Tate staring oddly at Santo, but whatever the expression was it didn't bother him. Over the last couple of weeks his concern and jealousy had burned off like fog. It seemed obvious now, however incomprehensible, that Santo had no designs on swiping Mary Tate back; and she had shown no signs of wanting to be swiped. She was happy on the mountain—she told Craig over and over that she had never been so happy. And neither had he. She had filled his refrigerator with Cokes and hot dogs and lemon pies, and his kitchen sink with unwashed dishes. She had littered his room with clothes and dirty towels, and on his desk now stood a huge, tacky, water-skiing trophy, all nickel and fake marble and scroll. But he didn't seem to care about any of it. He cheerfully used the trophy as a paperweight.

Shortly after she moved in he had taken her back to Ensley to get her car, and now each afternoon when he came home and saw it, a homely old green Ford parked in the circle in front of the house, the whole house could have been full of dirty dishes and underclothes and it would not have lessened his excitement. She would have been home for an hour by the time he got there and he always found her outside, always with some new shine of joy on her face—swinging in a pecan tree, chasing cows in the pasture, or in the garden. Her pleasure in the garden was so touching that he had hired a part-time gardener to replant and tend it for her. He would gladly have bought her a tractor to play with down there had she asked for it, for though he wasn't sure exactly what it was they were doing with each other he was sure he wanted it to continue. And just as it was. So far she had made no demands on him and Craig avoided thinking about what the relationship might develop into. But once in a while during these weeks (Mary Tate and Santo would be swapping rice or something; involved in each other) he couldn't help wondering what it was the two of them had in mind.

On the second Wednesday in July he got to the studio about five-thirty, just as Santo was finishing his stomach. Santo had on sandals and a pair of green shorts that said Ensley High School. His tee shirt with the bucking mustang on the front lay across a sit-up bench. His stomach from the sternum to the top of his shorts was flushed from the exercise and his abdominal muscles looked like short thick sections of hose. On the soft drink machine sat Newton, his face wizened as black leather, sullenly watching. Thor was reading in his office. A policeman named Andrews who came up often at night was working out with Santo, and Craig picked them up as they began the shoulder work.

Santo was "bombing" now for the contest which was only three weeks away—attacking his body with heavy weights and many repetitions to carve each muscle's outline cleaner and divide each muscle group into separate but connected territories. His workouts for the last three weeks had been grave and furious. Craig, using less than half the weight he used, could just keep up. And beer-fat Andrews puffed and strained and shook his head, one or two exercises behind them both.

"Santo," Andrews said, "someday you're gonna pull a gut up here and I tell you *one* damn thing, I'm gonna be here and I'm gonna laugh my ass off."

Santo chuckled and went smoothly on with a set of behind-the-neck presses. His deltoid muscles strained under the weight, round and dense as cannon balls at the top of his arms.

"Tha's all what Buminham need all right—a bunch of fat ass lazy cops," Newton said with a cackle.

"You little black turd. I ever catch you in the street I'll teach you how to talk," Andrews told him.

"You ain't bout to get your white-trash hands on none of me, offica."

Newton meant that. He and Andrews were not friends and Andrews had a grim reputation. The first thing Craig had heard about him (from Franklin) was that Andrews knew how to take out an eye with one finger, like popping an olive out of a bottle.

"You're getting behind, Andrews," Santo said. He was beginning his first set of seated presses with eighty-pound dumbbells.

Andrews lay on his back on the sit-up board sweating and panting. "Go on, man," he said, "I'm tired of this shit." He looked up as Craig took the forty-pound dumbbells from the rack. "What the fuck are you doing down here, Blake? Rich as cream and down here grunting and pumping iron like a poor man."

"I come down to see you, Andrews."

Andrews grunted and sat up. "You over-the-mountain smart-asses got a lot of mouth."

"He ain't stutin you, offica," Newton said in his shrill voice that made everything he said sound like an emergency. "He wouldn't speak to you if he saw you on the street. He buy you and sell you with the change in his pocket."

"I ought to cut your balls off," Andrews said and wearily rubbed the back of his neck with a towel.

After a few days of listening to it Craig had finally figured out that the violence and lechery, the ceaseless talk of cutting and pumping and stomping, were just polite conventions in the conversation at the Olympic. He hardly noticed it any more.

As usual Santo put on the Batman costume for his arm work which was mostly seated and required all his concentration. The mask made him inapproachable. No one spoke to him while he had it on, as he sat curling, or pressing from his triceps, looking strange and mythic and capable of calm superhuman deeds. Whoever happened to be in the studio then lay down their iron and watched quietly as the great arms expanded and contracted, stretched and bulged under the cape, and the masked, square-jawed face stared impassively back at them.

The workout ended about eight o'clock and Thor came out of his office to direct Santo's poses. They had grown steadily more massive since the first time Craig had watched. It was impossible now to imagine a larger arm, a broader back or a deeper chest. Yet all Santo's proportions were still graceful. Craig could squint his eyes at the poses and Santo would become a Renaissance goblet or an hourglass—some kind of a wrought, inhumanely balanced shape. The biggest problem Thor told him now, was skin tone. He told Santo to get less sun on his back and to start using moisturizing cream.

At nine o'clock they met Mary Tate at Myoto's. Over dinner Santo mentioned that the Mr. Gulf Coast contest was being held that weekend in Mobile and asked if Craig and Mary Tate wanted to go down for it. The contest was sponsored by Thor's Mobile Club. Thor was going down to present the awards and he, Santo, was on the panel of judges. Mary Tate was willing and Craig, who had never seen a body contest, said sure they would go. They would leave Saturday morning, said Santo, and come back that night after the contest. They could go down in Thor's air-conditioned Continental.

"Stewart will probably take it," he said. "He's big time now but he likes to win these little ones." He shook his head. "He's a good boy, Stewart, but he has practically no sense of style."

"Is that Mr. Mississippi? The guy you thought I worked for?"

"The same. I'm still not sure you don't."

"Joe won the Gulf Coast three years in a row," Mary Tate told Craig. "Till Stewart started raising hell about him working for Thor and it being Thor's contest and all."

Santo's busy hands were breaking little pieces off a fortune cookie and powdering them between his fingers onto his butter plate. "It's not a bad little contest. They've got a new auditorium and they pull a good crowd. They get a few good guys too. Lot of good backs down in that part of the country, and a lot of tattoos. There used to be a guy, three or four years ago. Name of Molloy. You remember me telling you about Molloy, Mary?" Mary Tate shuddered, remembering, and Santo laughed. "This crazy motha used to enter that contest every year and he had an *ear* on his chest—had it grafted on there or something. I mean it was growing there. Franklin says he took it off some guy down in Pascagoula." Santo had scooped the fortune-cookie dust into a little brown mountain on the plate. "He had a hell of a build but he never won cause of that ear, and he wouldn't take it off so finally he just quit competing. Old Molloy. He was a hell of a nice guy."

Santo put some money on his check and stood up, mountainous, still smiling about Molloy.

"You want a ride?" Craig asked him.

"Nope. It's a nice night, I think I'll walk. Besides y'all look tired. You ought to get more sleep," he said and winked at Mary Tate.

There was a gusty wind outside that scattered paper around his legs and stung his eyes with grit as Santo walked into it down Nineteenth Street out of town. At First Avenue he crossed over to Twentieth and followed it south toward Five Points, three miles away. On the way he waved through the streaked window of Young's Shoe Store at Henry, the black proprietor who had gotten rich selling whiskey and beer on Sunday. Tilted against the wall in a straight chair, Henry grinned his sleepy, bootlegger's grin and waved back.

He spoke to Phil who sold tamales in front of the Parliament House and then to the one-legged parking lot attendant who called himself Jeb Stuart. It was a beautiful night on the street. The wind was gusty and excited as laughter. It whirled scraps and bits of things like confetti above the sidewalk and they glittered in the creamy lights of passing cars. There were a lot of lights on Twentieth Street at night but Santo's favorites were high and distant. To the northeast, repeating the profile of the skyline was the cherry glow from the steel mill in Woodlawn that made him think, though he had never seen them, of the northern lights. The other light was four or five miles to the south, on top of Red Mountain in the outflung hand of Vulcan, the ironman, the mythical blacksmith and symbol of the city. The statue stuck up 180 feet, stark and narrow as a finger from the bare mountain, and showed the whole valley below a colored torch—red if somebody in Birmingham had killed somebody else that day, green if everyone had gotten through another day without being shot or stabbed or run over. The torch was usually red but tonight it was green, a healthy tropical color that Santo preferred to the red.

He jogged the last uphill blocks to his apartment, feeling wonderful, like another borne up part of the warm breezy night. It was eleven-thirty. He made another milkshake and drank it in bed as he thumbed through a *New Yorker*, a *Strength and Health* and an *American Horseman*.

He turned off his light before twelve and fell asleep, as he always did, immediately.

11

"THEY'RE VERY USEFUL things," Santo was saying.

He was turned around, his big arm strewn across the top of the front seat, talking about body contests into the back where Craig and Franklin sat on either side of Mary Tate. It was Saturday afternoon and they were busting down the four-lane highway to Montgomery in Thor's huge, ice-cold Lincoln. Thor was silent and scowling. Between his legs was a bottle of peppermint schnapps and bourbon, mixed half and half.

"Look, they make people see the body as something more than just a thing to carry your head around on, or be shot at, or screwed, or covered with clothes."

"Right," said Franklin, nodding. "Thas exakly right."

"The thing that inspired Michelangelo, Rodin, guys like that, was the human body. You take Reeves or Grimek or Park—those guys are walking art work. The fact that they don't know it or care doesn't make any difference." Santo turned around, drummed briefly on the dashboard. "In a way a bodybuilder is like the simplest kind of artist. He takes the only thing he really owns and develops it as far as it'll go. He's kind of a sculptor of himself."

"Uh huh," said Craig, who had started all this accidentally by asking what kind of weirdos came to these contests anyway.

"It's a living," Thor interrupted. "What line of work you in, Blake?" His voice was fuzzy and hostile.

"I sell real estate."

"For *Blake* Realty Company," Mary Tate added.

"Uh huh. You go to colletch to learn how to do that?"

"Well, yeah, I went to college."

"Fuck colletch," said Thor, lifting his bottle.

Santo went on as though no one had interrupted him. "It's easy to misunderstand a contest, to miss the point. People think there's something unnatural about all that greasing and flexing and everything. But when you watch a pose you shouldn't be worrying about any of that, or why the guy wants to be up there—you ought to be looking for what kind of *lines* he's put on himself."

"Cuts," Franklin said. "And proportion. Density, skin tone . . ."

"Franklin here is a connoisseur. He really knows how to look. It's like everything else—you dig around in it long enough, you're gonna find out where the joy is at."

Thor drove the curvy, two-lane road from Montgomery to Mobile like he was raping it. Flat out he roared through Hope Hull,

Georgiana, Castleberry. He slowed below sixty only once, in Brewton, where what looked like the whole population was draping banners and flags and colored lights over the town.

They made Mobile by six o'clock, an hour faster than Craig had ever heard of its being made before, and Thor stopped at a Dairy Queen on the outskirts of the city and bought them all hot dogs and onion rings and twirled ice-cream cones. He had finished his bottle and was not speaking at all any more.

While the rest of them were eating he walked unsteadily back to the car, took a pigskin valise from the trunk and disappeared into the men's room for twenty minutes. When he came out he was holding a fresh bottle of schnapps and bourbon by the neck and he was dressed in an incredible outfit.

"His big shot costume," Mary Tate smirked.

It was a jumpsuit made of purple velour with broad patches of sequins over each breast. With his stiff blond curls and his tanned, ingenuous face Thor looked a lot like a big six-year-old on his way to a party. He was suddenly in a benevolent humor.

"Can I get y'all anything else?" he asked.

"Show Craig the back of your suit, Thor honey," Mary Tate said.

Thor grinned and turned around, showing big letters the color of blood that spelled *Erickson's World-wide Health Studios and Spas* down his back.

"Gorgeous," said Mary Tate.

"Iss good for bidness," he said quietly.

The contest was being held in a new high school auditorium. It was a dim, cavernous place that smelled strongly of cleaning compound. It was already half full and filling fast when they got there, with a noisy, scruffy-looking crowd. In the flow of men in work clothes and women in shorts with their hair in rollers, the bodybuilders were not hard to spot. Though street clothes blunted them as they did Santo, enough to make all that carved bulk look like fat, they all had the same walk—a swinging, high-chested strut that bowed their arms away from their bodies.

Just inside the auditorium a big Mexican builder came up to shake hands with Thor.

"Jumbo Jimenez," Santo told Craig. "They call him The Vein. He took most-muscular at the IFBB Mr. Universe last year."

Jimenez wore a bright green double-breasted blazer, tight slacks, yellow pointed shoes and a floppy 1920 newsboy-style cap. Underneath the jaunty cap his face was thin, dour and scarred. With his left hand on Thor's shoulder he shook hands for a long time, staring gloomily at Erickson, then he moved his head to Erickson's ear and whispered something.

"Whassat you say, Vein?" Erickson asked impatiently.

"Plenny good brush at theese one," The Vein said, louder.

"That's right, Vein buddy. Look, we'll catch you later, hear," said Erickson and shouldered off through the crowd toward the stage.

Santo and Jimenez gave each other a friendly little poke in the stomach as they passed. "He's the guest poser. You'll get a kick outta him," Santo said. "Franklin, you take care of everything. I've got to get up there with the judges."

Franklin nodded and led Mary Tate and Craig to seats on the aisle of the third row. As they were going in, Jumbo Jimenez popped through the crowd at the edge of the stage waving and smiling a neat, mean smile, and was applauded mightily. At the same time, like an echo, came a separate volley of applause from the back.

Doug Stewart, Mr. Mississippi, had entered the auditorium.

Stewart was an extraordinary-looking person. He had brick red hair and very pale skin. He wore madras shorts, a white tee shirt and a black sombrero that was pulled down close to his nose and made him look cheerful and cruel at the same time, like a toy machine gun. He was followed as he bulled through the thickening crowd shaking hands right and left by a little boy who looked exactly like him and who carried a gym bag with Mr. Mississippi printed on the side. Stewart rumbled toward the front down the center aisle, his chest puffed out like a rutting pigeon and his little eyes raking the crowd until something next to Craig's head stopped them cold. Craig turned around to see Franklin locking looks with Stewart. They stared at each other until Stewart had swaggered past, with so pure a loathing that the air between them seemed to hum.

"Uh, what's that he's got in the bag, Franklin?" Craig asked pleasantly, sensing trouble.

Franklin was moving his feet on the floor in a dry, rapid shuffle. "His gear," he said after a moment, his eyes starting to come back to normal. "Baby oil, razor, posing suit, dumbbell . . . Look at that bastad now. Nosing Joe."

Santo was seated at a long table in front of the stage with three other men and a woman. Stewart was bending over him confidentially, one arm lying lightly over Santo's shoulder. As they talked the stage curtain above them parted suddenly and there was Thor Erickson, lounged over a microphone as though he were about to slide into song. Fifteen or twenty men were standing around behind him, arms bowed, staring at each other. At the back of the stage hung a black nylon scrim. Twenty feet in front of it, just behind Thor, was a posing platform covered with leopard-skin vinyl.

"Would all the contestants please come up now to be measured?" Thor asked resonantly and turned his inscribed back to the audience. The contest was underway.

There were nearly thirty contestants in all. When they had all been crowded onto the stage each was measured for his height and separated into one of three groups: shorts, mediums and talls. There would be a winner and a second place in each group, Franklin explained, and one of the winners, most likely the tall, would be chosen Mr. Gulf Coast. Erickson supervised the measuring, checking the tape and nodding each man into his proper group. Perspiration gleamed on his wide forehead and the sequins on his chest flashed like stars.

"He makes my flesh crawl," Mary Tate said, watching him. "I'm going to get a Coke."

"I like him. He's a little moody maybe . . ."

"Moody! Baby he's a snake. If he doesn't like you he'll have your arms broken—and he's not all that crazy about you."

"Me?"

"Well, he knows about us."

"Why the hell should he care about us?"

"He's been trying to get me to go out with him for a year," Mary Tate said. "He told me a long time ago that if I ever broke up with Joe he was moving in." She stood up. "The bastard *watches* me all day. He bored a hole in his floor over my desk."

While she was gone Craig thought about Thor hunched over a hole in his office floor watching Mary Tate at her desk. When he saw her coming back down the aisle, swaying toward him in her cool abstract way through the sweltering crowd of laborers, he felt nearly suffocated by pride and a sense of his own deficiency. She was his woman now. *His* woman. And he would have to protect her, broken arms or not.

After the builders had been measured they were herded off the stage into a big tent that had been devised on one side of the auditorium for a dressing room. The tent was actually a canvas screen about twenty yards long and eight feet high, running parallel to one wall of the auditorium and making a long cubicle with it that fed onto the stage. The screen didn't quite reach the floor and the contestants' feet were visible as they prepared themselves with quiet shuffling sounds like cattle in a boxcar.

Thor left the stage and was replaced by the M.C. for the evening—a small, slick-looking guy with candy-striped pants and a tenor voice. He tinkered with the microphone, cleared his throat and welcomed the huge hot crowd to the twelfth annual Mr. Gulf Coast Contest, sponsored again this year by the Mobile branch of Erickson's Olympic Studio and Spa. Respectfully, he introduced a few honored guests (among them Thor, a local Jaycee man of the month, the weather girl from a TV station) and then the judges. There was Miss Nina Patina, a renowned local entertainer (stripper, Franklin told them); an expert on macrobiotics named

114

Jess Gunn; the manager of Erickson's Mobile Club; Hubie Sellers, onetime winner of best abdominals in the Mr. America; and Santo —who drew the longest applause and was referred to by the M.C. as the Alabama Apollo.

During the introductions the activity behind the canvas had increased. Most of the feet were now bare. Craig could hear the clinking of iron and see dumbbells rising and falling rhythmically at the top of the screen.

"They're lifting *weights* in there?" he asked Franklin.

"Pumping up. Most of them bring a dumbbell and they do a few quick sets to pump before they come on."

"What else do they do back there?"

"Shave off all their body hairs, practice posing, grease."

"Grease?"

"They rub baby oil all over theirselves to bring out highlights in the spot."

"That's beautiful . . . you know that's Greek? Anointing themselves with Johnson's."

"Uh huh. Well, it's American too. A lot of 'em don't do it theirselves though, they got a greaser to do it. Stewart uses that little brother of his. I grease for Joe sometimes."

A hush had fallen on the crowd. The M.C. was introducing the guest poser.

"A few of these boys here today," he was saying, "if they train hard and develop, might well go on to MOVIE FAME much as our guest poser had done. Ladies and gentlemen—a man who has won more body titles than Carter has pills, a LEGEND in his own time, Mr. Everything—JUMBO JIMENEZ. With two minutes of routine."

The audience ruptured into shouts, whistles, applause.

"Movie fame?" Craig asked Mary Tate.

"Just commercials. But watch him, he's fantastic. He looks like he's been skinned."

The house lights of the Azalea Heights High School auditorium went off and two spotlights in the rear were trained on the leopard posing platform. At the edge of their light a flap at the end of the dressing tent opened and The Vein strode from it clad now only in a pair of silver posing trunks. He took the platform. He faced the dead-silent crowd, spread his legs, stretched out his arms like the Pope blessing Rome and with a sudden intake of breath locked into his first pose.

Every inch of Jumbo was flexed, from his flared Mayan nose to his curled feet, and he really did look *skinned*. He was transparent as a young oak leaf. It was the most whelming visual experience Craig had ever had—it was like looking at one of those subcutaneous charts that show the human body grotesquely naked of surface; that show the muscles as broad, striated ovoids, the tendons as eccentrically tapered cables, and over it all the mad red scampering of blood vessels.

Expertly, dramatically, Jimenez shifted through his routine, taking his time, holding each pose for a perfect duration, ignoring the rabid crowd. With each position he revealed from a new angle his unheard-of venation. He showed thick, pulsing chest veins, stomach veins, curvilinear back veins, veins that ran across the top of his feet and coiled around his arms and zagged like miniature lightning in his forehead.

The same thin, oiled skin that was driving the rest of the audience mad with delight made Jimenez's routine seem embarrassingly immodest to Craig—like someone displaying their intestines. He was relieved when the big Mexican finally fell in profile to one knee in a swooping finale, rose, bowed and walked off stage, looking discharged and limp.

"A FANTASTIC EXPERIENCE. Fantastic," said the M.C., clapping his little hands as the house lights went back up. "Thank you, Jumbo. Thank you from the bottom of our hearts . . . And *now*, ladies and gentlemen and judges, without further delay, I'd like to bring on our first group of contestants for the evening. The shorts. Let's hear it for the shorts."

"Never is nothing in the shorts," Franklin said. "I'm going to pee. Y'all want anything?"

"Bud Taylor is a short," said Mary Tate.

"I know Taylor is a short. He don't show me all that much."

"He's got the best *lats* you ever saw."

"He's got a lat on him, all right," Franklin conceded. "But he ain't in this contest."

"You said . . ."

"Aw honey, hush," Franklin chuckled and winked at Craig.

After Jimenez, the shorts were in truth not very impressive. They came on stage as a group first—about ten five-eights and under, sparkling with baby oil, innocent of body hair and spanking nude except for the brief posing shorts—walking lissomely as their stubby legs would allow, and stood in a self-conscious line like so many cigar butts facing the audience.

The M.C. read off their names, places of origin and titles if any (next in line is Buster Hannah, Jr., from Biloxi, Mississippi: Mister Old Spanish Fort of 1968). Then he requested that the group make a quarter turn to the right, to give the audience and judges a profile view.

In defense of the shorts they were nervous, being the first group out. About a fourth of them made the turn as directed, only to find themselves facing others who had turned the wrong way or, worse, the shoulder of somebody who had turned completely around to face the back of the stage.

"To the *right*, shorts," the M.C. said impatiently, "a *quarter* turn," and forced every one of them into more confused turning. The confusion had an edge of panic to it. The faces onstage looked as though they feared they might be up there turning all night like figures on a Swiss clock.

As the shorts struggled for the right position a shy tittering began in the crowd. It grew and then subsided and then, suddenly, was touched off into total hilarity from down front by a single giant of a laugh, a joyful thunderous laugh from Santo at the judges' table that took everyone in the auditorium, even the stumbling contestants, along with it.

12

AFTER FIVE MINUTES of pandemonium the M.C. finally managed to calm the shorts. Modestly they finished their turns, filed off stage and then returned one by one for two-minute individual posing routines under the spotlight.

Franklin gave a bored criticism of each routine and from what he said Craig began to understand the elements of the art. In two minutes a poser was expected to assume ten or fifteen positions that would show all sides of his anatomy to the judges. Timing was crucial. Each pose had to be held long enough to be properly judged and then cut off quickly before the muscles began to quiver from strain. Transitions between poses had to be smooth and controlled and to lead directly from what Franklin called the "line" of one pose to the line of the next. Finding the lines was where the talent was at, he said. Anyone could memorize a routine and get up there and flop around. But you had to be by God born with the ability to know the cleanest line of a pose and then stick your body onto it.

Each of the contestants included certain stock poses in his routine (the classic bicep poses, the Atlas poses, etc.) and he mixed those standards with poses of his own, called individuals, that showed off his particular strong points and obscured his weak ones. A man, for instance with good abdominals would put a lot of stomach up in front of the judges.

Short by short they came on, blinked into the spot for a moment, curved and strained through the routine, giving it all the art they could, and then left the stage, some of them by bowing sweetly to the applause like little girls after a recital. Throughout, Craig looked for some irony on the faces but couldn't find a whit. The expressions ranged from sensuous to truculent but not one was the least self-conscious.

The mediums were a more formidable lot. They were bigger, more self-assured and more expert in their posing. Mr. Mobile was among this group—a thick, surly-looking boy with acne on his back who nevertheless looked to Craig like the best so far. The applause during his routine was deafening.

"How will he do?"

"Probly won't even win his group," said Franklin. "That Wilson guy looked better."

"What's the matter with him?"

"Lumpy," Franklin said. "He's lumpy and his skin's bad. You haven't even *seen* the good stuff yet."

Franklin was right about that. As soon as the talls came out in line it was apparent that the class had just now hit the stage and, further, that the new Mr. Gulf Coast had to be either Stewart or the black man next to him in line.

"Oh goddam," said Franklin, punching Mary Tate and scraping his feet. "Oh Jesus Christ, look at that nigger. He might do it. Mary Tate *look* at that motha. He might take Stewart."

The man Franklin was talking about was fabulous. Among the other talls he looked like a peacock among rhinos. He wore lavender trunks and his oiled torso gleamed upward from it, shiny and black as a telephone. His musculature was refined and perfectly proportioned yet it seemed ornamental on him, as decorative and unfunctional as plumage. He didn't strut like the others but pranced across the stage behind Stewart, up high on his toes, making musical little motions with his hands. He had a Greek profile: large chiseled nose, fine mouth, and wide excited eyes that flicked shyly through the audience. As soon as he cleared the curtain a woman shouted huskily from the front row, "All right, Wayne, I heah you now, baby—bring it *home*," and he grinned down at her.

Towering over him in the line was Stewart, looking like a mammoth weapon, something developed to do wholesale injury. Underneath the Chicklet-pale skin his muscles were round and cruel-looking.

"You're right," Mary Tate whispered, excited too. "He really might do it. Oh God I'd like to see that cocksucker Stewart lose."

"He's put some fat on his midsection," Franklin said. "He never has been able to pose wuff a shit and I'm gonna tell you one thing, Bru—that spade is *good*."

His name was Wayne Latrobe. He was from Point Clear, Alabama, the M.C. said, and he had won one or two local titles. There was only scattered applause at his introduction, to which Latrobe made a small, graceful bow.

"You got it, baby. I *heah* you, Wayne," shouted the woman again from the first row.

The M.C. gave a lot of attention to Stewart's introduction.

After calling him the Mississippi Mastodon he named off some fifteen recent titles that Stewart had won, then he paused affectionately.

"Look at him," he told the crowd. "With a chest like that, ladies and gentlemen, can this young Alexander have further worlds to conquer?"

The crowd answered with nearly two minutes of maddened applause.

There were nine talls altogether. The first four to pose individually were good but spiritless. They knew they were in the wrong competition. Latrobe was next and he was magnificent. His routine was like ballet and was made up completely of individuals. He didn't do a single pose that anyone else had done. He was very musical, very lyrical—his movements had an almost embarrassing polish to them, a feminine sort of stylishness that made some of the audience titter. But Latrobe paid no attention to that, nor to the wild applause that followed the end of his routine. He looked out at a fixed point in the back of the auditorium, his face twitching oddly through a whole series of climactic little expressions, swirling his hands around his waist in preparation and then sliding into a new position so gracefully you hardly knew he was doing it. And there he would be—bent backward at the knees, or twined around himself, in some unique breath-taking pose.

The crowd started out cold and amused but during his routine it decided that it loved Latrobe and at the end of it the applause and stomping finally had to be quieted by the M.C. It was a hard act to follow, even for Stewart, and he came on looking peeved. His posing was as sluggish and perfunctory as heavy machinery being moved around but Stewart was still Stewart—the beer-keg chest and great arms that looked like they had been slugged full of sausage were impressive. Appropriately, the audience applauded him loudly but didn't really extend itself.

The last three posers slunk through their routines as fast as possible, aware that they were only holding things up. When the

122

last one finished the M.C. excused himself and went down to the judges' table to confer.

"They're might gonna have a pose for pose," Franklin said. "I believe they're gonna have one. You don't know how lucky you are, man. You don't see one of those every day."

"What's a pose for pose?"

"It's when the judges can't decide between two guys," Mary Tate said. "They bring them out together and make them pose off against each other."

"Side by side," said Franklin. "It's unreal."

"*Mano a mano*, huh."

"Say what?"

"Nothing. What are they doing now?"

"Deciding—three of the judges have to want it."

The M.C. came back to his microphone radiant with the good news. "Ladies and Gents," he drawled, "you're a very lucky bunch of folks (murmur from crowd). Our fine judges have decided (pause) to BRING BACK TWO OF THE TALLS FOR A POSE-OFF FOR MR. GULF COAST (crowd roar). The great Doug Stewart and newcomer Wayne Latrobe will now return for a five-pose POSE FOR POSE (sustained roar)."

Latrobe was delighted and nervous. Stewart followed him heavily, looking grim. The M.C. met them in the center of the stage and explained the rules of the pose-off. They were to begin and end each pose on command, they could do any five poses they chose, the judges' decision was final. Then he instructed them to climb up on either end of the platform.

"What do you think?" Mary Tate whispered to Franklin.

"I don't know . . . never has been a nigger won this contest. Stewart's got the bulk on him but the nigger's got the cuts."

The woman on the first row was shouting again, standing up this time. She was a middle-aged black woman dressed in an old tan rain coat. "Take yo time," she yelled to Latrobe, who grinned nervously from his end of the platform. "Take yo *sweet* time, honey."

Latrobe was doing just that. The M.C. had called for them to begin the first pose and Stewart was already locked into one of the standard chest poses, shoulders lifted, chest out, hands at the waist as though to hitch up his shorts. Latrobe cleared his throat, made a few musical gestures with his arms and slithered finally into a very quirky position. He tilted slightly backward at the waist, stuck his left leg out in front of him and commenced peering over the audience. His right arm strained out before him at shoulder level, forefinger pointing, and his left hand was held like a visor at his forehead.

It took the audience a long moment to realize what the hell he was doing—the line of the pose was so fresh that Craig thought for a second he was looking at a brand-new arrangement of the human body. Then everyone recognized it: right hand pointing out some wondrous, distant thing, the left shading the eyes from a new-world sun. Latrobe was in the old Land-Ho pose of discovery—the Cortez upon a peak pose, old as man. And he had rediscovered it. As Latrobe gazed out over the sea of laborers he might have been Ulysses or Balboa or Champlain, and the audience, looking back, knew it was seeing the true line of excitement.

"Sonofabich," said Franklin.

"Awright baby, keep it *going*," shouted the woman in front.

"Break," said the M.C. "Pose two, please."

For pose two Stewart went to an ordinary back position. Latrobe made himself into a spear thrower, shifting his weight smoothly back on his right leg, shoving his left arm up and outward and drawing back the right full of stiff sharpness.

Next he did a number on Rodin's "Thinker," down on one knee, deltoid swelling with concentration; then a very dramatic pose that was an exact duplicate of Michelangelo's "Rebellious Slave"—neck bent back, shoulders and upper arms and chest agonizing against bonds. That one nearly brought the house down. Stewart, staring down at his own bicep in one of the old Atlas poses, sensed the applause was not for him, glanced up at his opponent for the first time and nearly fell off the dais in surprise.

124

"Break," said the M.C. again. Then he asked for the fifth and final pose.

"Put it *togetha*, baby," shrieked the woman on the first row. "*Find* it, honey, *find* it for yo mama," she told him and Latrobe responded with what looked like a little fit of searching for his last pose. His feet scuffled against the vinyl, his head lolled, his hands leaped around with little plucking motions as if to pull the components of the pose from the air. Stewart, who had been watching all this with a superstitious expression on his dumb features, lost all concentration and stumbled off the dais looking badly shaken.

The mama was on her feet again, her voice hoarse and urgent: "Get it, *get* it, *get* it, baby," she pleaded. In a moment she was joined by a few other voices in the auditorium. Then more. "*Get* it, *get* it, *get* it," chanted Mary Tate and then Franklin and finally Craig along with a host of others. "*Get it, get it . . .*"

And all at once Latrobe did. He stiffened suddenly, locking his legs together under him, brought his arms up slowly, pushed his palms together over his head and became . . . a candle and flame, a spear, a cypress tree. From his feet to his fingertips, up his legs and out along the flaring latissimus dorsi muscles, Latrobe was one innocent and uninterrupted line, a shape lanceolate and pure as a leaf.

Down front Santo jumped to his feet applauding. The other judges followed him. Then the entire audience was standing, stomping and whistling and clapping deliriously as Latrobe held and held and held his lovely pose. And still held it longer.

"Incredulous to the eye," the M.C. said when the applause finally died away. "A very very great experience."

There was no doubt about who had won, but Stewart would not quit the stage. Latrobe bowed off to the dressing tent, the M.C. went down to the judges' table for the list of winners and returned and still Stewart stood, hands on hips, dazed and belligerent.

"What the fuck is this?" he asked the M.C.

"Folks," said the M.C., trying to ignore him, "we are fortunate to have with us tonight to present the awards, a man who needs no introduction, a long-time Titan of the iron game . . ."

"What the fuck is going on here?" asked Stewart. He grabbed the M.C. by the shoulder of his double-breasted blazer and pulled him to him as though he were opening a file drawer.

"I'm gonna get on that motha," said Franklin, rising and shuffling.

"Sit down, Franklin," Mary Tate told him.

"I'm gonna get on that bastard like baby doo on a wool blanket . . . that rotten sonofabich."

But before Franklin could clear the aisle Santo was standing by the judges' table, saying gently: "Doug, let him go, all right?"

"Stay outta this, Santo," Stewart told him. The crowd had begun to mutter nervously. "You and Erickson had this goddam thing rigged, bringing in this jig. Where in the fuck you find this freak? This is *my* goddam contest and I sure hell better've won it."

"You didn't win it, Doug. Latrobe won it. You didn't win it because you posed like a cow—now get on off that stage or you and I going to go round like we did in Memphis."

With a sudden sweep of the scrim Erickson appeared at the back of the stage. "Wait just a goddam minute," he said, stumbling toward Stewart. "Get the hell *offa* here! Get offa my stage."

"He's drunk as a skunk," Mary Tate said. "This is going to be beautiful."

Erickson made an enraged rush for Stewart who was still holding the terrified M.C., microphone and all, in his right hand. With Erickson just a step or two away Stewart reached out and swatted him on the shoulder, hard enough to change the big man's course without slowing him down. Erickson hurtled off the end of the stage as if it were a diving board, eyes wide, legs still working beneath him, and landed with a fruity thud in the empty orchestra pit.

"You dirty sons of bitches," Stewart shouted after Erickson. "I'm afta your ass now, you read me, Bru? And yours, Santo, and that little freckleface fart. You're a dirty bunch of crooks. Filthy! You read me? And I'm afta *all you bastads*."

Stewart was slathering and hysterical. He still had hold of the M.C. and was rattling him in punctuation. Unsure exactly who Stewart meant to be after, parts of the audience began to move out and the shuffling, muttering sound of panic began to well through the auditorium.

"Roger, where are you at?" Stewart shouted into the stirring crowd and the little boy with the Mr. Mississippi bag answered him from the canvas tent. "*Maveat mavee avin thavee bavack!*" Stewart yelled, dropped the M.C. in a heap and fled through the scrim.

"That's Russian he's tawkin—Oh my God, that's Russian," shrieked a woman in the crowd.

Everyone was standing. Everyone was trying to shove toward an aisle. A man pushed past Craig moaning, "What's he going to doo, what's he going to doo . . ." Only Mary Tate was still seated, weak from laughter, and Craig stood beside her, his eyes out of focus, stupidly wondering what the hell to do.

"Just sit down," said Santo. The tone of his voice sounded normal but everyone seemed to hear it. With the ex Mr. best abdominals he had just pulled Thor from the orchestra pit. Now he stood talking to the crowd with that friendly coach's authority of his, his tough face amused and with a quality in his voice that said "look, how could anything possibly be wrong when I'm standing here like a small hill telling you it's not?"

"You folks don't want to leave now—hurt Latrobe's feelings? After that beautiful routine he put on you. Mr. Stewart's gone and he's not going to bother anybody—he's just a bad sport. Now just sit down and we'll get everything straightened out."

He took on them like an anesthetic. They sat back down, and they did it silently.

Back on stage Thor Erickson brushed off his crushed velvet suit, steadied himself against the microphone and began presenting the awards. There was very little applause. The crowd seemed spent. Thor had just shaken the hand of the medium runner-up when a faint but steady noise began above them—a hissing sound like rain on concrete—and grew. Hisssss, it went; hisshissshissSShiSSSS-HISSSSSHHHHH. It was right above their heads. The ceiling began to vibrate to the noise.

"What the hell?" roared Thor. "What is this?" He was about the only one curious. The tranquilized crowd seemed not even to notice.

"Mr. Erickson. Uh, Mr. Erickson," said Santo, popping to his feet again. "I believe I know what the problem is—very small thing. If you'd just go right on with the ceremony I'll run up and check it out." He vaulted onto the stage and disappeared behind the scrim. Franklin began scrambling out of the aisle after him.

"I'm going with them," said Craig.

"Not without me, baby," said Mary Tate. And so they all followed Santo—onstage, through the scrim and out a backstage door that opened into a hallway. They caught him walking calmly up a flight of steps at the end of the hall.

"What'd he do?" Franklin asked him.

"Turned on the showers, I think," Santo said, and that seemed to be all he wanted to say. "We'll see."

They went through big double doors into a darkened basketball court where the noise was very loud, and through it toward lights at the far end.

The shower room was a mess. Stewart and his little brother had turned on twenty-two showers full blast and clogged the drains with toilet paper. Three or four inches of water, in which floated twenty-two bars of Ivory soap, was beginning to spill over into the locker room. Stewart was nowhere in sight, but he had left a message on the blue tile wall. With a bar of soap he had written, "take a Bath you filthy basterds, yrs. truly mr. mississippi."

"Sheeeat," said Franklin quietly.

Santo was pensive. His right hand massaged his chin. "Huh," he said. "Well, we'll have to clean it up."

It took them a half hour to do that after the awards were over (Santo, Mary Tate, Craig, Franklin and a night janitor, who was only supposed to lock up, picked at soggy toilet paper while Thor sat in a dry corner of the locker room, blearily watching and drinking steadily from a new bottle). It was eleven-thirty before they left the gym.

In the parking lot Santo came up behind Craig and took his arm. "Well, what'd you think? I'm sorry Stewart had to dick it for you."

"What do you mean? I thought it was great."

"What else?"

"Beautiful."

"Now you're on it!" Santo yelled at the moon.

"That boy just flat hates to lose," Thor said to himself.

"World's biggest prick," said Mary Tate. She was leaning on Craig's shoulder and nuzzling his neck, smelling of Ivory soap.

"I don't know," said Santo. They were at the car and everybody suddenly was as happy as he was. "I sort of loved old Stewart out there tonight. He's finally starting to develop a little style."

13

As soon as he was seated in the car Thor Erickson fumbled for a minute in his pants and then with a heavy sigh passed out. Santo drove.

"He's gone," Franklin said. "He'll drink a ton of that shit and stay right and then when there's nothing else to do he'll pass and stay out for a day."

"That's his way of relaxing," said Santo.

"I'm waiting to see it relax his ass for good," Mary Tate said. "Schnapps and bourbon. God. If he wadn't mean as a stra-ped snake it'd killed him already."

Franklin leaned up, looked at Erickson and chuckled. "Hey Craig, lookahear." Craig looked down where Franklin was pointing to a wide, unnatural bulge in Erickson's crotch. "That's his wallet. Sonofabich has to stick it down in his goddam jockey shorts before he can pass out."

"Or even go to sleep," said Santo. "He's been doing it long as I've known him. A man has to take care of what's important to him."

"How did he get all these health clubs?" Craig asked.

"By screwing people," said Franklin. "Tell him about the guy from Tanny, Joe."

Santo laughed. "He was screwing people a long time before that. He was what you might call a child prodigy. He started over in your neighborhood. Made his first big buck when he was fourteen, hitching over to Woodstream every day during the summer and begging as a blind man. He'd go from house to house dressed up in an old overcoat and dark glasses, tapping this red-bottom cane and holding out a hat."

"Tell about the umbrellas," said Mary Tate. She was curled sleepily against Craig as she had been on the trip back from Guntersville, this time with her hand lying light and familiar inside his shirt.

"Well he took the money he made begging and bought up two-thousand little dowel-stem umbrellas from a lumberyard. Cost him a nickel apiece. All the next year he'd go around after school whenever it was raining and hawk 'em for a quarter apiece—at football games, concerts, that kind of thing. He said he'd wear the grubbiest clothes he could find and an old pair of busted wingtips and stand around in parking lots, dripping, coughing and selling the hell out of them. He put everything he made in the bank. Then the next summer he doubled it by caddying."

"Caddying . . . golf bags?"

"He made it in tips. Old Thor was the most popular caddy in the history of golf. What he did was split the toe of his right tennis shoe into two flaps, so he could come poking up on a ball, pretending he was looking for it, snap that mother up between the flaps, carry it out to a better lie and drop it again. He made a lot of friends like that. And by the end of the summer he had around two thousand dollars."

"Then's when he come down on the body business with all fo feet," said Franklin.

"It was a few years after that, around 1950. Thor decided there ought to be a better place in Birmingham to work out than that ratty old Y so he took out some of his capital, bought some second-hand weights and a few benches and opened his own gym downtown. First year he sold enough memberships to pay his overhead and clear a thousand or so. And he thought he was doing all right until he found out how good Vic Tanny was doing. He found out this guy Tanny was making a *fortune* out of weights—chains of clubs, everything. Old Thor wanted to know how, so he quit his job, took out some more money and hired one of Tanny's top idea-men for five hundred a week."

Franklin was cracking up on the other side of Mary Tate. "Listen to this. You gotta listen to this."

"Thor got closer to this guy than skin, see. Ate breakfast with him, took him places, got him women—and all the time he was pumping him twelve hours a day. Then after two weeks when he knew everything the guy knew he fired him."

"Just flat *farred* his ass," Franklin whooped.

"Then went around kicking himself for not figuring out on his own what he had to pay a thousand bucks to find out."

"What'd he find out?"

"That the whole country is fat and doesn't want to be. That there are poor fat and rich fat and no profit in the poor ones. And that there are lots of ways to make the rich ones think they're losing weight, developing great bodies and adding years to their lives—all without having to do anything much. What he did was, he went to Dr. Elijah Wright, who was one of the guys he'd caddied for, borrowed some money and set up the studio where we are now. He started giving out health lunches at noon to businessmen, taking out ads about helping your sex life . . . all that stuff. And it strictly made the money. In two years Thor and Elijah were in the black and going to town—starting new clubs everywhere, buying up warehouses full of weight . . ."

"Then he got his dirty tail in a crack," said Franklin.

"Life whomped him from behind," said Santo. "He made his one big financial mistake. Molested a minor out in Chicago in the men's room of a Y and got caught. It nearly ruined him. It kept him from moving into the Midwest and he had to shut up four clubs down here. But he hung in and waited it out. He hired me to front and he's kept his profile low—stayed out of trouble. Now he's got all the old clubs back plus two and he's about to start moving for more."

Thor's dream, said Santo, was one hundred clubs. And personally Santo hoped he got them. He had sure as hell worked hard enough for them, and he didn't really get a lot of fun out of anything but that.

They were back in Brewton, where Thor had been slowed on the way to Mobile, and something big was going on here. It was 1:00 A.M. and every light in town was on. There were people all over the streets dressed like—cowboys? Carrying beer cans, shouting. Somebody was riding a yellow horse down a sidewalk.

"What *is* this?" said Franklin. "What's going on in this place?"

"Looks like some kind of fair," Santo said. He turned the car into the main street. Strung above it was a big banner with glittery letters pasted on it. "WELCOME," the banner said, "TO THE BREWTON ANNUAL RODEO AND FESTIVAL OF STARS. THIS YEAR'S STAR, SHORTY CRUMP, JOHN WAYNE'S PERSONAL STUNT MAN. MEET HIM IN THE FLESH SUNDAY, JULY 17, AT THE FAIRGROUNDS."

"They're hanging it out down here," Santo said. "Hell, they're having a ball—look at this place. Mary, hey Mary, wake up."

"Numph," said Mary Tate.

"You ever see a rodeo?"

"Uh uh."

"We ought to stay, you know that," he told Franklin. "We ought to stay down here and play with these people."

"Thor ain't gonna like that wuff a shit, Joe."

"He'll be out all night. What do you say?" Santo turned around to look at Craig, his face eager and excited as a trailing bird dog's.

Since the first night with him at the Three O'Clock Club Craig had been amazed over and over at how quickly and totally Santo could get excited, and how easily he could pass it on. It was a childlike, infectious thing that began in his face and always looked incongruous among the tough features. Now he was up again, prepping a carful of tired people, and Craig could feel his own enthusiasm rising.

"Yeah, I'm game," he said. "I used to ride a little bareback."

"We'll find a place, first," said Santo happily. "I'll explain everything to Thor in the morning."

They had pulled up to a traffic light in the middle of town. Stopped beside them in the other lane was a dusty Volkswagen bus with a pair of metal crutches strapped to the back. A thin-faced boy with long hair and a band around his head looked over at them from the Volks, smiled sweetly and made a V with his right hand.

"What is that thang?" said Franklin immediately and grabbed the back of the front seat. "Is that a man? That motha's giving us the *fanger*. Hey," he yelled at the other car, "you stay *right there*."

"Wait a minute, Franklin," said Santo. "That's not . . ."

"I'm getting me a *piece* of that bastad." Franklin was scrambling with his door. Suddenly he was out of the car and charging the Volkswagen.

"Wait a minute!" Santo shouted. He slammed the car into park and leaped out himself.

Franklin had both arms elbow deep into the car and was trying

135

to pull the whole boy out by his dashiki when Santo got there. Holding Franklin under the arms like a clothing dummy, he lifted him off the pavement and shook him until he let go.

From where he stood behind Santo Craig could see the boy's face as he eased himself back through the window—it was absolutely placid and unconcerned.

Santo whispered something in Franklin's ear and put him down over near the Lincoln. "Look," he said, turning back to the boy, "I'm really sorry." His voice was rich with sincerity and the boy smiled at him. Craig noticed for the first time that there were two other boys in the car. They were smiling too.

"No sweat."

"He thought you were giving him the finger."

"Nooo . . ."

"I know. Are you all right?"

"Fine man, I'm fine." He smiled steadily at Santo. There was a long pause. "Are you cats cowboys?"

"Nope. We're just here to watch. We were on our way to find a motel."

"No room, man," said the boy in the back. "No room in the inn."

"Thought if you cats were cowboys you could help my friend here," said the driver quietly. "My friend Willy here"—he gestured to the boy next to him—"he wants to *ride*, man—he wants to ride a bull and they won't let him ride."

"Who won't let him ride?"

Franklin had slipped up behind Craig and gripped his arm. "Ssst," he said. "You know what they are? They got a goddam Calafonia tag—I read about these pissants."

"Something about a card, man. Some ratshit about no card," said the driver. He had a thin ascetic face like an El Greco saint and a soft musical voice. He gazed down at the street, smiling slightly.

"You gotta help me find a rope. I gotta get a rope," Franklin whispered fiercely in Craig's ear.

"About the room, though," the driver went on, "it's like Pi says
—no rooms left in this town. But we got a place. Like a reservation. You can put in with us if you want to."

"And if they are hungry, feed them," said the one in the back.

"Yeah. We got refreshments."

"OK. We appreciate that," said Santo. He had picked up with
his mouth the exact curve of the boy's smile. "Hey, what do you
people like to do? What kind of things?"

"Far out," said the boy in the back.

"Lotta things," said the driver. He was staring at Santo. "We
can rap on it."

They followed the Volkswagen down the main street toward
the end of town. Craig woke Mary Tate and told her where they
were going.

Franklin was very agitated. "You don't know about these guys,"
he kept telling Santo. "I read a thing about 'em and they ain't
right. They do weird stuff."

"They're OK, Franklin. They're fine," Santo said.

"How the shit do you know they don't have a whole bunch more
just waiting to shoot your ass full of dope or something?"

Craig laughed. "We won't let them get you, Franklin. We won't
let 'em put a needle in you."

"Uh huh. Well Thor ain't gonna like *any* of this crap. Where
do them bastads get the coin for this place?"

They had followed the bus into the parking lot of a big, elaborate motel called The Frontier. The Volks went through the parking lot and pulled up behind the motel kitchen. The three boys
got out and stood by the bus with their hands in their jeans, smiling at the Continental. The driver and the one from the back were
tall and stringy. The other one, Willy, was short and birdlike. His
left leg was smaller than the right and turned away from the rest
of him as if somebody had screwed it in a quarter of a turn too far.
All three wore rumpled dashikis, long hair and headbands.

"Jesus," said Mary Tate sleepily, "where the hell did you find
them? Where are we going, baby?"

137

"Welcome to the reservation," the driver said. "Cowboys in town, Indians out here." He and Pi began pulling things out of their Volkswagen—sleeping bags, banjo, packs, a Bunsen burner —while the little one hopped around to his crutches on the back of the car. On the way he spotted Thor hunkered over like a huge wart on the front seat of the Lincoln.

"Hey Ruben, they got a wasted one in there," he said in a reedy, cheerful voice.

"What laid him out?" asked Ruben.

"He drank too much," Santo said. "He'll be all right."

"Evil stuff. We'll put him in the Settler's Cabin."

"Hey you, you got a rope in that car?" Franklin asked loudly.

"No, man, no rope," said Ruben. He looked at Franklin for a minute. "Ropes tie things *down*, and together. What you're doing with a rope is you're trying to catch life—you can't do that man, it's like a river. All you can do is stick your finger in it."

"Uh huh. Now look, motherfucker . . ."

"The man's right, Franklin, right as rain. Just relax." Santo opened the door of the Lincoln and slipped Erickson over his shoulder as smoothly as if he were an overcoat. "I'll tote Thor. Where's your place?"

Carrying the stuff from their car, the three boys led them down a dark, grassy slope behind the motel to a fenced yard. On the way down they could make out a group of unusual shapes in the middle of the yard that turned out to be two big teepees, a log cabin, a sandbox, two swing sets and a seesaw.

"This is beautiful," said Santo. "It's fabulous."

"Rent's low," said Ruben. "We been here three nights. We come in late and leave before the kids get here."

Pi built a little fire behind one of the teepees. Ruben and Willy lit candles and the Bunsen burner and laid out the sleeping bags inside the two teepees. With Santo's help they dragged Thor into the log cabin and left him heaped there on a blanket.

Outside in the shadows Craig and Mary Tate stood with Franklin, watching. "This is weird but I like it," Mary Tate said. She giggled and hugged Craig's arm. "I like them boys."

When everything was done the place was square as a hunting camp. Ruben knelt over the Bunsen burner in one of the teepees, slicing some little things that looked like brussel sprouts into a pan. Santo and the other two boys squatted around him.

As they started into the stucco teepee Franklin grabbed Craig's arm. "You *got* to help me find a rope," he said again, his eyes urgent. "I want to do something."

"Do what, Franklin? The guy told you you can't tie things down."

Franklin looked around. "Look. I tell you what." He paused. "I want to *capture* one 'em," he whispered. "Not to hurt him any —I just want to take him home and interrogate his ass."

14

"Now," SAID RUBEN, smiling around the teepee, "everybody's to-gether. We can break some bread."

He held out a rusty iron frying pan to Craig and Santo. In the bottom were twenty-five or thirty green-brown wafers. He had fried them outside on the fire and they gave off a strong smell like burned flowers.

"What is it?"

"Peyote," said Santo. "It's a cactus. Indians down in the Southwest use it for communion—they say it makes them able to see God."

"See that dude nose to nose," said Willy. He huddled over a handful of the wafers, eating them like potato chips. Against the back of the teepee Pi made a few soft chords on the banjo. There were just the five of them now in the tent. Franklin had gone back to the car for one of Thor's bottles and had sullenly retired with it to the log cabin. Mary Tate was sleeping in the other teepee.

"Are you going to have some?" Craig asked Santo.

"No."

"Go on man, fix up. It's easy stuff," Ruben said.

Craig took five or six of the wafers and put one in his mouth. It had a moldy rotten taste like the smell of compost that immediately made him nauseated.

"Just swallow them at first," Ruben said. "And hold your nose. What's the matter with you, man?" he asked Santo.

"I like to feel the knot."

"The what?"

"Man said he likes to feel the knot," said Pi.

"I ate some once in San Diego and then went outside and tried to yo-yo. I couldn't feel the knot. You know the slipknot on the string? It cinches up on the underside of the first joint and you have to *feel* that thing to control the spin. I couldn't feel it—it was like I had a glove on."

"That dude is weird," muttered Willy.

"How did y'all get down here?" Craig asked.

"Process of elimination," Ruben said. He lay out on the dirt floor and put a wafer on his tongue. "We been eliminated everywhere else. Had to get here sooner or later."

"Where you from?"

"City of Angels. Like we're refugees."

"Amen. Draft-dodging scum," murmured Pi from the back and strummed the first few bars of *Onward Christian Soldiers*.

"How long you been traveling?" said Santo.

"Oh bout a year, maybe two years . . . we been a lot of places. I lose track."

"You like it down here?" Craig had swallowed six of the foul little wafers and didn't feel any different except a little more like talking and a little more relaxed.

"It sucks," said Ruben. He lay on his back staring up at the night sky through the smokehole in the top of the teepee and harangued the South. He looked, thought Craig, like an exhausted monk— in the shadows his face had a cold metaphysical pinch to it. ". . . it's a rotten, vicious society down here, man—all these back- water Babtists, they gonna lift the balls off anybody who's black or don't cut his hair. It's a society of *cowboys* down here, man. They don't give a shit for anybody."

"Like that freaking friend of yours," said Willy. "Thas a *mean* dude." He had finished the last of the fried wafers and was slicing more and eating them raw. His hands seemed to Craig to move very slowly; his eyes looked big and dull.

"Why don't you ease off the buttons?" Ruben told him.

Willy stuck the knife in the ground and with his hands pulled his bad leg under him. "No sweat," he said, "I got it under control."

"Franklin's OK," said Santo. "He's like anybody else, he has to learn how to enjoy things."

By the touch of excitement in his voice Craig could tell Santo had something to say about that. He ate his last wafer. He was beginning to feel very comfortable and wise.

"People are afraid of what they don't know how to like—once they can enjoy a thing they're not afraid of it any more. They can handle it," said Santo.

"Lotta things you can't enjoy, man," Ruben said.

"A few, not many. You can find some joy on almost anything if you know how to look. There are a few bad honchos around but none of them started out that way. Something bends 'em out of shape: they get where they want to use and own things instead of enjoying them. This stonemason up in Vermont told me something once—said even a round rock has a flat side if you can find it."

"Right," said Craig solemnly. "My friend's exactly right."

"You take a guy like Hitler," Santo went on. "If somebody had just sat him down by a river, say, when he was seven or eight and told him, 'look, Adolf, you don't get off your butt until you've really learned how to *love* the way that current greases around that rock. And then we're gonna go do a hawk circling a rabbit, and then the Alps . . .'"

"I can dig it," said Ruben.

"The way I figure it the more things a man enjoys the fewer he's afraid of and the less time he's got for owning and using. After a while he's enjoying full time and he's not afraid of anything."

"Sounds like a crock of shit to me," said Willy. "Freaking communist conspiracy."

"It's good stuff. Go on, man."

Before Santo could start up again Willy's bad leg shot out from under him and kicked Craig painfully in the left knee.

"What the hell?" Craig asked him. "What did you do that for?"

"Never mind, man. Just ignore him," Ruben said.

Willy reached out and pulled the leg under him again. He looked at Craig with a confused expression of fright and anger. "Screw you, buddy," he said.

"What's the matter with you? What is this?" Craig felt an absolutely new kind of fear turn over in his gut. His head didn't seem to be working right. Things looked different and he couldn't understand what was going on.

"Oh God, oh God," moaned Willy and watched his leg shoot out again, this time in a flurry of kicks that pelted Craig all along his left side. Pi dropped his banjo and lunged at Willy. Santo jumped to his feet.

"Jesus Christ," whimpered Craig. "What's the matter with him?" He felt gorged with emotion. He was terrified and he wanted to laugh and cry at the same time. On his hands and knees

144

he scuttled for Santo and Santo pulled him to his feet and held
him.

"Relax," said Ruben. "Just cool it." Ruben sat as he had been,
shaking his head, while Pi struggled in the dirt with the writhing
Willy. Willy's leg seemed to have a life of its own. It jumped and
jerked with agonized fluttering sounds against the ground. "Sit
down," Ruben said. "He'll be all right."

"*Get* it. Hold it dowwwn," Willy pleaded and Pi, who was
stretched across him, managed to find the offending leg and pin it
to the ground with his right hand. Willy calmed then and just lay
under Pi, breathing raggedly.

"It happens about once a week when he's stoned," said Ruben
softly. "He thinks his leg is cutting out on him. Like it's running
off. It used to be worse when we was using speed. He'll be all right
now."

"All right?" Willy sobbed. "I'm not gonna be all right. I'm a
freak. I'm a fucking *dope* fiend." Pi had slid off him but Willy still
lay on the ground as though he were being held there. "I've got
more junk in me than any man alive. It's killing me—it's drying
me up."

He lay there sobbing by the Bunsen burner, his heaving chest,
narrow as a quail's, the only thing in the room that moved. Then
Santo walked around behind him and sat down. He took the boy's
head in his lap and held it there.

"I used to shoot two grams of speed just to be doing something,"
Willy said, looking up at Santo. His voice was a little steadier.
"Lookahere. Me and Pi one time got a bottle of Desoxyn and shot
up the whole hundred just to see what would happen—we was on
that run for sixteen days, fixin up every few hours and just floatin
around Long Beach. Fixin up round the clock." He smiled. "Shit
man. You know I got the record? The biggest hit ever—eighth of
an ounce of pure speed. I just shot it up and sat there laughing at
this spade I was with while I had this monster flash, like creamin
off in my head. That dude thought I was gonna *die* and I just get
up and walk right outta there." Willy was grinning now and his

voice was chipper and proud. "These kids now, they don't have a hair on their ass. I've done it all man, glue, *mush*rooms, twenty-*five*, turps, *Nem*butal, THC, *hash* . . . I been weird every way there is."

Craig huddled near the entrance to the teepee, watching Santo calm the boy and feeling like he'd been through a war. What the hell kind of people *were* these? And what was Santo doing down there fondling this junkie? He wiped his hand across his cheek and discovered he was crying. He wondered what the hell he was doing here all messed up in the head with cactus. He wondered what was happening to his life.

For fifteen minutes Willy talked and bragged and then suddenly in mid-sentence fell asleep with his head still in Santo's lap.

"Why the hell does he want to ride a bull?" asked Santo.

"I don't know, man. It's a weird thing," Ruben said.

"Wanted to for a year," said Pi, who was strumming on his banjo again. "Ever since we went to this big rodeo in Cheyenne. We watched this guy out there name of Jim Shoulders ride this bull name of Funeral Wagon and it was a beautiful thing. I mean he really *rode* that thing. Blew Willy's mind. He said it was like being synched into a natural force, you know. Like sitting in a hurricane? Willy went out and tried to find Shoulders after the rodeo—said he wanted Shoulders to adopt him."

"I told you it was weird. Willy's like a kid."

Santo looked up at Ruben. "Nothing weird about that. That's the way we're tied in."

He was stroking Willy's head as he would a cat's back. "Everybody sharing everybody else. This old guy in O'Hare airport taught me that in 1956. I was coming back from Korea, waiting on a plane. It was late and this janitor in a blue uniform and a brown sweater and these beat-up ventilated shoes was walking around emptying ash trays. He came over for one by me and I said, 'How're you tonight?' and he smiled and said, 'I'm fine now, but I'll be mighty tired tomorrow night. I got to play through one more game.' It was the tail end of the World Series see, and this old guy was playing all those games himself. He was sitting up in front of his radio in Des Plaines or somewhere using one guy's speed and another guy's arm and another guy's bat. And I thought, right—and one of those ballplayers, when he goes home he probably uses some movie star's smile on his wife. And that movie star might use something in a movie that he got from watching that old janitor. See how it is? How fucking close everybody is? Jesus, it knocks me out. It's like everybody ever born, all of us clear back to Adam are in one long line like paper dolls. Joined at the hand and the hip."

Santo looked down at Willy, musing. "We'll see can't we get him a ride," he said.

About four o'clock Craig fell asleep in a fishbowl of pink water. Thousands of multicolored fish swam lazily around him, changing shapes and burping clouds of bubbles. Above his head tall green sea fans and clumps of grass, fine as hair and tall as wheat, rocked to the stir of their tails. Barely visible in the recesses of the bowl were dark stationary things, shaped like torpedoes and sinister in their difference from everything else. They seemed to lurk there, black and striped by the grass, and Craig in his fear didn't know whether to swim from them or try to wait them out.

Near dawn he woke and it was raining—a fine rain that came down like a white tower through the top of the teepee. Someone had put him on a sleeping bag and the length of it was damp with his sweat. Against the back wall Santo was bent over Pi's banjo, singing. Ruben and Pi sat in front of him, their eyes fixed on his face. Craig had never seen it so intent. Santo looked as if he were trying to hear something a long way off.

" 'I didn't *knoww* God made hawn-keytonk Angels,' " he sang, " 'I should have knownn that you'd ne-ver make a wife. You ran ouut on the only one who loved youuu. And went baaack to the wi-ld side of life . . .' "

His voice was soft. He was chording simply with the banjo, just filling in under the lyrics. He sang *Walking the Floor Over You*

147

(I cain't sleep a wink   that is truuew). He sang *Too Late* (I *neeed* your loving   more than any*one*) and *I'm So Lonesome I Could Cry* (did you e-ver see   a ro-bin weep . . .)—old country songs of Hank Williams and Hank Thompson and Ernest Tubb; songs raw and bare as skinned squirrels. And his strong voice spread their lumps of loneliness and want like wool. It hovered on the sad low-down vowels and whined like a hit dog on the high notes. It sounded countrier than a five-acre red clay farm—countrier than the yahoo, slatternly, redneck, possum-poor, country South itself.

Santo sang and sang. He had all the right things in his voice and no one in the teepee moved. Craig lay on the sleeping bag listening and watching Santo's face through the column of rain for a long time before he fell asleep again.

15

FOR FIVE DAYS after the Brewton Annual Rodeo and Festival of Stars Craig Blake was exhausted—bone-deep tired, the way he had always been after hockey games in prep school.

He had fallen for hockey the first time he saw the Choate rink: the blue-gray color of the ice; the black fanlike tendon protectors on the back of hockey skates; the way a varsity wing named Brodie could juke defensemen out of their skates with a little crossover jog to his left. He had spent all of his weekends and every free hour during the week puck-handling, shooting and learning to skate. In his sophomore year he made the junior varsity team. He played dull, hard-checking defense in eight games that year and nearly collapsed after every one. Not so much from the physical exertion as from the struggle to do formally what everybody else was doing naturally, on a surface that they—his roommate from Fairfield, Connecticut, Brodie from Durham, New Hampshire—understood and he didn't.

On the trip back to Birmingham from Brewton he already knew how tired he was going to be, and he knew why. He had been trying since yesterday (God, was it only yesterday?) to play on the same ice with Santo and Mary Tate. It couldn't be done. Now, in the back seat of John Wayne's stunt man's maroon Eldorado he was being nearly smothered by a horny Mary Tate (her right hand worked away, businesslike, inside his pants; her mouth chewed away at his) while in front, Santo pumped Shorty Crump about stunting. Both still going strong, both still hungry. When all Craig wanted to do was go somewhere quiet and stare at a blank wall. When *all* he could feel, with toothsome Mary Tate plying him at both ends, was a weak inclination toward caution.

Caution because he was at least sure of one thing by now: he was on a faster turf than he knew how to run.

Any fool would have known that this morning on waking up in a stucco teepee to the following: full daylight, about eight o'clock, three long-haired junkies squatting like Apaches across a round expanse of dirt from where Santo—who is bare to the waist and who has sung country music and shot the shit all night instead of sleeping—is on his two-hundred and fortieth sit-up. He does them fast, hands locked behind his head, and with such ease that they don't even disturb his conversation:

". . . then I worked down in the Berry Islands oiling a crane . . ." he is saying.

150

Willy notices you, propped on an elbow, rubbing crazy, drugged sleep from your eyes. "He's got fifty-eight left to do."

"Well hey, buddy," says Santo, twisting at the waist on the way up for two hundred forty-three. His face is fresh as a rose. "Hope you got some sleep. We're gonna hang it out today. We gonna *celebrate*."

The rain has blown away. It is a bright windy morning. The air has a fresh texture and you stand outside trying to let it clean your head. Then you go over to the other teepee and wake Mary Tate who smiles, rolls over in her sleeping bag and wants to know what went on last night.

"Joined at the hip, huh?" is all she says when you finish. She unzips the bag, moves over in it and grins. "Why don't you and me try some of that, studhorse . . ."

Any fool would have known right then, if he hadn't known before.

Thor had been mad as a mink when he woke up and found himself lying next to Franklin on the dirt floor of a toy log cabin. He woke Franklin and when Franklin tried to explain how he had gotten there Thor cursed him. Then he went over to the teepee where Craig and Mary Tate had just joined Santo and the three boys and cursed all of them. He stood at the entrance to the teepee in his wrinkled velvet suit, raising hell about how he was too busy for this kind of crap.

Then he left. Drove back to Birmingham at a hundred miles an hour they learned later from Franklin, who, hung over and convinced that Santo wasn't going to let him capture anybody, left with him. Santo was sorry to lose them. He had wanted everybody to celebrate together.

About nine o'clock the six of them packed into the Volkswagen and drove downtown for breakfast. Everyone was hungry but Willy, who was very worked up about finally being able to ride a bull. Nobody, least of all Willy, wondered how Santo was going to get him that ride. He seemed to have developed quite a bit of faith in Santo since last night. ("That mother's OK," Craig heard Pi tell Willy as they watched Santo doing his sit-ups. "OK?" said Willy. "OK? He's freaking Superman is who he is.")

The center of town was roped off. It looked like all south Alabama was inside those three blocks. They left the car behind a church and walked down the main street toward a bright red chuck wagon that was serving breakfast to a crowd. The street was aswarm with people on horseback, high school cowgirls, men with pistols strapped to their legs and beer cans in their hands.

"It's like a movie," Mary Tate said. She glistened with excitement. Even after a night in sleeping bag and teepee she looked fresh and clear as spring water. "I want to ride a palomino horse. I bet they have a parade and maybe we could get some horses and ride in it."

Ruben looked at her and laughed. "You got the wrong man, babe. I don't ride that kind of horse."

"Amen," said Pi. "You said it right."

Willy darted around to Santo, lively as a sparrow on his crutches. "What do you think? You think we can get some horses?"

"Horses?" Santo cracked his knuckles. "You bet we will. They're long on horses here in Brewton."

The chuck wagon had BPOE printed on the side in gold. It had a big charcoal grille built into one end. Behind the grille was a smiling Elk in a chef's hat. He was cooking dollar-pancakes and thick sausage patties and giving them away on napkins along with steaming paper cups of coffee.

"This stuff free?" Ruben asked him.

"All you can eat," the Elk said and smiled at Ruben. He looked happy. It occurred to Craig that it would be hard not to be happy right then, there by the bright chuck wagon under the windy blue sky and warm sun, with the smells of horses and free coffee and sausage on the air. He closed his eyes, pleasantly voluptuous.

"You like it?" Santo asked.

"Could stay here all day . . ." he said.

But Santo was talking to a short, heavy man with a big face. The man had a cup of coffee in one hand and was gesturing with a sausage in the other. "Doing these fairs? It sucks cock. I'm not even sure which one I'm *at* right now."

"Brewton, Alabama," said Santo.

This was Shorty Crump—five feet tall, stunt man for John Wayne and star of this year's Festival of Stars. His left arm was in a sling and devil rum was on his breath.

Crump had just driven into town an hour ago from Memphis —tired, bitter from a fair the night before at which he had broken his left collarbone rolling a horse, and mean hung over from a bottle of Tennessee sherry. Jerez, Shorty called it. He was trying to coffee-up before he went over to the rodeo office to punch in, he said (Crump talked out of the side of his mouth with his eyes thin, but still didn't manage to look any more like John Wayne than you do), for another one of these catfucking rodeos.

Santo asked him how much he made at a Festival of Stars and what he had to do.

Crump said he made five hundred dollars and usually had to do a few stunts, but what with his collarbone he couldn't do any of that today and they'd probably try to cut him a C.

Santo asked how hard were the stunts.

Not too hard if you knew how to do them.

Then Santo wanted to know if Shorty had ever been in Brewton before and it dawned on Craig what he was doing.

"I ain't ever been in Alabama before," said Crump.

"But you don't look like John Wayne," Craig said.

"Neither does he," said Santo.

Crump gave a hard little grin. "You mean the Duke don't look like me." It was obviously a line he had practiced. It had authority.

The deal Santo made Crump was this: he would pretend to be Crump. He would do all the work and give Crump all the money save the hundred the rodeo people would have taken out anyway. Crump could sit in the stands and just watch it all for a change. Enjoy himself.

Crump gave Santo a hard look. "You individuals wouldn't be figuring on taking Shorty Crump would you, mother?"

"No," said Santo.

"Bigger studsenyou have tried it and got their asses wiped."

"Not interested," said Santo.

"I won't mess with you—I'll cut your ass."

"We wouldn't tamper with a man of your reputation," Santo said sincerely. "I need the exercise. And I'd like to see what it's like to be a star."

Shorty grinned. "Plenty of folks'd like to know what that's like. You know I pull down forty thou a year? I just mess with this chickenshit to keep my hand in between the Duke's pictures. I don't stunt nobody but the Duke."

Santo clapped him on the shoulder. "I tell you what, Shorty, I'll throw in a bottle of wine. I'll get you the biggest bottle of wine you ever saw to sit up there in the stands with."

"Jerez . . . You got a deal, hoss."

"Fine. You'd better tell me how to do a stunt or two. And I'll need some clothes."

"I got threads in the car."

While Santo and Shorty were talking Willy got very excited. "You see what he's doing?" he kept whispering to Ruben, to Craig, to Mary Tate. "I swear that sumbich is *God.*" When they finished he swung along behind them back to Shorty's car. Craig and Mary Tate stayed with the other two boys at the chuck wagon. Ruben was anxious. He didn't like Crump and he was worried about Willy.

"Joe won't let nothing happen to him," Mary Tate told him.

Just then, on the street in front of them, there was a drawdown.

A fat man with fancy tooled holsters came around the corner of the Brewton Trust Bank and spotted somebody in the crowd by the chuck wagon.

"Billy Ray," he shouted, crouching, chubby hands sneaking to his gun butts. "Come on you egg-sucking old dawg. I'm faster'n last year."

A peaked-looking individual who looked to Craig like a druggist stepped out from the crowd. His was a single army holster with the flap cut off. He wore ordinary street clothes and spectacles.

"You don't want none of me, Bubba," he said quietly.

"We're about to have one less cowboy riding the range," said Ruben. "I'll bet on the skinny one."

"GO FOR IT," Bubba shouted, drawing, and the druggist calmly shot him in the stomach. Bubba dropped his gun and looked at his belly where the wax bullet had splattered into a disc the size of a silver dollar just above his steerhead belt buckle. "I'll be gotdamn," he muttered, picked up his gun and waddled off down main street—where the pitch of things was rising.

A befezzed covey of Shriners pushed by, in a hurry; a red and black high school band was forming on the corner in front of the bank. Mary Tate asked someone in the crowd what was going on and was told that folks were getting ready for the parade. The parade began at noon.

When Santo returned he was carrying a Tex Tan presentation saddle and wearing yellow Nocona boots, orange chaps that reached just below his knees and a matching hat. Crump had found Willy a hat too and an old pair of chaps that hid his leg and made his limp look like something that might have come from a bad fall off a sorrel pony.

Crump was pleased. "Looks almost good enough to be me," he said approvingly of Santo.

Santo had with him five fifths of good Brolio chianti, a wheel of Port Salud cheese and a gallon of sherry. He was in a festive mood. "We got to find this rodeo office and get our hosses. How you like my saddle, missy?" he asked Mary Tate.

Mary Tate smiled and hugged his arm.

"I tell you what," he said. "You look so good I'm gonna find you that palomino hoss."

He did just that, and getting a palomino out of Seymour "Buddy" Hanes who ran the rodeo office was no mean trick. For one thing he didn't have one—he had to send to the other end of town for one and that meant walking across the office to use the phone which was a pain in the ass for Seymour who weighed 275 pounds and had a bleeding ulcer. Another one was to have your star (even if he did look twice as good as any star Brewton had had in the ten years Seymour had managed things) bring a bunch of strange-looking wine-drinking stunt men buddies into town with him. And Dale Evans' stunt woman. One star a year was plenty for Seymour. He had had one weird sonofabitch in 1966 that ate bricks. And then to have the star demanding horses to ride in the parade for two of the stunt men buddies and the stunt woman (who wanted a palomino for Chrissake); and to top it off, demand that the little one with the crutches, who looked a helluva lot like a kid he had kicked out of here yesterday but didn't talk like him, be let in the bull riding when it was already past the go-rounds (he didn't even have no RCA card; said Mickey Rooney's stunt man didn't need one)—well it was all just a king-sized pain in the ass. And while he was getting the horses saddled up and writing out Willy's permit to ride, Seymour decided he was going to get his money's worth out of this particular star.

At the head of the parade rode Seymour Hanes and the mayor of Brewton, sitting up on the trunk of the lead-off, goodwill Chevrolet convertible. Behind them were two girls in white hats and miniskirts on Appaloosa mares. One carried the Confederate flag on a long pole stuck into her stirrup; the other carried the American flag. And right behind them, with a couple of rodeo officials and a town councilman, rode Mary Tate, Santo, Craig and Willy, who was so excited he could hardly sit his horse. Pi and

Ruben had driven on out to the fairgrounds with the true Shorty Crump, who had already gotten very cheerful on the sherry.

The parade took nearly an hour to go the three miles from town to the fairgrounds. It was made up mostly of people on horseback, but there were also two bands, three convertibles, a covered wagon float behind four mules and, on foot, the Shriners and a sixth-grade class dressed as Indians.

There was whooping, blaring, neighing, honking and oompaahing from the bands. Quarter horses pranced and snorted and flicked their fine heavy necks like whips. The parade marshals all wore red armbands and rode up and down the length of the parade shouting with electric megaphones. The wind blew gaily, swirling dust and the strong good smell of horses, popping the banners and flags like firecrackers. The whole thing was loud and bright. Santo allowed it was the best parade he'd ever been in. Mary Tate and Craig and Willy agreed and Santo told the town councilman that it was the finest parade any of them had ever been in and offered him a drink of the wine he had in his saddlebags.

The fairgrounds was jammed with cars, buses, livestock and people when the parade got there. In the center was the arena—an old baseball outfield surrounded by heavy fence and bleachers. The parade moved inside the fence and around the arena once slowly to tremendous screaming and applause. Then Seymour Hanes's convertible pulled over and the two girls with the flags bolted into a canter. Everyone who was mounted followed whether they wanted to or not. The bands marched to either end of the arena and played *The Yellow Rose of Texas* as fifty cowboys and cowgirls dashed around and around the arena behind the flags. Craig followed Santo who sang with the band and followed Willy who grinned and clutched his pommel and followed Mary Tate. Mary Tate rode close to the roached mane of her horse, standing a little in the stirrups like a pro.

After four laps the flag girls pulled up in the center of the arena and the others stood their horses in a lathery line behind them. The bands played *The Star-Spangled Banner*.

At ". . . gave proof through the night" the drone of an airplane could be heard. As the last note of the anthem died away the drone stopped.

Almost every man, woman and child in Brewton looked up silently as a speck separated from the plane, floated on the blue air and sprouted. With a loud pop the speck suddenly flowered, yellow as a jonquil against the sky, and drifted for the arena. At one twenty-four a sky diver landed, not twenty yards from the girl with the Confederate flag, and the rodeo officially began.

16

The First Event was the presentation of the star.

Hanes gave Santo an elaborate introduction. He mentioned all the impossible stunts Crump had performed over the years, the barroom fights, the leaps from burning wagons, and promised the crowd that it would get a helluva sample later on. Then he said that anyone who wanted to could come up to the celebrities' platform and touch Shorty Crump or get his autograph. Santo looked properly humble and tough as the people swarmed around the platform. He shook hands and gave out autographs that said "Good luck, SC/js."

The platform was high above the arena, overhanging the east bleacher. With Hanes, the mayor and councilman and their wives, and the rodeo announcer, who sat at a table behind a microphone, there were ten of them up there on a space the size of three ping-pong tables. After the autographs Santo cleared the table of everything but the microphone and laid out the rest of the wine, the cheese and a huge garlic sausage that he'd picked up somewhere. He invited the people on the platform to help themselves.

"I never go to rodeos without garlic sausage," he explained.

"Forget it," said Hanes. "You ain't the worst—I had one one time ate bricks."

The Brewton rodeo was Rodeo Cowboys' Association approved, a part of the national circuit. That meant that the stock was all dependable and that there were some top hands around—cowboys who made their livings rodeoing, out of Smoot, Wyoming; Omak, Washington; Lemmon, South Dakota; Soda Springs, Idaho; Antlers, Oklahoma.

Lemmon, South Dakota took second money in the first event, the calf roping, to a local cowboy whose name happened to be Hanes, even though Lemmon seemed to have the fastest time.

Craig asked the announcer about it.

"Hard to tell," he shrugged, "unless you got one of these." He held out the official stop watch. "Sure is."

The bareback bronc riding was next and to everyone's surprise a rookie Brewton cowboy managed to beat out the field on style points, even Smoot, Wyoming, who was national champion of the year before. The rookie's name was Homer Wiley and the mayor's wife mentioned proudly that Homer'd always been her favorite nephew.

Homer did have a determined ride on a straight-away-bucking horse, raking the horse's withers so furiously with his spurs that he didn't notice the eight-second bell and had to be pulled off by a pick-up man. But even without it he was in the right rodeo. As it turned out, the mayor and Seymour Hanes were the only judges.

"That kid sure was in the right rodeo," said Santo when the winners were announced. He was leaning back in his chair, with Crump's fancy boots propped on the back of another one, eating cheese. "I liked Smoot, Wyoming, myself."

The announcer, Hanes and the mayor stared at him. So did the mayor's wife.

"Yeah, I can dig it," said Willy. "Lot more style. Wouldn't you just as soon they change that, Shorty?"

"You know, I would. I surely would," said Santo. "Just as soon they change the calf roping too."

"Now look heah . . ." began Seymour Hanes.

"Don't forget yourself, José," said Willy. "Don't forget who the hell the star is around here."

"*What'd* he say?" the mayor's wife asked the mayor. "What'd he call Buddy?"

"Who you got planned to win saddle-bronc and bull riding, Seymour?" Santo asked quietly. He offered a piece of garlic sausage to the mayor's wife.

Seymour Hanes turned the color of a radish. His little eyes glittered. "Who the hell you think you're talking to, son? You think some two-bit star can come in here and run my show?"

Santo was chuckling. "Calm down, Seymour. I got you by the short hair, old buddy."

Santo took a swallow of wine and went on to explain that he was not in fact a star at all. That he was only im*per*sonating Shorty Crump and could prove it by producing the real Crump. And that if they did not do as he said, to the letter, he would announce his true identity over that microphone yonder and tell all the good people of Brewton that they were being hoaxed by Hanes and the mayor.

"I'll tell 'em I'm really a homosexual plumber," he warned.

161

It was a horrified bunch of people that stared back at Santo. "You would ruuuin this grand tradition?" asked the councilman's haughty wife.

"Yessum," said Santo.

Hanes was disturbed but not entirely off balance. "Hoaxed 'em how?"

"Pocketed the five hundred dollars and got me free. Plus fixing the rodeo."

"They'd riot, José. Those good people would burn your ass," said Willy.

"I'd swear you tried to diddle me," added Mary Tate.

Hanes and the mayor did exactly as Santo asked them. They paid him the five hundred dollars, then, on the spot. They forced the announcer to announce that Lemmon, South Dakota, had won the calf roping after all, and Smoot, Wyoming, the bareback. They agreed to let Santo, Craig, Willy and Mary Tate help judge the saddle-bronc riding event. They even sent the councilman's wife out for more cheese and wine.

And, in a way, they got it all back out of Santo. Santo had intended all along to do a stunt or two for Hanes at the end of the rodeo, but nothing quite as grand as what he wound up doing.

The bull riding was the last event. There were eight riders who had gone through the preliminary go-rounds, and Willy. Willy drew seventh start and a big blue-white Brahma named Destruction. Before the event was announced Santo went with him down to the chutes. Ruben, Pi and Shorty Crump were waiting on them there.

"You really gonna let that little sparrowfart ride a bull?" Shorty asked Santo. He was coming up on pie-eyed drunk.

"Who you calling little?" said Willy. "You call me that again I'll kick your ass."

Shorty grinned and took him around to borrow the stuff he needed: spurs, bull rigging, bells. Then they all stood on the slats of the stock pen watching the first four big-humped animals being chuted.

Shorty explained how the bull ought to be spurred and where Willy should try to keep his weight. He showed him how to take a twist in the palm of his glove before closing on the rope to make it harder for his hand to pull loose. He showed him how to use his free arm for balance and how to keep the elbow of the riding arm in tight to his stomach.

Willy smiled as he nodded but his mouth was trembling. Once while Shorty was watching a passing cowgirl he whispered to Santo his mother's name and address.

"Think about Shoulders," Santo told him.

"Shoulders hell, I'm watching ass," said Crump. "Like two hogs in a croker sack."

Willy's bull raised hell when he was run into the chute. Using his stubby horns like a shovel he scooped a plank out of the gate and shattered it with his heavy blue butt. Shorty quieted him by twisting his ear.

"Bull's got a soft ear," he explained. "You mess with his ear he'll stop anything he's doing, I don't care what it is."

As soon as the fifth rider came out of his chute Crump began to get Willy ready. He cinched the rope up tight behind the bull's shoulders, adjusted Willy's spurs and helped ease him into position on the top slats of the chute straddling the bull.

As he worked he sweated and stammered. "Goddamit, I love this. I *love* it," he said. "Look, you gotta watch his horns, pissant. Sometimes he'll hook one of 'em behind him to grab you. Guy over there says this bull's a spinner. That means he'll come out and start kicking around his front feet with his back ones. Turning. So you're gonna have to lean outside and forward. Keep your elbow in your gut. And when you hit, hit that dirt running. Don't look around for no bull or no clown or nothing. Just scat for that goddamn fence."

The sixth rider got hurt. He was thrown under his bull and before the clown could turn the animal it had crushed the man's cheek like an eggshell with its hoof. As number six was being helped back to the fence, glassy-eyed and spitting teeth, Willy was announced.

"Out of chute number three, California cowboy Willy Ewing on Dee-struction." And Willy exploded from his chute—leaning outside and forward, raking the bull with his one good leg and yelling like a banshee.

Just as Shorty said he would, the bull spun in tight little circles near the chute. Hanging on with his right hand and waving the hat with his left Willy flopped around on the great skim-milk back like a rag doll.

"Ride him," shouted Santo. "Tear him up!"

"That's a Bramer-ridin fool," yelled Shorty Crump who was snorting and chuckling with excitement.

Then suddenly Willy was gone—down the far flank of the bull. The bull's head dropped and whirled with him.

The clown, whose job was to distract the bull, stood stock-still and yelled at the fence. "He's *hung*. He's hung up."

As soon as the bull bucked around they could all see what he meant. Willy's hand was hung at the wrist under the bull rope along the Brahma's right side, and Willy was being thrashed against the ground each time the animal bucked.

"Sweet Jesus Christ," said Pi.

"He's being killed," Ruben said. "It's *killing* him, Santo."

But Santo had already vaulted into the arena and was standing beside the clown, his arms out like a wrestler, watching the bull.

"Don't get that bastard running," said the clown, "or he'll kill him sure as hell."

For a long moment there was no sound at all, then Seymour Hanes's voice came over the microphone. "Folks," it said good-naturedly, "folks, that yonder is your star Shorty Crump out in the arena with that maddened animal, about to do a stunt. For *you*. Let's hear it for Shorty Crump."

164

Santo was crouched, crabbing his way toward the bull who whirled without bucking now, trying to hook the annoyance off its side. Willy had managed to grab the rope with his other hand. He was holding his head and chest up to the bull's belly as his lower body was swept along the ground.

As the bull turned away in one of its circles Santo took three quick steps and leaped. He timed it perfectly. Just as the Brahma's head came around, low and hooking to the right, Santo was on it. His left arm locked around the wattled neck, his right hand grabbed a horn. His legs went out stiff in front of him and the forward movement of the bull stood him up.

". . . Years and years of practice cain't reduce the danger of this stunt one bit . . ." Hanes was saying. The crowd was standing, breathless. "He's taking his life in his hands here, for Brewton."

The bull was frenzied. It stumbled, bellowed, tossed, twisted, kicked, and still Santo dragged his feet and hung on. Somehow he had turned his body in front of the bull so that his chest now seemed to be riding the animal's snout. And he had burrowed his head down between the horns.

On the platform Craig was standing in front of Mary Tate when Santo finally stopped the bull, telling the still-prattling Seymour Hanes in a quiet voice to turn off the goddamn microphone or get it busted over his head. Mary Tate was crying and threatening all of Brewton.

"He stopped the goddam thing," said Hanes, more to himself than to the audience or Craig. "How in the name of Christ . . ."

From the platform Santo, the bull and Willy all looked like one animal—Willy dangling from the center and Santo draped over the front, his head cleaved to the bull's. The strange-looking mass stood for a minute or two without a quiver as the clown came up cautiously, freed Willy and helped him back to the fence. Elegant as Theseus, Santo leaped away from the bull, arms extended, facing the crowd, grinning, spitting and wonderfully gory. From forehead to shirt collar he was covered with blood.

The crowd went ape. It rocked the bleachers with approval. Twenty feet away the bull stared at Santo, dazed and annoyed and bleeding slowly at the head. Santo had nearly bitten off its left ear.

All Brewton belonged to them.

Crump wanted to stay around and cash in on that fact but Santo talked him into driving him and Mary Tate and Craig back to Birmingham.

Willy, Ruben and Pi did stay. The last Craig saw of them they each had a gin and tonic in hand and were chatting to interested little groups of Brewtonites. This was at Seymour Hanes's barbecue after the rodeo, in honor of Santo-Crump.

"Stay hungry," Santo told Willy as they were leaving. Willy was unhurt except for a bruised tail and a few glamorous abrasions on his face, but he looked like a different man. The clown had told Santo at the rodeo that Willy had wedged his hand under the rope with the left-hand glove.

"I love you," he told Santo.

"Hang in there," Santo said and poked at his belly.

"Peace," said Pi.

Ruben smiled.

They took ten slabs of barbecue ribs in a sack and ate them in the car. When Mary Tate finished hers she leaned against Craig, tucked her legs under her and put her left hand up high on his leg. Her face was flushed and beautiful.

"I loved you today, Swamp. You had fun, didn't you?"

Craig's head was already beginning to buzz. His thoughts were going soft and he wanted to sleep. She kissed him slowly and quietly and he saw a thought distract her, saw it ripple over her eyes.

"How come that boy said he loved you, baby?" she asked Santo.

"Huh? Oh. He didn't mean me exactly," Santo said and went back to talking rodeo with Shorty Crump.

17

HE TOOK TO pulling the velvet drapes in the morning all through the house and leaving them closed until evening. All day the big Carrier in the basement thrummed cool, odorless air through vents in the floor.

The house stayed chill and dark and uncleaned.

He had all their food delivered. He went to work infrequently. He spent most mornings sleeping and mooning over Mary Tate and in the afternoons he slept again or worked out downtown with Santo and worried about her coming home.

The weeks of working out had made him stronger and bigger than he'd ever been before but despite that, in the two weeks following the rodeo, Craig was unhealthy. He felt bloody-mouthed and torpid as a grazing animal suddenly made to eat meat. And while the old diet of country club, office and Rotary now seemed impossibly bland, the new one, with Mary Tate as its nightly main course, was making him a sort of invalid.

It was not so much the rigorous schedule of sex with her that enfeebled him (though he had begun to wonder about his adequacy, his continuing potency; even, in the back of his mind, whether this much sex might not give you heart trouble or something) as the rate at which their relationship was changing. Like Santo, Mary Tate seemed to be interested only in ferocious engagements. And like Santo she plummeted into them, taking whoever happened to be around along with her.

It was the momentum that got to Craig. Seemingly overnight he had lost his distance. His life was different. He was involved.

"All you have to do," she woke him one night to say, "is just sleep, just lie there, just be, and I love you."

"Good."

"I'm yours. Completely all yours. How does that grab you?"

"Fine."

"I don't ever want anybody but you."

"How do you know?" he asked her.

"What?"

"I mean how about Joe?" He could feel her looking at him. "I just mean that's a long time, ever."

The next day she brought home a small gold necklace and fastened it around his neck. Engraved on the medallion was To PRINCE CRAIG. FROM ALL OF ME FOREVER, MARY TATE.

He grew fastidious. He still couldn't look at her without wanting her. But little things, little facets of the magnificent raunchiness that used to excite him filled him now with a sort of dread: her coming naked to the table for their haphazard dinners, her using the toilet without closing the door, her habit of waking him in the middle of the night with a finger under his nose that was tart with her odor.

But despite everything he was not unhappy. He felt a kind of animal contentedness. He watched his muscles grow. He daydreamed. He canceled his trip to Montana in August.

Hal Foss came up to see him one afternoon, very agitated. Craig had worked out at noon and was taking a nap when Foss rang the chimes. He grabbed a carrot off his dresser on the way to the door.

"Culver said to forget it. FORGET it. He's taking the whole deal over to Bly Realty. You had an appointment with the man, Craig. Who do you think you are? That's a thirty-thousand-dollar package you blew. The second one this month."

"Look, Hal . . ." he began. He wasn't in the mood to talk real estate.

"All right, forget it. That's not why I came up anyway. What were you, asleep?"

Craig just looked at him. Foss had on a double-breasted gabardine suit, a blue-striped Brooks shirt and a foulard tie. He looked neat and calm as a letter opener. Craig felt a momentary surge of jealousy.

"Three o'clock in the afternoon on a Wednesday and you're asleep . . ." Foss came inside and stood looking at the disarray: a half-empty Coke bottle, a bra of Mary Tate's, her yellow portable stereo. "Uh huh," he said.

"I'm sorry about missing tennis. I was out of town two weekends ago, sick last weekend."

Foss sat on the sofa, hitched up his pant legs to save the crease and crossed his legs. His blue ribbed stocking ran neatly, forever, up his calf. "You look like you're staying in shape," he said coolly.

"I've been . . . exercising." Craig chewed the carrot vigorously, his mouth open.

"Uh huh." There was a long silence. "Why are you eating that carrot like that?"

"Good for your jaw muscles. I eat eight or ten a day. Can I get you something? We've got some Cokes and tomato juice. A little scotch . . . carrots."

"Look, Craig—what can I do? We've been friends a long time and it bothers the heck outta me to see you like this. This house like this. I mean you come from one of the first families of the state. There's a certain—*name*. I mean with your parents dead . . ."

"I'm all right, Hal. I'm just working out a few things in my mind. I haven't had a chance to get the place cleaned."

Foss's eye flicked over the bra, around the room. He lit a cigarette and looked at Craig evenly. "Is it gambling?"

"Is what gambling?"

"What you've gotten into. These people you're seeing now, Craig. I might as well tell you. I asked around. That Three-O'Clock place is a known gambling den."

Craig laughed, thinking how much had happened since that night, feeling Foss's impossible distance. "I'm not gambling, Foss. Look, if there were anything you could help me with I'd tell you about it."

Foss cleared his throat. "You're one of my closest friends. We've always had everything in common, same background, same clubs, same friends." Foss struggled to continue. "This attraction of yours to, uh, other types of people has always worried me. It can get you into bad trouble. They have ways. I mean if you're in *love* with her that's one thing . . ."

"Ease off, Hal."

"They have *ways*." Foss was getting shrill. "How do you know they're not after your money? That Mr. Alabama guy and the rest of them could be *using* this girl. How do you even know if she's *clean?*"

"Ease off, motha," he said in Franklin's voice. He stood up and shadowboxed at Foss. "You're talking about my woman."

"Come on, Craig."

"I'll kick your ass for that, Bru." He skipped around in front of Foss, on his toes. "I know twelve places I could hit you, *all in the face,* and kill you dead as hell. They taught me how."

"That's not funny," said Foss. He was up and backing toward the door. "I came up here in good conscience, Craig."

Craig tapped him in the stomach. "Hook out an eye like an olive out of a bottle."

"Look, dammit, you're not acting yourself. Remember who you are." Foss was out of the door, backing down the steps to the driveway and trying feebly to block Craig's little openhanded punches.

"Break the nose bone right at the top, take the heel of your hand and shove it up into the brain . . ."

"You're a very sick person," Foss yelled at him from his car.

As he drove off Craig looked at his watch. He had one hundred and fifteen minutes to rest before Mary Tate got home.

He tried to tell her about Foss's visit while she changed out of the smock she wore at the studio. He tried to tell her about the funny expression on Foss's face when he first stepped inside the house, his concern, his fright as Craig shadowboxed around him. But Mary Tate, who had met Foss once and disliked him, was not interested.

"He's doing it more," she interrupted him. She was freshening her lipstick at a vanity that she had charged to him and set up below his gun rack. She was bare from the waist up and fetching in the soft afternoon light.

"Who's doing what?" he asked sullenly. Foss's visit seemed less funny after telling about it, and more like a significant, touching act of friendship.

"Thor. He watches me all the time through that hole. I can see his little beady eye up there and sometimes hear him breathing."

"Why don't you tell somebody?"

"Who's there to tell, silly?"

"Tell Joe."

"Joe wouldn't care. He probly wouldn't believe it."

"Call the police," he said and turned over on the bed.

"The po*lice?*" she laughed, her high obscene laugh. "You'd be surprised what goes on down there, babe. It ain't no Woodstream Country Club."

"What kind of things?"

"Just things."

"Come on, Mary Tate. You know that pisses me off. Don't bring something up if you don't want to talk about it."

"Well, Thor and Newton. They have orgies up there at night all the time. And some of the women who work out—boy, you wouldn't be*lieve* some of those women." She turned from the vanity to face him, her high breasts bobbing. As was his habit he forced his eyes to her face.

"Wouldn't believe what?"

"Well, just for instance, you know that leg-press machine? You know that shiny pole the weight goes on?" Craig knew. There was one like it in the men's section—plates of weight with holes in the center were slipped down on a two-foot, chromium rod that had about the same diameter as a banana. "Some of 'em use that to, well, they sit on it and screw theirselves."

"Jesus Christ," he said and turned over again. He stared at his oak wall, feeling sick.

"Well, you asked me," she said, coming over to him. "Craig" —she took his face in her hands—"you asked me, baby." She lay down on top of him giggling.

One hot, quiet afternoon near the end of July they took a rare walk together around the mountain. From the garden they followed the cow path down through the woods to the blacktop that ran alongside the pasture, and sat on the gate watching his uncle's heifers graze toward them. Up the broad sweep of front lawn above the pasture was the house, built of long, buff-colored stone and green wood. It seemed to float up there, on the clouds of fat English boxwood all around it.

Mary Tate shook her head. "Jesus, that's beautiful. And you grew up up there." She made it sound incredible.

"We moved in when I was fourteen. When my grandfather died."

"Where'd your grandmama go?"

"Stayed with us. She died too about a year later."

"And now it's yours. How come you need such a big house?"

"Need it . . . ?"

It struck Craig that she had never asked about his background before; that they had never talked about it. He didn't know if he could get the whole elaborate mess straight enough to tell but he figured he owed her a try. "Hell, I don't need it," he said. "It needs me."

His grandfather built it over a period of years. It started as a summer cottage, a place to buggy to out of the heat of the city. Then as the trail to it became a road it occurred to his grandfather that he might as well live out there. He bought the whole mountain as insurance against the same thing occurring to anybody else.

As chief justice of the State Supreme Court, real estate broker and mine owner he was a busy man but he went on adding to the house a little at a time the way you build a sand castle—dripping New Hampshire granite for the walls, Italian marble for the fireplaces, Chippendale furniture and Persian rugs for the inside, Tennessee walking horses and prize Jerseys for the pasture—until the house became not a house at all but reconstructed history, a realized dream of antebellum life.

Not until the house was completely furnished, the full-grown boxwoods and flowering shrubs and fruit trees planted, the animals grazing, did Judge Blake retire and move in. He was sixty-seven then, chronically constipated and mean.

For the six years before he died he rode for two hours every morning before breakfast. He read Carlyle every afternoon, sold prize turkeys and calves and referred to his home, to those few people allowed to visit it, as "our way of life up here."

Craig never remembered seeing him without a tie.

When he died in 1954 his will divided the mountain into four forty-acre plots, one for each son, and stipulated that none of the land could be sold outside the family. The highest forty, the way of life, fell to the oldest son, Walter, Craig's father—who wanted no part of it.

Walter was a stylish man who loved business, people and parties, who preferred gin to Carlyle and who hated horses. He liked living near town and near Blake Realty Company which he ran very handily along with younger brother Henry. To him the house on the mountain was just a property and an unwieldy one at that. But his mother, old Mrs. Blake, took it very seriously and told him so repeatedly in her last year. After a while so did his wife, who planted jonquils and softened the sterner lines of the house with ivy but otherwise left it respectfully alone. And after living there for a few years, Walter, too, succumbed.

"That mountain is part of your tradition," he told Craig one day, making a way of life traditional in a record six years. They were in his Lincoln, coming out from town. His father, as was his habit when annoyed, shot an elegantly-linked cuff. "It's not a bad tradition as traditions go—integrity, privacy, not hitting women . . . small tendency to drink too much."

Craig was twenty, home from college in Virginia. Depressed by the August heat he had mentioned that he couldn't wait to get his ass out of Birmingham for good.

"That place stands for something in this city, buddy. And when your turn comes around you should be proud to live there."

"Stands for what?"

"Achievement, civic prominence, gracious living. And the most expensively produced manure in Jefferson County . . . You'll have to keep all that up."

Craig had never learned how to doubt his father, so six years

174

later when Uncle Henry called him at his graduate student board-inghouse in Iowa City (he was drunk on bourbon, learning how to catch walleyes through the ice from *Field and Stream*) to tell him that a private plane with his parents in it had flown into a North Carolina mountain—he knew the shit had hit the fan. And when his uncle asked him in the same long conversation what he planned to do about the "place" (saying the word as if the house were a bereft child), Craig didn't even think. "Come home and live in the bastard," he said.

Mary Tate was squatting beside the pasture gate, stroking the spotted ear of a grazing cow. Craig looked down at the sun-streaked hair that hugged her head like feathers on a duck's back, at the beautiful elemental curve of her position, and realized that none of what he had said could possibly make sense to her.

It was depressingly hot and still.

"Well, I'm glad you came back to live here," she said. She smiled earnestly up at him. "And I'm glad you got this house. I'd rather live up here than anywhere else in the world."

Walking back up the hill to the house, Craig watched his Uncle Herbert's sleek green Buick drive up the private road from the highway. From a distance it looked more like a yacht than a car—judicial, plump, composed. Halfway up the road it turned mas-sively off the road into a driveway, causing Craig to remember that it had been over a month since he had seen any of his rela-tives, any of the blood kin with whom he inhabited this hill.

Back at the house Mary Tate turned on the television and Craig walked around for a while, picking up ash trays, looking at silver, until he could no longer resist an urge that had come over him as suddenly and powerfully as nausea. He put on a pair of gym shorts and tennis shoes. He ate two carrots and a glob of peanut butter. He coated his entire body with Vaseline to retard sweat-ing and rubbed Sloan's liniment into the backs of his thighs and calves. Then he left the house quietly and ran.

For thirty minutes he ran without stopping, aimlessly at first, along the ridge of the mountain behind the house, then down the mountain's east flank along the back edge of familiar lawns. Lights were going on in the houses. It had grown dark enough to make him want to stay as close to them as he could without being seen.

The liniment burned his muscles. His body felt fired and light with energy.

At the powerline he cut cross-county through a thicket of pines where the red smudge of remaining sun was lost completely. When he crossed the road again his legs were heavy, his damp hair was in his eyes and his throat was dry. He flailed past the stone bear guarding the driveway of one of his cousins, jumped a hedge and pushed himself uphill for a quarter of a mile then down again, over the last cropped expanse of lawn, across a drainage ditch— and pulled up finally, gasping and heaving at the lip of the bluff that dropped off to the highway, ending the mountain. He stood there, at the farthest edge of the Blake property line, panting and blowing mucous from his nose, with no place left to run.

18

People down south hate social equality. You take your average mill-worker—seeing all this would make him happy, just to know that a few miles over the mountain from his house there's a bunch of people who are prettier and smarter and richer and more carefree than he is. Down here if you didn't have a bunch of people like that you'd have to go out and find one.

JOE SANTO, Woodstream Country Club, August 6, 1968

Which is exactly what Birmingham had to do. The city started late in the nineteenth century without the advantage of a social

177

roof—a top layer of descendants of prewar planter families—like Charleston's or Nashville's, say. It was a tough industrial city and didn't think it needed one. But no southern city can get by for very long with only part of a class structure, so Birmingham imported and invented a roof. Threw it together so to speak.

Cy and Amy Walterson were in the invented category. The success of his chains of barbecue restaurants and parking lots, her success in making virtually everybody feel smarter than she, his civic work, her charity work and interest in shrubs—those things got them in and kept them there, together with their annual party.

The party was a huge formal dinner dance, held on the first weekend of August at the Woodstream. Of the more than five hundred inventeds and importeds invited about three hundred and fifty usually came. The top three hundred and fifty: families of the men who chaired the boards, commanded the mills and published the print that kept Birmingham chugging toward its magical destiny—to become the Pittsburgh of the South.

Amy had held the first one seven years ago as a sort of coming-out party for herself when she and Cy were finally allowed membership to Woodstream. She had hired Guy Lombardo to play in the ballroom and Nat King Cole to sing intimately in the grille. And when someone reminded her that she had missed the dining room, she hired, at the last minute and for a pittance, an authentic Tennessee mountain mouth-organist. What he did was attract more attention during the party than Lombardo and Cole together.

She had had somebody authentic in the dining room every year since—a jug blower, a clog dancer, a warbler, a one-man band from Joplin, Missouri—and every year he was the main attraction, no matter that he was smelly and hairy and usually spoke with an accent.

It was not Amy's way to wonder why that was. It was a good thing and she kept it going. But subliminally she knew why *she* liked the authentics. Ever since she became an aristocrat she had enjoyed feeling *in*authentic—like some exotic tool, a cookie cutter

178

maybe, ornate, oddly sharpened, inappropriate for ordinary work. ("Amy can't even boil an egg," Cy would say proudly. Amy would shake her little curls. "I don't even know where to get one.") And being around an authentic once in a while, as he demonstrated some blunt proficiency for five hundred dollars cash money, heightened that pleasure for her.

On Friday afternoon, August 6, at the very moment that Amy was deciding with Mr. Brodie, the manager of the club, where her authentic for this year would stand or sit or crouch in relation to the tables of shirred eggs and quail, he, the authentic, was in his own club pushing four hundred pounds of iron off his chest and talking about Amy.

"I don't care how rich I was, I wouldn't pay me five hundred dollars to sing for three weeks every day. I told her that on the phone."

"What did she say?" Craig asked him. He was standing over Santo, spotting his bench presses. Santo finished the set with three more repetitions, got up and slid a twenty-five pound plate on either end of the bar.

"Said she always paid that. To 'you people' she said. Said it would throw the whole party off to change it now."

Wall Street and Hump were working out with them. Franklin, on duty and in his smock, leaned against the cold-drink machine watching. There were five or six other men in the gym. It was a hot windy afternoon and the fire escape door over the alley was open. The wind brought in noise and the smell of hot dogs off the street.

"I told you how much she paid when I first asked you about it last month," Craig said.

"I must of thought I was worth it that day."

"If you're gon dance you got to pay the piper," Wall Street said mysteriously.

"You flat better take it," Franklin said. "After Sunday you gonna need all you can get."

179

"What for?"

"You gonna be famous, Joseph. It costs money to be Mr. Southeast. You gonna need new threads, a new car. You got to travel, got to go places."

"Got to win it first," said Santo.

"Sheeat. You look bettern Steve Reeves ever looked. Who the fuck's gonna beat you?"

Craig had wondered the same thing. Santo's summer-long training and dieting had turned him, just two days before the big contest, into a spectacle, a . . . curiosity. Craig wondered if in the history of the world there had ever been a body as thoroughly exploited as Santo's was now. It was massive as a bear's but carved with figurine-like intricacy. The proportion of the parts, down to his fingers, was perfect and the skin that covered it all was taut and smooth and flawless as an apple's.

"You might make Johnny Carson," Wall Street suggested.

"In a jockstrap?" said Santo.

"I seen it once when they had Paul Dickerson on there."

Hump looked at Wall. "Paul Dickerson? That fat shit? If they had him on there once they ought to have Joe on eight times. What can he do but pick up some weight?"

"He can whip yo ass," Franklin mentioned.

"Joe can *sing*, jerkoff."

"From Woodstream to Johnny Carson," said Santo. "I wouldn't mind that. I always wanted to be a singer. I started to stay in Bora Bora once. Guy down there offered me a full-time job singing in a club. For a good buck. Lie on the beach, collect some sea shells . . . build me a shack like Gauguin. I shoulda done it." He stretched back out on the bench.

"Gogagne?"

"What time we supposed to be there?" Santo asked Craig.

"She said to have you there about seven. Come on up and we'll go together."

"You talking about Larry Gogagne from Roebuck?" Franklin wanted to know.

"I think I'll meet you out there. Then I'll have a car if they run me off."

"They're gonna love you. Put a little of that authentic country on them."

"I'm not just crazy about that word." Santo rocked the bar off the metal holders and did three smooth, flatback reps with four hundred and fifty pounds. "Is Mary Tate excited?"

"Hell yeah. She bought a new dress and she's been practicing how to talk clean. She says she's nervous as a whore at a wedding."

"Hey Joe—Gogagne build that shack in Roebuck?" asked Hump.

"Yeah." Santo stared at the ceiling. "I'm nervous too."

"What the hell for?" Craig asked him.

"Because I know you, old buddy. You're gonna try to show me off," he said.

The truth was, Craig was nervous too. He had not been to one of Amy's parties in three years. Usually this was his week on the Madison River in Montana and more than once that evening as he dressed (in his father's bedroom; Mary Tate's things were sprawled all over his) he wished he were there, about to be talking trout and flies at Wiley's grille in Ennis, instead of shepherding Santo and Mary Tate through legions of tinkling, odorous people whose names he had a hard time remembering.

It no longer seemed amusing, the picture of Santo there. He regretted having called Amy when Halsey first mentioned the party and having talked Santo into doing it. And there was Mary Tate. Who the hell would she *talk* to? After all he did do business with a lot of those men and there was no point annoying their wives.

Mary Tate yelled from the bathroom that she had lost her toothbrush and wanted to borrow his. "Christ," he said to himself and didn't answer her.

He put his father's ruby studs in the ruffled shirt front. The air-conditioning vents in the room were closed and he got hot struggling with the studs. This summer seemed to be taking a very long time.

He slipped on patent leather pumps and a gray silk dinner jacket. He patted his cheeks with Canoe, put on his solid black dinner watch from Lucien Piccard and the ring that was three interlocking gold bands from Georg Jensen. He folded fifty dollars and his driver's license into a moneyclip and put it along with mints and change in his back pocket. Craig never carried a wallet with evening clothes; it ruined the hang of the trousers. Then he checked his nails and the lie of his hair and ran his shoes under the electric buffer. He would try to leave early. He would get down two or three drinks in a hurry and find somebody to talk to Mary Tate who didn't care who they talked to. They could leave early and let Santo take care of himself.

"You look beautiful," he said, and she did, but little as Craig knew about women's clothes he knew there was something wrong. The dress was hot pink organza with a cloud of paler ostrich plumes along the bottom. Pink spaghetti straps held it on her shoulders. The neckline dipped almost to her sternum and the feathers at the bottom of the dress curled just above the middle of her thighs. She had on a pair of high, shiny shoes dyed to match the dress and in her hand was a rhinestone-crusted purse.

She did look beautiful; she looked radiant. But she did not look like the Woodstream Country Club.

"So do you," she said coming to him and holding his face in a way she had so that her cool small palms cupped his chin. She smelled faintly of vanilla as she kissed him. He loved her. He would not tell her about the dress.

"Boy, I hope Joe does good," she said, still holding his face.

"He will. He'll do fine."

"Is he coming here?"

"We're going to meet him there. We've got to go."

"Baby."

"Huh?"

"You know you're everything to me. You're like a mama and a daddy and brothers and a best friend all rolled up in one."

He stared at her blunt, lovely, country face and didn't know what the hell to say to that. "Good," he managed finally. "That's fine, baby." He smiled at her and steered her toward the door.

The club was decorated entirely in red and yellow, the colors of the Walterson's family crest. A huge likeness of the crest itself hung above the front entrance to the club, and beneath it scurried nine white-suited door-openers and car-parkers. Craig and Mary Tate arrived at seven-twenty, forty minutes before the party was to start, and the club was already filling fast.

They found Santo standing by the coat-check room, his arms folded on his chest, gazing calmly over the elegantly dressed people, the urns full of long-stemmed red and yellow roses, the comfortable beribboned expanses of the club's central hallway and nether rooms. Santo looked as though he knew and loved it all.

He was dressed in an outlandishly fringed buckskin suit, a purple shirt, scrolled cowboy boots and a wide-brimmed straw hat. There was no doubt that he looked vaguely authentic. But it was hard to tell exactly as what.

"Where'd you pick up the duds, Shorty?"

"Rented 'em, mister," drawled Santo, looking over the crowd. "How're you, Mary Tate?"

"So scared I could wet my pants."

"They're beautiful aren't they?"

"What?" Craig asked him.

"These people, man. They've got taste." He drew the word out and let his look come around to Craig and Mary Tate for the first time. Craig saw his eyes and hoped Mary Tate did not.

"What's the matter, baby?" she asked him.

"Isn't that dress a little . . . loud for this place?"

Mary Tate looked down at herself, her mouth open. "What's . . . oh shit, Swamp, is it wrong?"

It was the first cruel thing Craig had ever heard Santo say and he couldn't help thinking he must have a good reason. So he said, "Well, I don't think you'll see anything else like it."

Mary Tate looked at him and then at Santo and then back at

183

Craig. He watched her put her face together, the hurt mouth, the eyes, until the features were set and cool. Then she turned them to the filling hall and tossed her head. "Well, that's fine with me," she said.

Amy Walterson met them at the entrance to the ballroom. She was a short, pudgy woman with a porcine face surrounded by swirls of streaked, bouffant hair, and the nickname Angelfinger. She was sheathed tonight like a sausage in a floor-length midnight-blue Givenchy, and had already managed to fix her face into the vague-eyed, tremulous look, her party look, that immediately made strangers think her ingratiating or retarded or tight.

"We're delated to have you and your paramour with us this e'nin, Mr. Santo. Crayag, you were such a muffin . . ."

"Me and my what?" asked Santo.

"Your little friend here," said Amy, indicating Mary Tate with a pufflike gesture.

"Miss Farnsworth is Craig's little friend, Mrs. Walterson. In the interest of clarity," Santo said with dignity.

"You better believe it," added Mary Tate.

"Grand, grand . . ." Angelfinger looked confused.

In the corner of his eye he could see lank cousin Rose Nell swaying toward them and suddenly the unlikeliness of the whole situation smote Craig like a double whiskey across the head, relaxing him.

He would enjoy it.

"Yes indeed," he said, "my paramour for some time now. Rose Nell Debencourt," he said, taking his cousin by her reedy arm, "Miss Mary Tate Farnsworth, Mr. Joseph Santo, M.A., and of course your hostess . . ."

"Delated to see you," said Angelfinger.

Santo was to begin picking his guitar and singing at ten o'clock sharp when the guests moved into the dining room for supper. Amy Walterson showed him where to stand, arranged for a jug of cider to be placed on a nearby table, handed him his check in a

184

pink monogrammed envelope, told him he could wander freely about until ten o'clock and asked him if there was anything else he needed.

"A rib."

"A rib?"

"A sparerib with my cider," said Santo and winked at Craig.

"Got to have the rib, Amy, or my man can't perform."

"Why, all right, Crayag, I'm sure Mr. Brodie can find a rib. You mean—well a cooked one?"

Then Craig took them downstairs for a drink.

There were fifty or sixty people in the grille, eating in quiet clusters at the gleaming wooden tables or drinking at the bar, but so quickly did the eyes of anyone entering ignore all of them but one that they might as well have been reflections of her shimmering presence at the bar.

Her name was Zoe Mason. She was six feet two inches tall and had the hands and feet of a man but nothing else. She owned a monumental beauty, a stunning rightness of heroic parts to the whole that thickened the tongue of anyone who saw her. There was so much more of her and it was all so breath-takingly arranged that around her, smaller beautiful women looked like single shrimp beside a seafood platter. She was also rich (three times married to huge fortunes and three times divorced, she was reputed to be wealthier than anyone in the state except the governor) and she spent most of her time traveling from one of her tropical homes to another, depending on where the fishing was best. Zoe Mason held light-tackle records for white marlin, sailfish and wahoo, as well as the female records for tarpon in every line class.

Craig had not seen her in over a year and was not sure he was glad to see her now. She had beaten him too many times at tennis and once, guiding for herself, had outfished him three fish to one for a whole week in the Keys. Talking to her always made him feel, for some reason, as though he were faceless.

He looked at Santo, saw him notice her and saw, incredibly, his eyes pass on around the room.

"Jesus, what a room," said Santo. "Look at that ceiling, Mary Tate."

But Mary Tate was staring at Zoe Mason and chewing on her lower lip. "You know her?" she asked Craig.

"Yeah I know her."

"She's the most gorgeous woman I ever saw."

Craig ordered their drinks and when he looked up Zoe Mason was looking at them from down the bar. "You're about to meet her," he said.

They watched her toss a word over the head of the little dumpling of a lady she'd been talking to and start down to them. Everyone in the grille watched her move. She had on a white sheath, flared like a tulip at the bottom and a diamond choker around her long nut-brown throat. Under the high German forehead her eyes coming toward them looked as if they stared at fire all day long.

"Hello, lovey," she said to Craig. "Who's your friend?"

Santo was leaning back on his elbows, almost reclining on the bar, still studying the ceiling of carved wooden panels.

Zoe Mason punched him lightly in the stomach. "Hey. What are you looking at?"

"The ceiling."

"Why are you dressed like that?"

"I'm part of the show."

"What's your name?"

Santo dropped his eyes to hers and stood up. They were almost precisely the same height. Craig felt something clear and sharp as glass pass between them.

"What's yours?"

"Come on," she said and took his arm. "I'll show you around this dump."

19

AFTER ZOE MASON led Santo off, Craig threw down three straight Jack Daniel's in as much time as it took Chub to pour them. Mary Tate stood beside him at the bar looking nervously around and holding her champagne cocktail as though it were a bouquet. From the ballroom a strange, sad rendition of *Blue Velvet* floated down and hovered over the bar on a cloud of Chanel and Prince Matchabelli.

After the third shotglass of whiskey Craig ordered a civilized-looking bourbon and water and was signing his check when Foss, Halsey and Packman came bouncing down the stairs into the grille followed by three women, one of whom was Dorothy Stephens.

"The little water-ski thing," said Dorothy Stephens to Mary Tate. "How are you?" Craig was the only one who smiled.

Halsey sighed through his nose. "We have a table. I think we'll get a steak down here instead of waiting till ten for those damned little birds. Why don't you join us?" He was staring at Mary Tate.

"We'll sit down for a drink," said Craig.

"That's what I meant."

"How's it going, Hal?"

"Fine," said Foss. "Missed you at work again today."

"Uh huh. I got tied up."

"Look, meet me for tennis tomorrow. I've got some things I want to say to you."

"You've gained a lot of weight, haven't you, Craig?" asked George Packman. Of the three men Craig had always liked him best and trusted him most. Foss's and Halsey's distance didn't bother him, but the cool set to Packman's athletic face did.

"Where's your table?" he asked, and thought screw all of them.

Halsey's wife was a thin, breastless girl named Rhoda. As soon as they were seated she asked Mary Tate how she liked the club. Then Brenda Mathews, Packman's fiancée, who was president of the Junior League and the Woodstream book club, who was plump and henlike and affectionate, wanted to know how Craig and Mary Tate had met.

"At the Three O'Clock Club in Five Points," said Mary Tate.

"Oh," said Brenda Mathews and that was that.

Dorothy Stephens sat across the table from Craig, glancing at him occasionally with a haughty, pitying look. Foss ignored him and talked to Halsey about land development. Mary Tate tried hard to be charming; she put a stiff smile on her mouth and kept it there as Rhoda complained about the difficulty of finding reliable help and Brenda Mathews told about how the ocean was eating the foundation out from under her parents' beach house in Fort Walton.

Speaking of beach houses, said Packman, he had seen Zoe Mason upstairs, dancing with some very strange-looking person. "He was talking about the ceilings or something and she was asking him if he wanted a job."

"He's a friend of mine," said Craig. "He's singing in the dining room tonight."

"He asked me if I was enjoying myself," said Packman.

Chub the bartender had come over to the table and was standing behind Halsey trying to get his attention.

"Who is this guy, Craig?" asked Halsey. "Where'd you find him?"

"Mr. Halsey—Can I get y'all something else?" asked Chub.

"He's Mr. Alabama and he's about to be Mr. Southeast and then Mr. America."

"Joe? Joe's here?" breathed Dorothy Stephens.

"What?" said Foss. "You brought that freak to the club?"

Craig saw Mary Tate go rigid.

"Easy on the names, big fella . . ."

"Yes *suh*," said Halsey, laughing. "That's old Blake for you. Just ask him to get a singer. I've got to go see . . ."

"Mr. Halsey," said Chub again. "Can I get . . ."

Halsey whipped around in his chair. "You can shut your goddamn black face is what you can do."

"Pete!" said Rhoda.

"Who the hell does he think he is, interrupting me?" Halsey's skinny patrician face was enraged. Chub, who had handled dozens of these situations, turned easily and left. "If that ape messes with me again," said Halsey loudly, "I swear . . ."

"Would you hit him or what, Pete?" Craig asked.

"Uh, where is Joe?" Dorothy wanted to know.

"I'll tell you what—I'll bring him down, OK?" Mary Tate looked dangerous and Craig wanted to get her away from the table. Also the idea appealed to him. He felt a little lightheaded and excited.

"I'll introduce him around—you can get his autograph." He stood up, lifting Mary Tate by the elbow.

"I heard those guys can hardly move," said Halsey.

"He can make it down here all right."

He guided Mary Tate toward the bar, feeling gayer than he had in weeks. "They want an authentic, by God, they'll get one," he told Mary Tate. "I'm going to show the bastards what authentic is."

The upstairs of the club was choked with people. One end of the long hall opened into the ballroom and the other into the dining room. The entire space was shaped like a huge bar bell and it was completely full of wandering, smoking, chatting, drinking, reaching, laughing, tinkling, hand-shaking, cheek-kissing southern gentry. Craig pushed Mary Tate ahead of him, smiling and speaking as he went, to the ballroom.

It was a huge, round, vaguely seedy room with a high vaulted ceiling, old gilded chairs along the circumference and bewigged seventeenth-century men and women minueting away on its wallpaper. Santo and Zoe were not hard to spot. In the middle of the dance floor they seemed fluorescent. Surrounding them the other elegantly muted couples might as well have been shadows.

"Are you really going to interduce him to those shits downstairs?" Mary Tate whispered in his left ear as they pushed across the floor toward Santo.

"You goddamn right I am. How're you, Admiral? It'll be good for them."

Three couples away they could hear Santo's happy voice saying something about your average millworker. ". . . You'd have to go out and find one," he was saying as Craig put his hand on the buckskin shoulder. "Right, buddy?"

"Right. I've got some people I want you to meet."

"Forget it, lovey," said Zoe Mason. "He's staying with me."

Craig smiled at her, thinking she was kidding. She was not. "You come too, then."

"We're talking." She had a low serious voice with an authoritative trace of German accent. It was not a voice that played.

"Let's go," Santo said to her. "I told him he was going to want to show me off." He turned to Craig. "Miss Mason was telling me about tarpon fishing in the Keys. How they jump and all. Used a very colorful figure of speech about what they look like when they come up out of the water."

Craig looked at the Olympian face, hoping for a blush. Zoe Mason stared coolly back at him. "Craig has seen them," she said.

Mary Tate turned quickly and headed for the door.

On the way back to the grille, as a sort of warm-up, Craig introduced Santo to about twenty people, whomever he happened to see whose name he could remember. He introduced him grandly as Joe Santo, present Mr. Alabama, soon to be Mr. Southeast, Mr. America, Mr. Universe.

("Are you really?" Zoe Mason asked Santo after the first introduction. "Yes." "Will you take your shirt off?" "Now?" "Jesus. Mr. Alabama. They ought to be paying you to take your shirt off, not to sing.")

Santo met Alfred Croft, the Pepsi-Cola scion and his breasty wife, Wanda; Snake Snell, the ex-Auburn All-American and present alcoholic stockbroker; fabulously wealthy Lester Brewster and his Spanish wife, Consuela, whom, it was said, he had picked out of a Barcelona whorehouse. He shook hands with the Chaddy Caldwells and Horace Dennickers, who were always together and always calling each other "dearie." He was handled like a broiler chicken by Hattie Jewett, the city's obese cultural autocrat who married Birmingham money after an obscure history with a steel band from Trinidad. On the steps down to the grille he met Packman's mother and father, who owned seven hundred thousand dollars' worth of impressionist paintings but never could remember who had done them; and at the bar, Charlotte Stafford, a shrewd sexy author of "mature novels," who looked at Santo with cool flat eyes and asked if bodybuilders were good in bed.

"Keep your tacky writer questions to yourself, Charlotte," Zoe

Mason told her. Throughout the introductions she had stood beside Santo, lightly holding his arm, glancing disdainfully at the proffered hands, looking proud and owned by him and bored by everything else.

By the time Santo reached the table he was thoroughly practiced in being introduced as a celebrity. He shook hands with dignified nods of his head and a slight smile. He met Dorothy Stephens' unashamed joy at seeing him with calm, brotherly affection and inquired about the Junior League. As Craig talked on about his past and future achievements he took on a properly humble, inattentive expression and obligingly crossed his arms in a way that emphasized the width of his chest.

Like everyone who had been introduced to him, Halsey, Foss and the others were oddly subdued. They avoided his eyes, fidgeted and glanced at each other. Craig read these things as symptoms of awe. There was an image in the back of his head that he could barely keep from blurting out—"This guy," he wanted to inform Halsey, in the interest of truth and because he suspected Halsey and the others didn't realize it, "could crush you like an eggshell."

He was euphoric as he talked. People were turning around and he considered tapping a glass and introducing Santo from the table to the room at large, telling everyone there about the rodeo, the Mr. Gulf Coast Contest, the national white water championship . . . He was on the point of doing it, in his monologue somewhere around, "in addition to the finest latissimus dorsi probably in the country," when Mary Tate tugged at his sleeve and her look of suffering stopped him cold.

"I'm going upstairs," she said and flew.

"Pleasure meeting you people," said Santo. "I've got to set up for my performance." He followed Mary Tate, and Zoe Mason followed him. Craig stood looking at the familiar, unsmiling faces and felt himself go down like a punctured beach ball.

There was a long silence.

"I hope he doesn't mind that," said Foss grimly.

"Mind what?"

"Being made a fool of like that."

"A *fool?*"

"A spectacle. It was ab*sud*," added Halsey.

Dorothy was blushing and fooling with a sliver of carrot.

"You can't bring a person like that into . . ." Halsey continued. He was fingering a new scotch mist on the table in front of him. Before Craig knew he was going to do it he had shoved the glass into Halsey's lap.

Halsey jumped to his feet, stained from cummerbund to crotch and furious. "You're sick, Blake, you worthless sonofabitch."

Packman was standing too, pale-faced, asking, "What the hell's the matter with you?"

"I told you," shrieked Foss. "Didn't I tell you?"

"Who do you think you're *messing* with? Who do you think you're *pouring* drinks on, some hick goddamn redneck bodybeautiful?" Halsey was ranting. Others in the grille, almost everyone, were watching them. Packman took Craig by the arm and started moving him away from the table.

"He could crush you like an eggshell, Halsey," Craig got in weakly as he left. "Just pick you up and crush you like a goddamn eggshell."

Chub smiled at him as he left the grille and he stopped long enough for a new drink to take upstairs.

It took him quite a while to find Mary Tate. He went first to the dining room where phalanxes of servers were getting supper into chafing dishes on the long tables to ask Santo if he had seen her. Santo was fooling with the amplifiers to an electric guitar. Zoe Mason was sitting in a chair nearby watching him. Her legs were crossed and she was smoking a thin black cigarette.

"You have someone else you want to show him off to?" she asked Craig and there was a touch of war in her deep voice.

"No. I'm looking for Mary Tate."

"She said she was going for a walk," said Santo. "You overdid it a little bit, didn't you, buddy?" He was looking at the back of the amplifier and Craig couldn't see his face.

"I'd better find her."

"Yep," agreed Santo. "I think you'd better find her."

She was near the entrance to the club, being held by Chester Bartlett. He was holding her by the upper arm and talking into her ear. Chester Bartlett was a prominent young man. His family had brought the machine-tool industry to Birmingham and still controlled it. Chester was in charge of one of the company's larger factories and he took his tooling and dieing seriously.

"What do you say, Chester," said Craig, taking Mary Tate firmly by the other arm.

Chester looked surprised. "Hello." He looked at Mary Tate then back at Craig. "Is Mary Tate here, uh, well is she with you?"

"I was working up to that," said Mary Tate. She had a high, unnatural color in her face and Craig noticed with some scorn that Chester was trying to hide an erection.

"How's it going, Chester?"

"Fine. Everything's fine. Jap tools are a problem," said Chester, shifting his legs again.

"Better than fine, I'd say," said Mary Tate. "A hell of a lot better than fine. You see this?" She pointed to a diamond-shaped pin in Chester's lapel. "Read that." The pin said ZERO DEFECTS. "Zero defects," said Mary Tate. "*Zero* defects. Chester hasn't got a goddamn one. They're only five other men in the state with that pin."

"Is that right, Chester? Congratulations."

"Well, I just got it, actually. Our company gives them out, you know like NASA. My factory earned one at the same time I did."

"Great. Great, Chester. Look, will you excuse us? You look like you'd better go sit down somewhere and rest for a while anyway. Say good night to Chester, Mary Tate."

"What did you do to him?" He was pressing her toward the door.

"Kiss my ass," she said.

"You put your hand in his pants?"

"What do you care? You've been ignoring me all night. You've been *really* ugly."

"What did you do?" He squeezed her arm.

"I talked a little dirty to him is all. He wanted to be sexy and didn't know how."

Craig found that he was aroused himself. He was pleased by that since it fit so well into his plans to leave early. "We'll go home and you can talk dirty to me."

But Mary Tate stopped cold and pulled her arm free. "I don't want to leave yet," she said. "I want to take a walk and then come back and have you be sweet to me in front of your friends."

"OK," he said, knowing he would have to gentle her. A walk was better than arguing in the foyer of the club. "We'll take a walk."

The night air had two immediate effects on Craig. It made him realize how drunk he was and it made him horny as a toad. He decided not to wait until they got home—he would ravage her on a lounge chair by the pool.

They walked around the pale, looming front of the club, down the flagstone walk past the golf shop and along the north flank of the eighteenth hole. He held her hand and listened to the click of her high heels against the stones. It was a still, cloudy night and he could make out only the shapes of things.

At the walk's lowest point where it crossed a brook he stopped on the crumbling wooden bridge and tried to kiss her but she pulled away and walked on ahead of him toward the lights of the pool.

Embarrassed, he thought. She's just self-conscious from the party. He smiled, thinking how glittering and fancy it must look to her and felt a gentle surge of affection. He wanted to soothe her, to make her feel at home.

When he caught up to her at the edge of the concrete skirting the pool he put his arms around her from behind and kissed her neck. "You don't have to be uncomfortable around these people, baby. Most of them aren't like Halsey—they're all right. A little too rich and spoiled maybe, but that's the cream of Birmingham down there."

"Shit."

"No, really." He felt offended and he retreated pompously: "Those people stand for a quality of life, a kind of dignity and grace . . ."

"Dogshit," said Mary Tate.

She freed herself and walked to the edge of the pool. The illuminated water was green and calm as a yawn in front of her. Beneath their feet the concrete and tile were still warm with the day's sun and redolent with the peculiar daytime smell this place had—a complicated, cloying, almost human odor like blood, made up of chlorine and ketchup and hot children that Craig knew so well it might have been his own.

She turned around to face him, her strong blunt hands working at her side, her face tear-streaked; fragile, desirable . . . There was an unreality to her being there above that place where he had learned to swim, clothed in her fantastic dress and simple scent that at the time depressed him and refired his lust. He forgot completely about defending the people in the club. Throbbing in the crotch, he stared at her exotic middle, at the pink pucker of waist above those skilled country hips, and found himself wanting to screw her on the diving board.

"Craig?"

"What honey?"

"Why did you do that to Joe? Why did you make him meet all those goddamn people? He looked so . . . so *little* and miserable."

Breathing raggedly, he came over and put his arms around her again, pulled her crying face to his chest and held her tightly, as you might a bag of groceries. "I did it for them, baby. Sweet baby. I wanted them to meet him, and you too, because you all are so *real* and so different. I . . ."

He had the reason, the real one, on the tip of his tongue. He probably would have spoken it then, confused as he was by old smells and whiskey and lust; spoken it and told them both. But he waited, and by the time he had it straight she had broken his grip and was gone.

196

20

"ITSALLRIGHT . . . itsallrightbaby," he had repeated for ten minutes now like some idiot talking doll, as he took the hilly curves between the club and his house on two wheels, knowing that it was assuring neither Mary Tate—who sat stiffly and as far away from him as she could get, wearing her stony silence like a chastity belt—nor himself. It was anything but all right. He'd be lucky if they ever let him in the club again. But he didn't really care about that now; the only thing he cared about was screwing Mary Tate, and as quickly as possible. There was a storm of want in the pit of his stomach. He could not remember ever wanting anything as badly, or feeling as perverse about wanting it.

It had been bad in the club and the worse it got the more he had wanted her, so that at the end of her tantrum, as he led her out of the battlefield mess she had made of the dining room, down the rows of outraged faces, he could only wonder in his glands about the availability of one of the bedrooms upstairs . . . the ladies' room? the kitchen?

He found her in the dining room after chasing her back down the walk, his patent leather shoes slipping on the old stones, through the men's locker room and the cardroom and into the body of the club. She was much quicker than he and had disappeared by the time he got upstairs. But he had no trouble finding her. She was tearing through the club like a small tornado, looking for Santo. In the dining room there were still fifty or sixty people eating their quail and eggs sedately from china dishes when Mary Tate burst in. When she saw the guitar, the microphone, the amplifiers and Santo himself all gone she hurled herself at the diners as though they might be hiding him in the fancy forest of legs beneath the tables.

"Where is he?" she wailed at a table of six.

"My God, who?" asked Lester Brewster, his rich mouth half closed around a bite of quail.

"Joe, you prick. *Joe Santo*, goddamit." With one tug at the old Irish tablecloth she sent the china, the silver, the crystal, the wine, the food clattering to the floor. Then she turned and repeated the question menacingly to Peter Halsey senior's table. His lower lip trembled as he assured her he did not know the gentleman in question.

"You shook his haaand," she cried. Pull. Crash. "You shook his fucking hand!"

By the time Craig panted into the room, swollen pecker and

all, she had swept three tables and the serving table, had over-turned a bathtub-sized silver punch bowl, and was standing in the middle of the debris like Alaric in Rome telling a terrified Angel-finger Walterson that if she didn't tell her where Santo was she would pull her streaked hairs out one by one.

"Crayag," moaned Angelfinger, "look what this trashy young person has *done*. I told her Mr. Santo left. He sang and left about twenty minutes ago with Zoe Mason."

"Left? Left where?" Craig asked her, feeling vaguely deserted himself.

"He gave me my check back and left before half my guests had *seen* him. He said"—Angelfinger's bosom began to heave—"he said to send it to the United Indian Fund. Oh God, where is Cyrus?"

"I'm going to pop her one," said Mary Tate.

The dining room was full again, of bewildered, indignant gentry attracted by the noise, and Craig knew he had better get him-self and Mary Tate out fast. As she started for Angelfinger he grabbed her around the waist. He was expecting a struggle but Mary Tate went suddenly limp as a noodle in his arms and shook her head.

"Do you know where he went, lady?" she asked Angelfinger, her voice languid. "Do you know where Joe went?"

"Went?" said Angelfinger. Her eyes were glassy with shock. "He went to Flahida. He said they were going to Flahida to watch some fishes jump."

Optimistically, Craig decided to view Mary Tate's total silence as a good sign. She was probably regretting her behavior. She was ashamed. Dumb with desire herself.

"It's all right, baby," he said, slowing automatically as he turned into the road up the mountain. "It was your first party like that—everybody has a right to be edgy. We'll forget it. Who needs those people?" He looked at her through the dimness of the car. "All I need is you."

But he said it nervously. Looking at her lonely, serious profile brought back a dream he had had several nights before and forgotten until now. He and Mary Tate had been invited to his cousin Virgil's house for an afternoon trap-shooting party. There were eight or ten people in wrought-iron chairs around the trap in Virgil's five-acre back yard. Fine double-barrel guns stood in a gun rack, their blued metal and oiled French walnut gleaming quietly: there was a slight breeze, a blue afternoon sky, the scent of fall in the air. Dressed in Bean shooting jackets, pheasant feathers in their hats, everyone was drinking sangria out of silver goblets and talking softly—everyone but Mary Tate. She sat apart, legs drawn under her, staring at a black, far-off line of trees. Craig felt separated from her by a huge distance and pretended to anyone who asked that he did not know her. He drank his sangria and chatted, and every once in a while turned furtively to study her serious face.

He had forgotten to leave any lights on. The house was black. Mary Tate didn't move when he turned off the engine, so he walked around and opened the door for her. Still she sat, glaring into the dark.

His groin aching, he helped her out of the car and up the stone steps. Inside he leaned her against the door as he fumbled for the lamp chain and accidentally remembered the first night she had stood there while he looked for the light. Remembering, he turned back to her with a lump of tenderness in his throat but she wasn't there. He found her in the bedroom, sitting straight-back on the bed, her hands folded in her lap.

He dropped to the floor beside her and kissed one knee then the other. He pushed the ostrich feathers up her legs and kissed her thighs. Holding and pressing her hips, he moved his open mouth across the nylon of her upper legs, nibbling and licking as he went. Her hands rested idly on his back. With his head pressed into her lap he unzipped the dress and peeled it off between them.

Nuzzling her belly he reached for her bra strap, but with a clean shiver like a horse getting rid of a fly she shook off his hand.

"Craig." It was the first word she had spoken since the club.

"Huh?"

"Craig, get offa me."

He looked up and was dumbstruck by her face. There was nothing but pain and anger there, bunching her features into knots. It was a different Mary Tate he was looking at and he felt a cold wash of fear at not recognizing her.

She was staring at the wall opposite them with unhealthy concentration. "Those pictures. All those animals and fish. They're experiences, you said. You own 'em, you said. What you want is you want me up there." She said this flatly, rapidly, her voice like a growl.

In the face of something he could tell was going to be bloody he found himself weirdly admiring her figurative thinking. "Now wait a minute . . ." he began.

"Both of us. Joe too. I *loved you*," she screamed at him and stood up, shucking him like a husk. "I'm no motherfucking picture and neither is Joe, you bastard. I want to go *home, home, home*."

Then she exploded—breasts lurching from the half cups of her bra she flung open the glass doors of the bookcase and ripped out handfuls of calfbound James, Tolstoy, De Maupassant, Goethe; she pulled the drawers out of his rolltop desk, knocked the wood duck's head off without so much as trembling her trophy, spilled his pair of stuffed quail and flung the hen through the glass front of the rod cabinet. Craig stood and watched helplessly as delicate Orvis fly rods shivered and fell from their hooks like rain, something about the coupling of her near nudity and rage rooting him.

She attacked his dresser next, shouting, "Goddamn you, Craig, god*damn* you." She swept the top of it clean with one long stroke of her arm and then scientifically began to destroy the photographs. She jerked each off the wall and in a continuous motion cracked its face against a sharp corner of the desk. She was five pictures into the slaughter and was reaching for Craig and his fifteen-pound steelhead taken on a dry fly when he finally became unglued.

He tackled her. Screaming and turning as she fell, she whacked him on the ear with the picture. As he crawled up her body toward the pelting hands she kneed him twice in the crotch, bit his arm and scratched at his eyes but Craig couldn't feel any of it. Finally pinning her he looked crazily around for . . . an ax, a fire extinguisher, some emergency tool—he had to get her out, away—and then noticed that Mary Tate was laughing at him. Kneeing methodically at his back, her held arms writhing, her face gleaming and crinkled with fury like a wad of crushed tinfoil, she was laughing.

"You dumb fuck, you're scared. You're *scared.*"

He raised his right hand far enough to dab at her face a weak, openhanded blow that glanced off her shoulder, then immediately heaved it back. But she curled under him, still laughing and clawing and threw him off balance long enough to wriggle free. He caught her at the door, adrenalinized and indignant now, threw her to the bed and held her there while he scooped up her clothes. Then he threw her head-first over his shoulder and panting, aching in the nuts and realizing dimly that what she had screamed at him was true—if this were Dorothy Stephens, say, he would try to calm her down, but this was Mary Tate Farnsworth and he was *afraid* (what mean Opp blow, Lord?)—he ran for his car.

He drove like a madman for Ensley and Mary Tate wailed beside him, wailed with a pure agony that terrorized Craig's mind and flogged him down the dark streets and through the soft rain that had begun to fall. There was something about her furious pain that blanked him out. He felt barely able to control the car, much less the situation. He felt himself sort of disappearing—diminishing with every mile, with every lamp post and spotlight becoming less and less the man he had invented for her. His joints creaked with the shrinkage and he didn't know how to stop it. His old prim and orderly ability to deal with things had fled in the face of this avalanche of primitive emotion, leaving him unable even

202

to work up any emotion of his own beyond the tentative impulse to protect himself.

Mary Tate raged all the way to Ensley as he cowered and sped and tried not to look at the dingy neighborhoods they were passing through.

At a stop light three blocks away from her apartment he put the car in park and said, "Look . . ."

But she was out of the car and running down the sidewalk before he knew what he wanted to say.

"I need you . . ." he yelled through the open door. Then he sat for a moment, feeling lost, his ear and groin and back beginning to hurt. "Baby . . . baby, what about your stuff?" he yelled.

She turned around, distant in the misting rain, barefoot, her dress half-zipped and gestured to him. In final defiance her middle finger snared a gleam of light from a discount shoe store window and blazed at him down the block like a candle.

21

He slept pitifully—dozing, and waking in starts to find himself clutching his mouth and moaning. At seven he got out of bed and sat at his pillaged writing desk, his mouth furry with hangover, his ear swollen, and his head for the first time in three years scrambled with verse.

"If it were true, lady," he began on a yellow legal pad,

"That you loved me as you say—

That you loved me out of sight
Of where you loved before
As, learning how to crawl, some infant might
Outdistance first the bed, then the door . . ."

He stopped, recognizing the stupid formality of address and petulance of tone that had wrecked his poems in graduate school.

He threw a bathrobe over his shoulders and picked up the morning paper from the front steps. Then he went out to the kitchen and brought back three carrots and a jelly glass half full of twelve-year-old cognac. Propped by four pillows on the bed he lay looking blankly over the ruins of his room and tried to determine calmly what he was going to do with that day, and the next . . .

All he had really ever wanted to do, besides enjoy himself, was write poems. No, to be a poet—preferably without having to write anything at all. Not your pale academic variety, but a poet in the mold of Raleigh or Herrick—an adventurous, jobless man of action who decorated his hyperthyroid sport with deathless couplets and quatrains.

While he was an undergraduate at the University of Virginia, Faulkner had stalked around the halls smoking his pipe, looking prevailing, and Craig had taken literature seriously. As soon as he graduated he went to Dublin, disliking what he had heard of Paris, and for eighteen months he drank a lot of Guinness, wrote a few cavalier poems about the South, and fell in love with various Irish institutions: turf fires, salmon fishing . . .

When *Poetry Ireland* accepted one of his poems he decided he might like to become a professional writer. His father wanted him to come home and go to graduate business school. Out of the same respect for professional training he did come back, but went instead of Wharton to the Writer's Workshop at the University of Iowa. There, for the next two years, Craig found out how profoundly he did not want to be a writer.

He nearly went crazy in Iowa City. The simpering, gentle, dirty students, the unending talk of perception and resonance, the indoor pallor of everyone, the sitting down—it all turned him savage. He refused to speak to anyone in the workshop. He wrote and read only what he had to to get through the courses. At night he played pool in country bars and ate pork tenderloin sandwiches with corn farmers, or lay on his bed reading copies of *Field and Stream*, getting drunk on bourbon.

But if his nights were lonely his days were driven. In season he fished for anything that swam and shot at anything that flew—he became a walking grid map of county roads to farm ponds, marshes and bird cover; he had to rent three freezer lockers for the fruits of his days, for the pheasants and snipe and bass and trout and ducks and quail and perch and geese and squirrels. Out of season he took up watching waterfowl, ice-fishing, shooting carp with a bow and arrow, canoeing—anything that kept him outside, tired, muddy and away from talking and inventing fantasy. He would go to classes stinking of duck blood or bass slime, in his field pants and boots, and try to turn the quiet droning discussions of poems to talk about the corn crop or the skinny Iowa quail. He developed calluses.

When he learned of his parents' death Craig couldn't get out of Iowa fast enough. Secretly he was joyous over the nitty-gritty responsibility it pushed on him, excited as hell to be all of a sudden half owner of the South's fifth-biggest real estate company and delighted to be forced into the manly world of business. He wired his uncle that he would like to go to work immediately. His uncle shrugged and put another Blake name on another door.

He was joyous, excited and delighted for about four months in Birmingham, handling his affairs and working for a broker's license. Then as the cottony Alabama summer packed around the city he began to feel stuck—with a house, a job and a life that he hadn't chosen. He took a trip and then another, and another: elaborate catching and shooting trips, to Honduras, British Columbia, Argentina, Labrador. He gave up studying for his broker's license just then and read travel brochures in his office. He dreamed of all the experiences he had not yet had that might teach him something, might move his hand closer to the pulse of things. With them in mind he planned out each day, and then the next.

He finished the cognac, went to his desk and tore up what he had written, chewing savagely on a second carrot to keep from crying. He needed to take a crap but was reluctant to go through the necessary steps. He didn't feel able to make anything but the simplest motions.

The air in his room was cool and preservative. The drapes were pulled across the tall windows, shutting out all but a thread of light. Looking at them, Craig noticed for the first time how badly they were frayed. Actually the whole house was coming apart. Above his bed were mauve water spots where the plumbing was beginning to leak, and many of the walls were patched with flaking plaster and peeling paint. The furnace would have to be replaced; the roof needed work . . . All of this had depressed Craig for months but he did nothing about it. Now, looking at the dusty, algae-colored drapes, he allowed himself a dramatic image—of the fine old house as a rotting body and himself a casual parasite draining off the last of its vitality.

He finally made it to the bathroom. Heaping himself on the toilet he thumbed through the newspaper to the society page. In the "Jotter" column, where he knew it would be, was a description of last night's party. His eye skimmed the italicized names, looking fatally for his own. There was Angelfinger Walterson, "hostess with the mostess, dressed fetchingly in a gorgeous Givenchy" and the Horace Dennickers, whose "swingy steps kept pace all evening to the tuneful tantrums of the band." Lester Brewster was there, "with his symmetrical Spanish spouse, Consuela, in green domed silk hat with cocktail coat and dress of the same"; "dashingly refined young civic leader Chester Bartlett" was there, and Foss and "the scintillating Halsey clan"—but no Craig, no Mary Tate, no gory scene in the dining room. The society page had ignored all that.

The phone got him off the toilet before his bowels could relax.

It was Foss. Foss's voice was hoarse and tense. He wanted Craig to meet him for tennis. He had some things to get off his chest, he said, and for Craig's own good he suggested that Craig be there.

"I don't feel much like playing tennis," Craig told him, knowing he would go.

"Just be there," Foss said and hung up.

He felt a need of Foss. He felt a need of some good-humored friendship, and even of the dressing-down and advice he knew would come first, Foss being Foss. So he dressed, picked up his racket as an afterthought and went.

It was a damp, oppressive day. The rain had stopped during the night but sullen banks of clouds still brooded over the windless heat. He was sweating heavily by the time he got to the courts.

Foss was doing knee bends, holding the top of the first court net. There was no one else there.

"You got me up from a good crap to come out here," he said. He wanted to be light with Foss, to have fun with him. He hoped Foss wouldn't ask about his ear. "There'll be vengeance in my forehand."

"How do we stand?" Foss asked without looking at him.

"Stand?"

"In tennis. You figure you're a few sets up on me this summer?"

"I'd say no more than about fifty."

Foss was still doing knee bends. Obligingly Craig did a few with him on the other side of the net.

"More like five," said Foss. "But it doesn't matter. From now on it's all me." There was something viciously sure about the way he said that that rattled Craig.

"Look, Hal, about last night . . ."

Foss stood up and walked toward his service line. "You're through beating me, Blake," he said without turning around. "Ever. Now let's play tennis."

Foss murdered him.

He beat him at the net and in the backcourt; beat him with

whistling second serves, delicately placed dropshots and ferocious down-the-line and crosscourt volleys. He smashed back Craig's best serves and forehands and riddled his backhand. Panting and sweating and unbelieving, Craig forced the slaughter to five sets but could win no more than two games in any one of them.

They played silently. Foss stalked his court, unsmiling, playing each point with terrier determination, meting out each game as though it were punishment. At the end of the fifth set Craig's feet were blistered and his legs were rubbery. His head was light and he was having a hard time seeing the ball.

"You had enough?" asked Foss.

"One more," he said, hoping he could make it. But halfway through the second game nausea drove him to the side of the court and he knelt there retching brandy and chunks of carrot into the Har-Tru as Foss stood over him, ruddy-faced and breathing evenly.

"You didn't even do as well as I thought you would," said Foss. "I've been taking lessons, you bastard."

Foss said more than that. For fifteen minutes, as Craig sat on the green sand with his head between his knees, Foss tongue-whipped him as steadily and mercilessly as he had beaten him at tennis. He said that Craig was finished and he hoped he knew that. That no one in town cared any more whether he lived or died. They had all given him chance after chance—oh God had they given him chances, because of his parents, his position. But Craig had blown them all. He had shamed his parents and his position, he had humiliated fine warm people like Dorothy Stephens and Amy Walterson—and for what? *For what?* To play around with a bunch of illiterate degenerates.

Craig, said Foss, could neither shit nor get off the pot. He was socially useless. And he, Foss, was going to by God beat him out. He owned his own damned Chevrolet convertible, by God, free and clear; and his own boat on Smith Lake. He had money in the bank that he had by God earned himself. Nobody had ever died and left him with a fucking thing, not a dime. He, Foss, he said, was going to win out. He, Foss, was the future.

Craig sat and stared at the drying puke for a minute, unable to speak. Finally he looked up at Foss. "Will you help me?" he asked, his voice breaking. "Will you help me for Chrissake, Hal? I've made some mistakes . . . I'm all broken up, I'm *tired* . . . Look, would you just help me up?" He got his legs under him and reached out his hand to Foss. "You're right, what you say . . . I . . ."

He stopped, realizing Foss wasn't going to take his hand. Foss stood above him like a Prussian, nostrils flared. He slammed his racket into its plush blue and white Davis cover and made his eyes thin as fingernails. "Fuck off, Blake," he said. "I hope you stay down there all day." Then he turned quickly and walked off up the hill toward the parking lot, up through the comfortable glade of boxwood and pine, through the formal, needled quiet, his white shape stiff with pride. And Craig sat and watched him go, dizzy with defeat, adrift, hardly recognizing the hillside.

22

THE LAST MOTHARAPIN straw, Newton called it, in a mutter as his fingers flew over Flower's mostly naked body, pulling, slapping, kneading the squishy white flesh. The *last* gotdam straw—this was it.

He had been at it for two hours now and the girl had calmed down some—a stupor had crept over her dumb eyes. But still he kept her bound to the table and gagged, for still there were noises coming from the gym—an uproar of giggles, grunts, curses, clanking weights, and once a scream, that meant neither Thor nor the other girl, Mae Ruth, had passed. And as long as Thor was conscious Newton knew he would have to stay at this, even all night, so he paced his hands into patient little midriff chops and kept himself mad, which was easy enough, just by looking at the stupid white-trash girl and thinking about the night—the last, the very last motharapin indignity he would ever suffer from Thor.

If he'd of had any sense he'd of seen it coming that afternoon while he and Thor were playing Chinese checkers, and would of scatted then. Jesus knew he'd seen that mood coming on enough times before, the no talking, the scowl, the pulling at bottle after bottle of bourbon and peppermint schnapps. He had even taken a game off Thor, which was no gotdam help.

"Don't worry about it," he had said, picking up his marbles in a hurry lest their victorious position turn Thor violent. "He be back. The contest ain't till tomorrow night. He probly went to see his mama and daddy."

"I had somebody check that out you stupid shit—he ain't up there. Don't talk to me. And if you beat me again I'll cut your dick off."

"I got lucky, you'll win this un. Did you ax Mary Tate?" knowing Thor couldn't find her either, or the dude from across the mountain, or for that matter and luckily for them anybody else he had looked for that day, except him, Newton.

"What'd I tell you, nigger?" yelled Thor slamming down his pint bottle only inches from Newton's fingers. "Don't talk to me!"

Right then is when he shoulda said, "I'm going for a dog," and scatted his young ass out of there.

Course he couldn't blame Thor for worrying: there it was five o'clock Satdy afternoon, a little more than twenty-four hours before just about the biggest contest of the year—one that worried Thor anyway ("I can't help this one," he had told Newton, "they got all these hot shit judges coming in this year from Atlanta,

Nashville—it's too big") and one he needed (Thor was in bad debt, even Newton knew that; his last two clubs were starting slow and he had blown a lot of money recently in a shopping-center deal with Dr. Wright)—and there was no sign of Santo. Santo had disappeared. And Thor with his good nose for trouble sensed something weird. It wasn't so much, Newton knew, the chance that Santo wouldn't show at all that worried Thor—Santo had never even been late for a contest before in his life and he, too, needed what he could make at this one to get a little farther out of Thor—it was mostly just not knowing whether Santo was drinking his milkshakes and eating his food supplements, not knowing what bad air or lack of sleep was dulling his skin tone or the sheen of his hair. That was enough right there to make Thor foul as a fart to be around.

And it din't help Newton's nerves any either to have five thousand dollars worth of prize money for the Mr. Southeast Contest just laying there six inches from his hand in an old shoe box. Because Thor had put up the biggest part of it, the two thousand dollars first place money, he got for the third year in a row to make the awards. But there was Atlanta money, Charlotte money, Memphis and Miami and Tampa and Roanoke and New Orleans money in that box too, already translated into greenback hundred-dollar bills for presentation, and those boys who put it there didn't play. But Thor just let it lay there on his desk, smelling it, looking at it, where anybody who wanted to could come in and snatch it—drunk as Thor was getting he sure as hell couldn't of stopped em.

The money worried Newton; it was because of the money that he didn't even leave the second time his good sense told him to— when Thor lurched up around six o'clock and said he was sick of this shit, they was going to the fair.

Fair?

Thor had read about a fair coming in town out to the fair-grounds and they was going. Right then.

"I believe I'll go for a dog," he said. But it was too late for that.

"You going to the fair with me, Bru. I get you a gotdam dog all right. We gon do some screamin."

"How bout this money—you gon leave it sittin out here fo anybody who wawnt it?"

Thor was reeling toward the toilets, jabbing at his curls with a comb and Newton could have scatted then, knew he should have, but instead he looked around for a place to hide the shoe box (the money wadnt none of his; he couldn't care less which of them apes wound up with it, but as long as it was here in this studio it was in *his* place, where he stayed, and wadnt nobody gon mess with it if he could help it) and by the time he got it stuffed behind a file where a bird dog couldnta found it Thor was back, zipping up his fly, ready to go.

"We gon get girls this time—*two* of em. And white," said Thor. He grinned unkindly and Newton had felt his stomach drop out.

There wasn't *ever* any changing his mind once Thor was drunk, Newton knew that. The only way to stop him doing something then was to hurry up his drinking, the fierce process that always led sooner or later to Thor's being stone cold out—to hurry up the change from mean-drunk Thor to passed-out Thor. And Newton tried. All the way out to the fairgrounds he kept asking for pulls on the bottle though he hated the stuff, partly to calm himself down but mostly because he knew and trusted the reflexive greed that made Thor take a large swallow right before and right after handing the bottle over to Newton for a small one. It was a new bottle, the third of the day (the fourth lay between them on the front seat) and Thor seemed to be getting wobbly—but you never could tell with that cocksucker. Newton had seen him go through five and stay on his feet.

Thor drove slowly, straddling and concentrating on the center stripe of Eighth Avenue through the concrete desolation of the northwest city toward Bessemer. This was Newton's turf. He had grown up out here and he knew every house. He had watched the red land, that twenty years ago when he started remembering lapped at the very center of downtown Birmingham, pushed farther and farther away by unarguing dozers until now even this area, his always poor and unenticing area of dirt streets and scraggly squirrel woods and country stores, was a part of the used-car lot, Dairy Queen, junk store waste that spread around the city like a poisonous film fifteen miles in every direction.

Newton wanted to go to the country. He flat wanted to go. He had some people in Moulton, upstate where the nights were cooler and there were chickens scratching around in the back yards. For two years he had wanted to pack his grip for Moulton—massage, pump gas, he didn't care, just get his ass shut of all these mean streets, all these mean-drunk city sumbiches: he knew, he'd been whupped and he'd been cut; he was tired of that shit. And it seemed to him now, in his gut so he knew it was true, if a little weaker than before because of the poison in that bottle, that if he had even half a brain he'd be trailing his thumb up Route 65 right now toward Moulton instead of headin at God knows what kind of trouble with the meanest drunkest sumbich of 'em all.

"Hep me out," said Thor. He had parked slantwise at the edge of whirling lights and calliope music in the center of the fairgrounds. It wasn't even a parking place.

"You gon get a ticket you leave this fatass car here. Stuck too—thas mud."

"Hep me out I bust yo ass," growled Thor. He had poured the rest of bottle number three into a huge Dixie cup and filled the cup out of bottle four.

Newton helped him out.

"Here we *are*, snatch. Wheresasnatch?" Thor bellowed at the fairgrounds.

"We go ride a bumper car, ride the farris wheel, get a dog, we gon see some nice stuff," Newton babbled. Unable to pass him out he could maybe distract him.

"Where you *at*, snatch? I got the king of the voodoo lovers heah

—Haw haw*yeah*, mama. I'm gon tell you *one* thing, got a cock like a rattlesnake."

"Sweet Jesus," said Newton.

Thor grabbed him by the arm, wrenched the thought right out of his head and stomped on it in the mud. "Don't you *think* about goin nowhere, don't you *think* it, Bru. I'm gon put some hair on yo ass tonight. This's white snatch night."

Then wandering around for three hours maybe four shooting at things, throwing balls and rings and darts at things, Newton speechless now, walleyed with fury and fright, Thor sipping discriminately at his Dixie cup and seeming to sober some with the cut-down intake, dropping cash and watching arrogantly from the top of his big-chested strut every girl that passed whether she was with a man or not, looking for the right look back. And finding it finally in the middle of a plastic lake full of electric boats, it coming from two half-wit pigs in short shorts and halters who puttered by all scrunched up together in a blue boat hardly big enough for two kids and had bad luck enough to smile back idiotically at Thor's leer.

Newton was a little way off, holding some cotton candy Thor had bought him and staring glumly into a sort of amphitheater where a bunch of dressed-up monkeys were tearing round and round a track in little cars: the monkeys were chained in their cars but they didn't seem to mind. And Newton saw the pigs bump their boat into the plastic just below Thor, saw them giggling hysterically and Thor leaning down full of good-natured nautical advice—and knew then that it was all over.

The short fat one with broken teeth and red-brown hair like a fox, the one who he heard giggle (as he walked over to them after the fourth time Thor yelled at him) "I never had no nigra date before; my sister has but not me"—her name was Flower. The other one was fat too but had big tits. Her name was Mae Ruth.

"This ain't no ordinary nigra," said Thor, taking him sweetly above the elbow. "This here (and this is what Newton couldn't believe, not then, not six months later) is Buck. Buck's a gotdam *jungle bomb,* honeypot. Got all these things to turn you on—rhino horns, dildos, stuff like that. I tell you one thing, baby, he's got more ways to wind your clock than you got hairs on your head."

Flower's stupid eyes got big. "Where we going?" she asked.

But Mae Ruth wasn't sure. She popped her gum, hands on her hips. "Now wait a minute, we might not be goin anywhere but crazy. Who are you anyway, honey?" she asked Thor. "I think I've saw you in the papers or something."

"I been in there," said Thor. "Plenty. What you might say I'm head of the physical culture industry in this adjoining area. Buck here's one of my assistants."

"Me and Flower don't go out with nobody we don't know, but I knowed I've saw you in the papers."

"I don't wawnt *none* of this shit," he whispered fiercely into Thor's ear. "Who you think you messing with—I knows too much."

The last thing he could think of to try so he tried it, but Thor just looked at him blankly for a minute then bust out laughing. "Ole Buck here's hot to trot," he whooped. "Come on y'all, less air this place."

So what he decided on the way back to the studio (with Flower laying all over him and Thor mouthing off above the radio about his bidness in New Orleans, his bidness in Miami, his bidness in Atlanta) was to leave finally—to last out this night somehow until Thor bellowed his last and collapsed, then cut out for good. For Moulton. Because if Thor could do this to him after everything they'd been through there wadn't no point in staying: in not knowing, ever, what way that motha would twist and run.

"Huh?" he said.

"I said where you keep all that stuff—them horns and stuff?" Flower asked him. She smelled like a telephone booth.

"I'll show you," he whispered into her stiff hair. "I'll show you when we gets there. Just leave me alone till we gets there."

"I'm good anyway—I come twelve times one night."

Sweet Jesus, you graymeat whore, thought Newton, feeling licked, feeling desperate. Then all at once, in a flash, it came to him what he would do. "Uh huh, well fine."

"Yeah, Mr. Alabama, I own him," Thor was saying. "He's in my stable."

(Scared and mad as he was Newton couldn't help snickering, thinking about it.)

"He's gonna be the next IFBB America—there ain't nothing he can't win."

"Where's he at?" asked Mae Ruth, looking interested.

"He's uh . . . he be around." Thor stepped on the gas. "You come around the auditorium tomorrow you see him. And see is *all*."

In the back seat Buck laughed out loud. Flower giggled with him and struggled to spread more of him with her soft expanse.

Thor let the two girls get up the stairs to the gym ahead of them and grabbed Newton's arm, his face popping and twitching with excitement.

"Look, I'll get you a queen. I'll get you fifteen of 'em outta the park next week, only don't mess this up, you hear. I been in the mood for this." And Newton, terrified as ever in the pinch of that huge hand, nodded. "We'll do some stuff in the gym—mess around a little with the weights. Now go get yours undressed."

Because that's what he liked better than anything, Thor did— to have the woman or man or child, whatever it was he was violating on a particular night, work out with him: hand him weights, maybe struggle a little itself with some dumbbells. Thor liked 'em sweating, naked and ignorant. And the more of 'em there were around like that the better he liked it. Newton could remember plenty of six- and seven-people nights and one last spring with twelve—a real fiesta where as Thor put it, color, sex and age was each person's own bidness, where every chrome weight and machine in the place had been put to use and there were gallons of Thor-produced Thunderbird wine, where nobody made a move to leave—except one scared-shitless Caucasian male who snuk out in the early morning after Thor asked him, just joking around, if he liked bullwhips—until two o'clock the next afternoon. That had been one, like Thor said, to hang up on the wall and remember.

Newton didn't mind that kind of party—the more people there were the less attention Thor paid to him, and the freer he was to wander around and take up with whoever the hell he wanted to take up with. But with four it was different. And tonight if he was going to make his plan work he had to get Flower off somewhere by herself and keep her there (he had no idea how to do that: if Thor wanted to he could come through two feet of concrete).

So he prayed and said, "I'll get her nekkid all right but I'm gon keep her back in the massagin room."

"Forget it."

"Then the office."

"I said forget it. Now get yo skinny ass up them steps."

If crying woulda done it he'd of cried; if shouting woulda done it he'd of shouted, or begged or even jumped out the window onto Second Avenue. But he knew Thor too good for any of these, so when he was saved, and not even by anything he did himself, it seemed like not only the first piece of luck he'd seen all day but also like maybe Somebody was looking out for him for a change.

"I don't mind learning about lifting them weights," Mae Ruth said—she had one fat hip cocked out, finishing off the second glass of bourbon-schnapps that Thor had given her, and they were all standing around like in some weird bar waiting for Thor to get down to business; she was also putting on this "I'm hot taters and you gon have to go some to get me" grin—"But I'm sure as hell gon have my privacy, Mr. Big. Flower too."

"Tha's right," said Flower. "Me an Buck want to be alone."

"What's fun for two is more for four," said Thor, grinning but, Newton knew, feeling mean as hell.

Newton prayed again.

"Come on, Flower," said Mae Ruth. "We thank you, genalmen."

"Hold up, baby. It ain't no *big* thing . . . lookhere, Buck. Why don't you show this un your room back there."

Mae Ruth switched her hips triumphantly. "Uh huh. You be a good girl, Flower. And my *glass* is empty, Mr. Big."

So he had it—and he was so nervous with having it after not thinking he was going to that he nearly messed it up.

"OK, get up there on that table," he told Flower as soon as he had locked the door and stuck a chair under the knob.

"What all we gon do, hon?"

"You gon do what I tells you and shut up," he said, too nervous to think about his tone of voice.

"Now *waiiit* a minute," said Flower.

"I didn't mean it. I didn't mean nothin," scuttling to her and patting her rouged cheek. "We gon have a good time. I just got to find my stuff."

"You want me to get nekkid?"

"Sure. Sure, get nekkid if you wawnt to, honey. Only cept leave yo pants on. And lie on yo stomach."

Then he had to pray one more time, that he could find everything he needed—that piece of old nylon sash cord, that tore-up undershirt for a gag—which he did, and that he could keep her still and quiet long enough (she outweighed him) to get it on her, which he didn't have to worry about because as it turned out he coulda told her he was gonna nail her with a battleship and she'd of said come on.

"We gon have fun," he crooned, puttering around her, taking up slack here, checking out a knot there. "You gon *love* what I got," and finally slapping the gag over her dumb mouth and tying it up quick and tight; waiting till then to say, relaxed now, leaning on the table and happier'n he'd been all day, "Now, graymeat. Now. What you *think* you gettin you can get off anybody crazy enuff to mess with you. I'm gon give you somethin you cain't *find* nowhere else." And then, as she struggled heavily against the rope and made noises on the gag, dousing her all over with liniment —not the strongest one but strong enough so you knew you had it on—and wading in with his best stuff, the toughest stuff he knew, a whomping, kneading, pounding loosening-up massage.

He was four hours into it. He had caught a second wind (he knew now he could go all night, all the next day too if he had to; he couldn't hardly believe the strength in his wrists and arms; it seemed like he'd been storing up strength for this for years) and was riding high on his own rhythm of flutter punches, reverse stretches, buttocks sweeps, on the fine clatter and slap of his hands over the now inert girl (who had whimpered and lurched for an hour or so but since then had lain still as a corpse, breathing raggedly, her eyes glazed and unblinking) when Thor banged on the door.

"What you wawnt?" he croaked, terrified again.

"Lemme in."

"What you *wawnt?*"

"I want in and I'm coming *through* that door if you don't open it."

"Wait a minute, just wait. I got to get up." Frantic, he started whistling, tore the clothes off himself and the pants off Flower. He snapped his fingers in front of her eyes and when she didn't even blink whispered, "Don't you say a wud, bitch, not a wud," and jerked off the gag.

"We been goin to town," he said.

"Hotdam," said Thor, pushing past him and not even glancing at Flower. "That one out yonder'll curl your hair. Where'sa electrical massager?"

Thor was nude, pink, sweating and ravening drunk.

"Bottom drawer," Newton told him. "She wawnts it like this dontchasee. Made me tie her up soon we as got in here."

"Uhwaw," said Flower, looking goggleyed at Thor.

"This here's a night you can hang up on that gotdam wall. Taught me tricks you wouldn't believe . . ." said Thor.

"Uhhwawwn," said Flower.

"Wheresa gotdam thing?" He was ravaging Newton's neat

drawer and making great slurping heaves against his cabinets so Newton reached around him and handed him the massager.

"Gotdam tricks you never *heard* of." He weaved around the sunlamp, clutching the massager against his stomach. "I got to get outtahere . . ." He ran into and backed off the table with Flower on it without even looking down, then crouched like a lineman and threw himself through the door.

"Omigod," murmured Flower.

Newton closed the door quietly and picked up his clothes. He knew he had it in the bag now. He could massage as long as Thor could stand up, enjoy it even, beat him at it, then whoosh—he'd be up to Moulton. Gone.

He didn't even bother to lock the door.

23

A FEMALE WHOSE voice Santo had never heard before answered the phone. She said, "Huhumph," dropped the phone and then hung it up.

He called again. This time it rang fifteen times before the woman answered.

"Let me speak to Thor," he said. He could hear Thor's slavering laugh in the background and had a pretty good idea of what was going on. "This is Santo. I'm in Islamorada, Florida. Who is this?"

This was Mae Ruth in Birmingham, Alabama, the voice told him, if it was any of his bidness. "There ain't nobody here—now quit ringing this gotdam phone."

She hung up again and Santo gave up. He had tried to call Thor at seven and eight and ten when no one answered, and now at eleven when nobody but a hostile woman did. He figured Thor knew who was calling and why. He was probably mad that Santo hadn't called sooner.

He chuckled, imagining what was happening in the gym, and sipped from a third glass of mango juice.

"What's funny?" asked Zoe Mason. "Did you get that Thor person? God what a name." She stepped onto the patio from the kitchen, a gin and tonic in one hand and a silver platter of fresh-peeled shrimp and key limes in the other. In a terrycloth Pucci jumpsuit she was, all long bare legs and tumbling hair, iceberg beautiful, looking like she had spent the day ministering to her pores and nails instead of standing shirtless in the 110-degree bow of an open boat fighting tarpon.

"He won't answer the phone. Look, I need to get to bed."

"I've got a snapper baking, lovey. It takes time to do it right. Start on these." She put the platter down on a table beside him and sat on his lap, curled him like an anaconda. "Do we really have to go back for that contest?"

Santo, in Jesus sandals and the same pair of baggy Bermuda shorts, house shorts Zoe Mason called them, that he had fished in all day, mouthed a shrimp thoughtfully. He sucked it for the cold iodine taste and the tart bite of the lime. "Got to," he said, sucking. "Owe it to Thor. And I need the money."

"You don't need anything any more," she growled in his ear. "But me, lovey. And whatever you owe I can handle." She moved his hand around the long slope of her haunch and kissed him, her mouth open and pouting.

The crescent patio they were on extended halfway around Zoe Mason's house. The house was oval and built like a conch shell or a rat maze. The inside was one long spiral corridor, tightening toward the center, with twelve curved rooms opening subtly off of it. All of the rooms were smoke-colored and furnished with Barcelona chairs and couches and obscene Eastern statuary. At the center of the house was Zoe Mason's bedroom. It was cold orange, had a ten-foot mirror over the bed, a mineral-water pool in the center, and in the bathroom a small waterfall for a shower. When Santo first walked through it the night before the house had made him feel dizzy and trapped.

"I feel dizzy and trapped in here," he told Zoe Mason, standing in the center of her bedroom, the center of the center of the house.

"Get used to it," she said. "I'm thinking about locking you in here."

Zoe Mason liked to make love standing up and often. Between that and the dangerously-colored room Santo had not slept much.

On the stretch of lawn between where they sat and Florida Bay were twin lighted fountains from which two tumescent cherubs made water into each other's pool. Below the cherubs was the dock where Zoe Mason's seventeen-foot Mako—with its raised casting deck and beveled gunwales and line wells and hundred-horse Johnson—bumped to the tender, scented air. They had spent the day on that boat, celebrating. From the pure Keys' dawn until six that evening. Mike Curry, Zoe Mason's laconic, pecan-colored guide had poled them over acres of grass and sand flats, through milky-green channel mazes and around mangrove islands, while Santo stood in the middle of the boat clutching a nine-foot glass fly rod, learning things, and Zoe Mason stood on the casting platform, bare to the waist, her eyes ploughing the water ahead, teaching them.

Santo had learned how to tie blood knots and nail knots. He had learned how to strip a fly line and double-haul a cast. He had learned the difference between saw grass and Chinese sea grass.

227

He had learned to recognize ospreys, herons, cormorants, Cuban pigeons, frigate birds and flint-head cranes; and how to tell a shark from a ray just by the wake it made. He had even learned what he had come down here to learn, that hooked tarpon do indeed come up out of the water exactly as Zoe Mason had described them, like great gleaming erections.

On the fourth one he hooked Santo got his hands doing the right things and after twenty minutes brought the fish in to Mike Curry's lip-gaff. Leaning over the gunwale he studied the forty-pound tarpon, handled it and finally kissed it on its coin-silver head before releasing it.

"God they're beautiful."

"They're better than that," said Zoe Mason. "But not as beautiful as you are."

The breeze on the patio was limp with salt. It smelled of lime and oleander.

"You could work for me then," she was saying. "*Earn* the bloody money."

"It's nice of you to offer."

She pulled back and looked at him. "You're really turning it down."

"I don't like that orange room."

"I'll paint it."

Santo stood up and shook his head at the dark Florida Bay. "We have fun together . . . that's important."

"Look, money is nothing. Take the money, or work for it and pay back this Thor person. All I want is your being here. Or we can go somewhere else. Places—Aruba, St. Marten, Andros . . ."

The names floated by like scents on the night air. She stopped talking and the only sound left was the cherubs in their fountains, peeing gently onto each other's legs.

They fished on Sunday until nine, then drove to the airport in Zoe Mason's twelve-cylinder Porsche 917, eating papayas that they bought from a vendor along A1A. They flew out of Miami International at eleven o'clock in her tangerine-colored Lear executive jet and were in Birmingham by one-thirty.

"The measuring-in's at five," Santo told her. "Why don't you meet me at the auditorium? I've got to get my stuff and change these clothes." He grinned. He was still dressed in the buckskin suit that he'd left Amy Walterson's party in.

"I go where you go, lovey," Zoe Mason said. "I want to be sure you make your plane after this chickenshit pageant. I think we'll spend tonight at the Palm Bay Club. Then Chub Cay for a week . . ."

She sat in one of Santo's three chairs and smoked as he made and drank a milkshake, changed his clothes and threw his gear together in a gym bag: fifty-pound dumbbell, baby oil, razor, Vaseline, make-up, posing trunks. With a phone in the hall he tried to call Thor again, and again no one answered. Then he called Franklin at home and told him to meet him down at the auditorium at four.

"What time do you go on?" Zoe Mason asked.

"Contest starts at seven."

"How long will it last?"

"Two or three hours."

"You sure you'll win?"

"Sure I'm sure."

"Mr. what is it again?"

"Southeast, hon. Southeast. Try to remember."

On the way to the auditorium Santo talked about what he was going to do after he won this contest and maybe one or two more —the barbell endorsements, the television commercials, getting the debt to Thor off his back and then, he said, he thought he might like to turn camp counselor—work at some camp on a blue lake in the mountains where he could teach people to sail and canoe and play volleyball.

Zoe Mason smiled to herself, tapped out a rhythm against the arm rest with her nails and kept glancing down at a diamond watch on her strong brown wrist.

The municipal auditorium had about a thousand seats, nearly half of which were filled when Zoe Mason and Santo got there. All those people were watching the Southeastern Power-lifting Championship which had been lurching along for five hours. Onstage, under the scrolled proscenium, great taped and belted men struggled beneath squats and bench presses, and heaved erect with dead-lifts. The super-heavies were onstage now—each a shuffling, no-neck of around twenty stone—and the great hall reverberated with their mammoth grunts and sucks of breath.

Craig Blake sat in the back, on an aisle by himself, with a day-old hangover and a two-day beard. He had been there most of the afternoon brooding, through the 165-pound class, the 181s, the 198s, the heavies and now the supers, waiting for Santo and noticing the clanking and heaving onstage peripherally through his misery as he might have noticed noises through a fog. He was aware of the door though, and as soon as Santo came through it he pounced on him, wringing his hands and oddly out of breath.

"God, I'm glad to see you. Where have you *been*?"

"Florida," said Santo. "You don't look too good."

"Had a bad night." He looked up through blurred eyes for Santo's pity and noticed dreamily that Santo didn't look too good himself. "She's left me, Joe. She's gone." His lips were trembling and this embarrassed him.

"Who?" asked Zoe Mason. Craig, noticing her for the first time on the other side of Santo, couldn't place her for a minute.

"You're uh, still around, huh?"

"You bet your ass," said Zoe Mason.

"Where'd she go?" asked Santo in a tired voice.

"I don't know. I've been looking for her since yesterday afternoon. I went to her house to take her stuff back . . ." he dribbled off. "Not there. She's not anywhere."

"You blew it, huh?"

"Uh huh."

"She'll show up. She wouldn't miss the contest."

"I don't know, man. I just don't know."

Santo curled his mouth as though he had something sour in it. "Don't worry about it. You must have had to do whatever it was you did. Look, I'm going to be busy, why don't you two go take a drive?"

"I'm staying here," said Zoe Mason.

"I, uh . . ." Craig started and faltered, teary again.

"Come on then, for God's sake," said Santo.

They followed him down the aisle toward a backstage door. Zoe Mason eyed the stage, looking rich and exotic as turtle soup in the dingy bowl of the auditorium.

"What are they doing?" she asked Santo.

"Seeing who can lift the most weight. It's not much fun."

Backstage Franklin was waiting on them, among a dozen or so bodybuilders who were walking around silently, their arms bowed.

Franklin was frothing with excitement. "You know who all's here?" he whispered at Santo. "Homer Lurid from Memphis, Jack Kael from Tampa, Sonny Culross . . ."

"Yeah I know, Franklin. This is Mrs. Mason. Franklin Coates."

"Hiyou," said Franklin, noticing Zoe Mason for the first time, staggering a little.

"Fine, thank you," said Zoe Mason with a chilly smile. She glanced at Franklin as though he were some sort of uncertain mushroom.

"I'm Joe's greaser," said Franklin affably.

"Where's Thor?" asked Santo.

"Ain't he here?"

"Maybe he is, why don't you look around. Nobody answered at the studio."

"He be around, he's got all the cash."

"See can you find him. How about Mary Tate—she around?"

"I haven't saw her either," said Franklin. "What time you want to grease?"

Santo looked at his watch. "The measuring-in's not for an hour. Contest starts at six-thirty . . . so around six, I reckon. Two hours."

"Djeatjet?"

"Just get me some peanuts. That's all I want."

Franklin shot his eyes around the dim, cavernous backstage area that was filling with bodybuilders. A semireligious expression grew on his face. "Jesus," he whispered, "Culross, Kael, all of 'em. And you're gonna take it. I'm so excited I could shit my britches, I swear to God."

"Uh huh. Just go get the peanuts and see if you can find Thor. I'll meet you back here around six."

Santo took Zoe Mason by the arm and started leading her toward the door. Craig followed them.

"God, what a funny person he is," she said. "Where are we going?"

"I'm going to take you home until this is over."

She pulled her arm away. "I told you I'm staying, lovey. I'm good luck. And besides this is interesting in a seamy way. Why don't you introduce me and Craig to some of these people. I'd like to meet Mr. Wewahitchka, for instance, or Mr. Wetumpka . . ."

Without his usual humor Santo explained that those guys wouldn't be here, this being a major, pre-screened contest. But he did introduce them perfunctorily to Jack Kael, Mr. Florida; Rolfe Heinz, Mr. Iron Man; and the fabled Sonny Culross, who had at least fifteen titles including Best Back in the '66 America.

The backstage was filling fast now, with bodybuilders, greasers and club owners. A measuring platform was being set up along one wall where the forty contestants would be divided into shorts and talls. In an alcove were three full-length mirrors and in front of them three or four builders with their shirts off, and one already in posing trunks, were flexing, posing and studying themselves.

The one in trunks was huge. He was turned sideways to the mirror, balancing a full glass of water on the puffed-out pectoral

232

muscle of his chest and bouncing his right tricep up and down the back of his arm like a tennis ball.

"Who is that gorgeous one?" asked Zoe Mason.

"Mr. Mississippi," said Santo. "What do you say, Douglas?"

Doug Stewart looked up at Santo and Craig and Zoe Mason in the mirror. The tricep stopped halfway down his arm.

"You're looking better than in Mobile."

"You and that fat frien of yers got a special nigger this time too, Santo?" Stewart went back to watching the muscle bounce.

"You lost some ugly fat around your waist."

"Won't work this time, Bru. They got straight judges this time and I'm taking this one *home*."

"You got more than Latrobe to worry about in this one," Santo told him pleasantly.

Stewart looked at him in the mirror like a gun firing and the water glass on his chest shook. "I got friens, Santo. You and Erickson mess with me again I'm gonna get you dirty bastids wasted, you read me?"

"I read you, Dougie . . ."

Just then a fat girl sidled up from nowhere, grinning and shuffling her feet and addressed Doug Stewart.

"Hey, are you Mr. Alabama?"

A second fat girl with stiff red hair like a fox's stood behind her, looking shell-shocked. They were dressed in matching halters, short shorts and sneakers.

"I didn't know who you was when I tawked to you las night on the phone. We know a *frien* of yours. Guess who?"

There was a mad note of hysteria in her voice, a foreboding quality that rendered Stewart dumb. He just stood there quivering and staring at her.

Suddenly the girl shot out a chubby, desperately quick hand and touched Stewart's massive arm, tumbling the water glass. "I TOLD HIM I'D GET MY HANS ON YOU," she squealed triumphantly. With that she whirled and the two girls bolted like frightened sows for the street exit.

"Wait a minute, where is he?" shouted Santo, starting after them, but Stewart stopped him with a beefy hand in the chest.

"Awright, Santo. *Now what is this shit?*"

"Get off me, Stewart," said Santo, sounding dangerous.

Doug Stewart looked genuinely pained. "What are you trying to *do* to me? Whaddayou got planned?"

Santo looked at him for a minute and his face softened. He chuckled. "It's a plot, Dougie," he said. "It's a *hell* of a plot. Latrobe dreamed it up. You thought . . . you thought she just *touched* you, right, Dougie? She *poisoned* you, boy. That was essence of nightbane she had on her hand . . ."

Santo was busting up now. He clutched Doug Stewart's shoulder for support.

Stewart looked down at his arm and back at Santo. "Goddam," he said quietly.

"You know what nightbane'll do to you?"

Stewart whirled, looking wildly around. "Wheresajohn? Oh Christ, wheresajohn?" he shouted and tore off into the crowd.

"Too late," Santo gasped at the scuttling Stewart. "It'll shrink you right down, Bru. You won't weigh fifty pounds in an hour . . ."

He looked like a new man as he ambled back over to Zoe Mason and Craig, thumbs in his belt, still chuckling—relaxed and clean of the pursued look Craig had noticed earlier.

"Nicely done," said Craig. He felt somewhat buoyed himself.

Santo patted Zoe Mason on her tight and shapely tail. "I got to go to work, baby," he told her. "Craig'll take care of you. Y'all look out for Mary Tate and Thor. And don't worry about anything, we got this one in the bag."

Zoe Mason started to say something but Santo had already turned and was walking, swaggering really, toward the measuring platform. It was nearly five o'clock.

24

At FIVE-THIRTY when Mary Tate found him—sprawled naked and florid, up to his nipples in the Vesuvian mineral bath and looking like some fat Polynesian god under the great plaster shell—Thor had been out for nearly six hours. Newton, with enthusiastic help from Mae Ruth, had dragged him to the bath and plopped him in; and then had had to restrain the wild-eyed girl from pushing Thor's Grecian head under. Newton had no intention of being dragged back from Moulton by the state police.

235

He had left the studio just as it was in his hurry to get the two girls out of there and himself pointing north, so what Mary Tate found in the gym was an incredible shambles of clothing, whiskey bottles and barbells. She had let herself in the locked front door to pick up some things—a sweater, a framed picture of her little brother, a mascara kit—waiting until an hour before the contest began even though the bus to Opp left at six because she was sure that by then everyone would be at the auditorium, except maybe Newton who was the only person she cared anything about saying good-by to anyway. Silently she shoved the things in her handbag and left. But as she stepped onto the sidewalk and turned to lock the door, maybe the loneliest feeling of her life swept her and suddenly she *had* to tell somebody good-by, even if the somebody were Thor.

There was no one in the office and for a minute she thought maybe Thor had stepped out. But he never left lights on when he did, so she went to the back and found him.

At first she thought he was dead—had finally drunk himself dead as a mackerel. But when she slapped him, taking this chance to by God enjoy it, he made some kind of subhuman noise and unaccountably she found herself glad he was still alive. As she slapped him some more she thought to herself that maybe it was because at least he had wanted *her*, just her, a simple enough want that nobody else around here seemed able to feel.

"Wake up, fatshit," she ordered. "Aren't you sposed to be down to the auditorium?"

"Glull," said Thor.

"You got the money don't you?"

She went into the massage room and filled an enamel bowl with cold water. She took it back and splashed it over Thor, then another one. When she came back with the third Thor was licking his lips and muttering to himself, his head lolling against the back of the pool.

"Get up. Wheresa money? Wheres Joe's prize money?" She

grabbed him by his curls and shook his head. "The *contest,* you idiot. You remember the contest?"

Thor's eyes popped open, staring wildly and crimson from twenty-two hours of drinking. "Whassay . . . *Hey.*" He flicked out a hand, grabbed one of her wrists and gaped at her, his eyes blank and savage as raw meat. Caught by the huge hand and bloody eyes Mary Tate felt a sure intimation of danger, thin and cold as an ice pick.

Thor grinned. "Whausay baby. *Hey.* Gon more screamin . . ." He splashed and wallowed in the bath, trying to stand. Mary Tate jerked her arm free.

"The contest starts in forty minutes. You're making the awards, you've got the money, Joe's money." As she spoke Thor cleared the bath and moved like a fat, pink roach across her path to the door.

"Go put on some clothes," she told him, trying to stay calm. "Go put on your nice velvet suit."

Thor belched and stared at her, his head lowered like a bull. "Cum . . . ere Maai Ruth, we gon scream little bit." He laughed briefly.

She realized with a chill that he thought she was somebody else. "It's Mary *Tate.* I'm staying right here. Go put on your suit, Thor."

Thor lifted his head and looked unsteadily around the ceiling as though he were listening for something on the wind. He studied her.

". . . Maai Tate . . . *Hey,* baby," swaying for her. "Lissen, we got time . . . little fucky-fucky. That whatchu want? *Knowed* you been crotch-watchin me." He made a soft almost gentle sweep for her with his right arm. She ducked under it and backed out past the office into the gym.

Thor followed her, a gentle, lopsided expression on his face, stepping gently, gently babbling: "Didn't mean to say fucky-fucky . . . didn realize who you was . . . now come on. Come on

237

. . . I'll treatcha right . . . *know* how to treatcha, baby . . . I needja darlin, I'm 'on buy you things."

Mary Tate was in the middle of the gym and had grounded herself on a rack of shiny little chrome dumbbells before she quit being scared and got pissed-off.

"*Come on?*" she said to Thor, who had stopped too, a foot away, visibly aroused now. "I wouldn't let you lay a hand on me if you was the last man alive, you pig. Now get outta my way. I gotta ticket to ride."

She scooped up a ten-pound dumbbell and heaved it at him, at the same time breaking for the stairs. Thor didn't even notice the dumbbell bouncing off his chest, he moved when Mary Tate did, grabbed her by the top of her skirt and whirled her around. But she kept turning and broke his grip. She darted toward the rear of the gym, the only direction open to her, off of one foot like a dancer. Thor scuttled and grunted after her, around one of the naugahyde benches, a bicycle and the Total-Tone machine, leering through the brilliant confusion of pulleys, bars and plates.

"Don't hurt me—I want to go home."

"I loveya . . . God I NEEDJA. I GOTTAHAVEYA!"

Using her quickness and the myriad objects in the room, Mary Tate might have stayed out of his reach indefinitely, but the hemorrhaging greed in his voice then panicked her and she ran flat out for the steps. Thor caught her before she made six steps. He carried her kicking to the lifting platform along the back wall of the gym, threw her down and proceeded to mount her.

As he clawed at her pants, forcing his engorged and stubby member between her legs, Mary Tate bit his left shoulder, the only part of him she could reach. Gagging on the smells of lust and sweat and mineral salts, she chewed on Thor's meaty shoulder as she would a flank steak and after a moment it got to him. He rolled toward the pain and she shot a knee into his hip to help him over. He still had her by the calf but she made it to her feet by pulling up on the drapes drawn across the long plate-glass window overlooking the street.

Her face was pressed against the cool, greasy glass; she breathed, and began to turn, and only heard what happened to her after that—a crash like plaster falling from a roof as Thor, who had risen too, backed off and charged, blasted open the jagged hole that she fell headfirst through.

It was not a long fall, two stories, but it was long enough. She landed badly and Thor, looking down to where she lay, in and out of shadows as the Joe Santo sign blinked off and on, knew by looking that the shit had hit the fan. He seemed to know this with a wonderful detachment, as if he wasn't really there.

Naked, bleeding slowly from the shoulder and in calm, even spurts from halfway up his ruined right forearm, he was conscious of people forming like flies on meat on the street below. He knew they might as well be forming to watch his club, all his clubs, burn down, but for some reason he didn't even care.

First Franklin shaved him: armpits, legs, stomach and chest—using six blades and a Weck hospital razor. Santo stood in his gold posing trunks, watching abstractly and eating peanuts. Then he rubbed the make-up over the stretch marks at the top of Santo's rib cage and under his arms, working the buff paste into the skin until the edges were lost. Finally, with quick circular sweeps of his hand Franklin covered every visible inch of Santo with a film of baby oil. When he finished, Santo's color and finish were very much like waxed cordovan.

Franklin circled around him, looking for flaws.

"Be sure to pump your traps."

"I will."

"And get your lats far down as you can."

Santo put his hands on his burnished waist and began doing slow deep knee bends.

It was six-thirty. Onstage a beaming, lusty announcer was introducing judges and present notables, and welcoming the sweltering hundreds to "Dixie's finest show of strength, this Spectacle of Southern Supermen . . ." Behind the scrim, in a fidgeting line near the stage-right entrance, stood seventeen glistening 5'8"s and under, ready to roll. Most of the talls were off to themselves in lonely corners backstage, anointing themselves or pumping up as Santo was doing.

He finished his legs and began pumping his upper body with the dumbbell. Franklin, Craig and Zoe Mason leaned against a water cooler, watching.

"Iss almost a waste," mumbled Franklin.

"What?" said Zoe Mason. Neither of them took their eyes off the bulging Santo, who was growing in slow, complicated increases like a sand dune.

"There's nobody here can touch him. I doubt if there's anybody alive can touch him but I wish this was America or Universe. Least he'd have some competition."

"You better let him win them one at a time, don't you think?" said Craig. He was feeling hopeless, dirty and peevish. "God, it smells like hell back here."

Franklin looked at him. "Why don't you just hustle your ass out front."

"I'm waiting for Mary Tate."

"I'll tell her where you're at."

"I'll wait, thanks."

Franklin did his little shuffle and checked his watch again for the third time in five minutes. "Don't bother me, man," he said. "I got a lot on my mind."

Franklin was not the only one worried about Thor. Doug Stewart was very worried and he had gotten other people worried, including his manager, Moe Zwick. Zwick had put up a grand for this contest and not knowing where it was or the guy who had it made his balls itch a little. Zwick didn't believe with his boy that Erickson would even think about heading for the men's room with the prize money—Erickson was a pro; he knew the percentages—but still, Zwick would have just as soon had him where he could see him. All afternoon Stewart, who was temperamental anyway and could flat hold a grudge, kept worrying him about it: Erickson had had him poisoned, Erickson had gone to Mexico. Zwick didn't want anything on Stewart's mind to maybe make him forget a pose, so he had sidled up once to Santo, once to Franklin, asking over his cigar, "Wheresa man?" in a good-natured way as if he had just missed him.

"He be around," said Franklin and walked off.

"Don't know," said Santo. "Doug upset?" "Upset? Naw man, he's not upset, we was just wondering. Sorry I missed you fellas in Mobile." "Look Moe, about that . . ." "No word is necessary," said Zwick solemnly. "I saw the nigger later and you was right. Life goes on."

But finally when it got to be six-fifteen and there was still no sign of Erickson (his boy had begun picking nervously at his greased chest, jerking at the slightest sound and psyching the other talls with whispered hints about plots and "night-something") Moe Zwick decided to find out what he could.

He couldn't spare anybody with any sense, so he had to ask Stewart's half-wit little brother, Laverne, to run over to the Olympic and check things out. The boy never wore shoes and wouldn't talk in anything but some crazy language that just Stewart understood, but he was a sneaky-shrewd little mother. "Break in if you have to," Zwick told him. "Find out if he's gone."

"Ravight," said Laverne, grinning like a dog.

Craig sat in a metal folding chair watching the shorts file on-stage. Three feet away in another chair Santo was doing curls with the dumbbell. Zoe Mason was standing behind him rubbing his neck. Franklin squatted in front of Santo, rapturously watching the sheath of his arm fill and empty, fill and empty. It all looked dirty from where Craig sat. All of it. He felt drained, leached, bloodless. He couldn't take his eyes off the smudged, splayed feet of the last departing short, a nervous, funny-looking kid. Everything around him seemed to be the color of dirty bath water.

"Oh God," he murmured, pressing his temples with his finger-tips.

"It's not that bad," said Santo. "And I've got something I'd like to say on that score." He dropped the dumbbell. "Franklin, find Mrs. Mason here a good seat out front and stay with her until the awards."

He took Zoe Mason's wrists and pulled her around to face him. "You be a good girl and sit out there so I don't get a hard on look-ing at you."

"OK," she said. She kneeled in front of him and kissed the back of one of his hands.

"You make me feel like a secretary . . . Joe? You know what time the plane leaves. I don't want to beg." She said this with Nazi control—softly and unselfishly.

The thing that made her beautiful, Craig realized, looking at her little-girl crouch, her positive knees, her rich hair and Berg-dorf suit, was an ornate greed in her face—not on the surface, but locked mysteriously into the features. It made her look always on the verge of some intricate kind of orgasm. It was not there right now. She looked simply like a rich wolf.

"I know," said Santo and kissed her on the forehead.

She stood up impressively, brushing down her skirt, remaking her face, and walked off with Franklin.

Santo watched her go. "Nice niche as niches go," he said.

"You going back with her?"

"Nope."

"Why not?"

"Being comfortable's like a profession or a religion or uh, a philosophy. You get in there you can't get out. You get fat. Like those rat traps they've got over in China or someplace, that are full of rice and have a hole big enough for a hungry rat to get in but too small for a full rat to get out."

He stood up and stretched. "Let's talk about you. Little tacky back here for you, is it?"

"Don't pontificate, Santo, you jock. I don't feel good and there's a lot of preening going on around here."

Santo swung up the dumbbell and began doing piston-quick tricep presses. "Your 'strenuous tongue' a little sore?"

"Say what?"

"From bursting Joy's grape against your palate fine? You been doing a lot of bursting lately. That's my favorite poem, by the way, Keats."

Santo was beginning to irritate him. "I think I love her, Joe."

Santo made a hybrid noise, half laugh, half grunt.

"I'm apeshit over her and I don't know what to do about it. Would you mind putting the fucking dumbbell down?"

"Quit thinking," said Santo, pressing right on.

"Uh huh."

"Thinking's what messes you up. Trying to decide how to fit everything in. I'm talking in parables here for a minute, old buddy, and a minute only. Trouble is you don't eat it like a grape at all. You eat it like a grapefruit, section by section . . ."

"Look, I don't need this." Had he hated Santo all along? He wondered.

"With a little silver, pointy spoon. And get out of that house. It's dusty up there. And the air's too thin . . ."

Santo had more to say but that was as far as he got. Suddenly the heavy metal door to the street flew open and there under a red exit sign was some barefoot urgent child whom Craig remembered from somewhere before, shouting gluey, Rumanian-sounding phrases, holding the door open, his eyes big as lemons.

Santo listened, the dumbbell poised over his head like a spear. Everybody backstage listened paralyzed to the echoing, pubescent voice: ". . . *thavers covops avall ovovover thave plavace*," it wailed.

Santo dropped the dumbbell and raced for the door. On his heels came Stewart ("They're doing it *again*. Goddamit Moe, I *tole* you . . .") and after him Moe Zwick. Sonny Culross looked at Jack Kael who looked at Jim Gagne who looked, for lack of anyone nearer, at Craig Blake—who lit out for the door.

Who knows why they all followed, all twenty-three talls, six managers and nine relatives, greasers and friends? Maybe because somebody else did. Or because in the face of this horribly garbled emergency (Fire? Nuclear attack?) running seemed to have something to do with protecting themselves. But follow they did, and all at once, in a flailing crunch of Herculean bodies.

Onstage, short number seventeen had just made a quarter-turn to the right with his sixteen stubby brethren when he saw the entire backstage area empty of people as suddenly as if some giant vacuum cleaner on Eighth Avenue had jerked them out.

This short was only sixteen years old, had no titles and was skinny. He didn't want to be up on that stage at all, and wouldn't have been but for the fact that his daddy, who was Thor Erickson's partner, thought him unaggressive and liked for him to compete.

Watching all those huge people being sucked unexplainably outside terrified the already shaky Elijah Wright, Jr. He went totally to pieces. He forgot sticking out his chest, looked madly around at the M.C., the crowd, the other shorts, and knew that they were all somehow horribly stranded.

"EEEHHHHHH!" he said.

25

DR. ELIJAH WRIGHT fidgeted in his seat. He had been antsy with presentiment for some time, and that on top of not wanting to be in the smelly auditorium in the first place had him radically uncomfortable.

"If you're going to make the boy strut around with all those queers the least you can do is go down and give him moral support," his wife had said. So he was there, in the middle of his sour hour, trying to avoid looking at Elijah Jr., and itchy with foreboding when the boy suddenly cut loose and screamed pitifully from the stage. Dr. Wright knew that scream had something to do with his own sense of hurrying disaster and he didn't wait around to find out what had spooked the boy. His sixth-sense-times-pi, as he called it, told him where to go. He headed there running.

Between the auditorium and Twentieth Street was leafy Jefferson Park. Arriving in full stride at the glass doors of the auditorium, Dr. Wright was brought up short by its contents. He studied the scene in the park for a moment, hand to chin, and was moved to note to himself that what he saw probably bore a very close resemblance to approaching apocalypse; that the world might very likely end with half nude people running witlessly through trees.

He could make out Craig Blake around the middle of the pack. Already out on Twentieth Street, moving like a miler, his bare torso winking through the dusk, he recognized Joe Santo, and a hundred yards or so behind him the cloud-pale skin and red locks of Doug Stewart. His Buick Electra was three blocks behind him in the museum parking lot. It was only six blocks to the studio, so despite his distaste for exercise, given the certain and pressing abnormality of the situation, Dr. Wright elected to run too.

As he chugged through the park, choosing a zagging sequence of pebbled paths to avoid the sickly summer grass, he computed possibilities. By the time he hit asphalt again Dr. Wright saw things whole and saw them clear.

Puffing onto Twentieth Street he passed a knot of six or seven talls who had unexplainably stopped flight there and were mixing oddly with pedestrians and evening traffic. There was an expression on their faces . . .

A block down the street he passed some others, then a group of five, and four more between Fourth and Third Avenues—all with the same expression, all moving in the same eccentric way. At the corner of Twentieth and Second Avenue he came on the last three builders, among them Doug Stewart, who stood with one hand on a parking meter, fairly reeling, his eyes glazed with a primal ecstasy.

Dr. Wright stopped and caught his breath. "Nice afternoon," he mentioned to the other two, checking their reactions. These went on staring marvelously about them, as though they'd been dropped into an enchanted forest. Dr. Wright moved professionally to Doug Stewart. He reached up, took the great burnt-sienna head between his hands, held it to the light and studied the eyes for a moment. Then he turned and walked up Second Avenue. Two blocks away he saw the swarms of people, police cars, disappearing ambulance—all exactly as he had imagined it except for someone sitting on the sidewalk, an annoying detail.

He stopped, shot a forefinger to his nose and pondered for a moment. "Transcendent self-awareness," he termed it finally. Then, satisfied, he hurried on down the block toward the wrapping up of this particular misadventure.

Doug Stewart wasn't conscious of Dr. Wright holding his head. He couldn't even remember how exactly he came to be there—in front of Sax Brothers Department Store, downtown Birmingham, Alabama—but he flat knew he was there. And he knew too, or rather sensed, along with twenty-three other talls, that this was the biggest goddamn moment of his life. That this was it, Bru. They were *outside*. After years of exposing themselves darkly in auditoriums and gyms to piddling, meager, niggardly crowds, here suddenly they were: with a whole frigging city for an audience. All along Twentieth Street cars were stopped, horns were blaring and people, thousands of them, were looking, *gaping* at the talls who were strung out like so many Christmas lights over six blocks.

After the first few stunned minutes of realizing what the hell the story was here, Doug Stewart felt himself fill with an overwhelming, gaseous sense of his own worth. God, he was huge and beautiful and people were digging that. He giggled, let go the parking meter and tried a confrontation.

There was a young business type eying him agog from fifteen

feet away. Stewart strutted to and then around the man, crouching lewdly, heaping his trapezius muscles up around his neck like two huge scoops of vanilla ice cream.

"Uh huh," said the man quietly. "Oh my God."

Stewart stopped in front of him and touched him experimentally in the belly, just below his striped tie: not belligerently, just testing his reality.

"My God, what's happening here?" asked the man, not moving a hair.

Slumping suddenly, Stewart laid a back and tricep pose on him, practically nuzzling him with one extended elbow.

"Look," said the man, "my name is Hal Foss and I'm a *friend* of one of you people, the one on the sign . . . I have money if that's what you want."

Stewart didn't hear him. Across the street he saw Homer Lurid, on one knee in a chest pose before three nuns, and suddenly got bored with his man. He felt . . . God, he felt fantastic. He wanted to pose for Governor Wallace, for the President, for every living soul in Alabama . . .

He skipped across the street. "I got this deltoid pose I been working on," he told Lurid who was grinning mightily at him. "You mind if I try it on your nuns?" He loved Lurid and didn't want to offend him.

"Hep yourself," said Lurid sweetly.

Stewart looked at the terrified nuns, imagining he could see gratitude in their cowled faces. "Here we go then," he said and began finding the line of the pose. He put it together beautifully for them and held it, radiant with generosity, happier than he'd ever been before in his life. His grandmother had been a Catholic.

(One block up the street Sonny Culross had found a rhythm. He was in the lucky group of builders who had wound up between Third and Fourth Avenue. Most of the east side of that block was taken up by the Beef an' Brew restaurant, whose fifty-six customers and thirteen employees were separated from the sidewalk by nothing but windows. Culross and the other three talls had audience on either side of them, but the very richness of their situation had created the problem of how to gratify both flanks equally. Culross had solved it by revolving slowly like a pig on a spit as he shifted rhythmically in and out of poses. Smiling to his private cadence, he pawed the cement with his bare feet and circled himself like a Hopi Indian. Two blocks up from him, Jack Kael, a three-hundred-pound weight lifter turned bodybuilder who still thought posing a little candyass, was doing feats of strength instead. Kael bent a yield sign double and straightened it out again. Then he invited three or four medium-size pedestrians to jump up and down on his supine self, and followed that by leaping up to lift the front end of an Opel Kadett. All up and down the street transported talls sported deliriously, singly and in groups, moving through the halted traffic, confronting and performing with such exuberance and precision that to some pigeon five stories up on a cornice the whole thing might very well have looked choreographed.)

Doug Stewart went from the nuns to a group of delighted school children, to a woman who threw a shopping bag at him and fled across the street, to an old couple in an automobile who nodded and applauded as though they were watching Lawrence Welk. He brought to each encounter a mumbled "Here we go," a pose and a soft inward smile, and with each his generosity grew. He tried poses he had never tried before—Wayne Latrobe's candle flame, Joe Santo's looking-at-the-sun—feeling puffed up not only with protein-stuffed tissue (he had the sure knowledge that he was bigger just then than he'd ever been before or ever would be again) but with some airy, internal thing that kept busting out of his rusty head in whoops of laughter. Doug Stewart felt immortal and protean. He felt bigger, more generous and dazzling and restorative than the Mediterranean.

He had just floated up to a plum-assed, curly-haired secretary in a short shirt when the cops moved in, nervously with helmets and night sticks. Stewart had expected them and was not upset.

"Do sumpin with your laig," suggested the secretary.

"OK, here we go," Stewart said. "I got to hurry so look close."

"Ahhhh," sighed the girl to the incredible convolutions of Stewart's flexed legs.

Two of them were moving for him, night sticks raised. With his time run out Stewart felt overpowered by a final, Vesuvian impulse to give himself. He looked at the cops, laughing wildly, then back at the secretary. "You don't have to look," he told her. Happier than he'd ever been before, insanely happy, Stewart jerked down his leopard posing trunks and swung his preposterous arms wide open. "Come on and take it *all*."

The person sitting on the sidewalk in front of Erickson's Olympic Studio and Spa, interfering with Dr. Elijah Wright's vision of the scene, was Craig Blake. He was still there despite the effort of several people including Wright to get him to move, because J. L. Andrews, a member of the Birmingham Police Force and an acquaintance of Craig's, said he could stay.

"He don't see me when I talk to him," Andrews lied to Dr. Wright. "It says to leave them where they're at when they're like that. Besides," Andrews felt constrained to add, "he don't look it right now but he's from over the mountain."

Andrews had been stationed on the sidewalk with instructions not to let anyone in the studio when Craig came loping up. It was Andrews who had told him the story—about how they had had to scrape that little secretary offa sidewalk, how Erickson had blowed his cork, locked himself in the studio and nearly bled to death from a cut artery before anybody could get to him. ("When I come up he was standing in that broke window yonder yelling to everybody to go fuck theirselves. Nex thing heas keeled over. Say that motha bled a ton!") Then Andrews had to arm Craig a little to keep him out of the Olympic. Finally, when Craig flopped down in the middle of the sidewalk, Andrews just stood over him, not knowing what else to do, and watched out for him.

"Hell," he said to Craig's bent head, trying to soothe what he figured was probably just a weak, over-the-mountain stomach, "I seen 'em a heap worsen this. When they go out twenty, thirty stories is when you got a surenuff mess on your hands."

Craig could hear Andrews but he had no idea what the cop was saying. He was concentrating too hard on Andrews thick black shoes to listen. He was concentrating on the shoes because it seemed to be the only place he could look without getting dizzy. Whenever he looked up, the street spun out on him. Clumps of people, automobiles, whirling red police lights, buildings, glass, pavement—all mixed, blended and spun out, the way a wall will when you're drunk. He looked at the shoes and clung to the pavement like a mollusk as wave after wave of feeling broke around him. After a while the dizziness went away and he could look up, his senses going soft as butter in the carnival shift and glance of lights, movements and noise.

"You got some people I can call for you?" Andrews asked him.

"Where is Santo?"

"Gone to the hospital," said Andrews softly. "I tole you. In the second ambulance, with Erickson."

"What do you like to do, Andrews? What sort of thing?"

"Huh?" said Andrews.

"What sort of thing do you like to do . . .

"Uh, he say anything? Santo, I mean. You know the one." He looked up at Andrews and saw that Andrews was looking back at him, his face sort of melted, like sand that's been rained on. He couldn't look at that long. At the end of the block a guy in posing trunks was walking dreamily toward them and for some reason the sight made Craig nauseated.

"Well, there's bowling," said Andrews.

"What else?"

Just then the door to the studio opened briskly and out came two policemen followed by a little man in a business suit who looked like a ferret. The little man talked to the policemen for a moment. When they left he bent and picked something pebble-sized out of the gutter. Then he came over and squatted down by Craig. He looked at Craig, nodding sadly.

"Shame. Well, so it goes; wages of bad management. Stealing from me too, actually for some time . . . shame though—our dream of nation-wide good health, beautiful bodies making beautiful bodies; boxes in boxes. Still don't want to move, eh?"

Craig was watching Dr. Elijah Wright flip the thing he had picked from the gutter as though it were a poker chip. It was small and bright.

Dr. Wright noticed him watching. "Well shaped," he said, holding out on his tiny palm one of Mary Tate's white and perfect teeth. "Tarter free as well. Lower first bicuspid." Dr. Wright stood up and pocketed the tooth. "Shame," he said again. "Well, live and learn." He walked off.

The bodybuilder passed them in the street carrying himself strangely, up on his toes, his eyes cutting around like somebody lost and proud of it. The lights flashing off his lubricated body made Craig think of armor: creased greave of calf and cuisse of thigh; the biceps, rerebraces; pauldrons for shoulders; breastplate and besagew of chest . . .

He vomited quietly in his lap. When he had finished and wiped his mouth he asked Andrews again if Santo had said anything.

"I tole you that too. He said tell you to hang loose. Which you ain't doing. We better get you cleaned up, little buddy. Don't you have nobody I can call, or what?"

Craig leaned back against the imitation marble wall of the studio, feeling better. Above him the sign of Joe Santo blinked on and off, on and off, on and off. He lifted his eyes over the heat-squashed buildings of Second Avenue to the darkening outline of hills in the south, and the change of focus cleared his head. He followed the gorge of the highway cut out to Red Mountain, then up past the vulgar statue of Vulcan with its lickerish crimson light, and east to the mountain he lived on. Though it was too far to be sure, he thought he could make out the lights of his house, a calm semicircle of yellow beads at the near crest of the slope—dim, distant and cool. Looking at them Craig was struck suddenly with a dumb, ineffable aching for simplicity and peace—a yearning like some ailing animal might feel for a pasture where it learned to walk. He gave the feeling a little moan and told Andrews no, there was no one in particular.

26

He took the last two weeks of August and the whole month of September off and traveled.

He went to Mazatlán, Mexico, and sat around the docks there drawing deep breaths and eating squid. He caught steelhead from the Babine River in British Columbia and brown trout from the North Platte near Encampment, Wyoming, where he spent two weeks at a dude ranch. Back home for three days he sold some stock and struck out again in the other direction: Miami, Cat Cay and St. Thomas.

Originally he had had a vague intention of not ever coming back to Birmingham—of telling his uncle to kiss off and selling his house, all by long distance, to become, say, a fishing guide somewhere. But nobody offered him a guiding or any other kind of job and after six weeks he was tired and all his clothes were dirty, so he did come back to the house and he went back to work hawking lots and warehouses.

For the next few weeks he lived quietly. He had some work done on the house, hired a full-time maid and saw a lot of his relatives. Then toward the end of October he took up field trials.

From an ad in *Hunting Dog* magazine he bought a $1500 liver and white pointer, a runner-up in the National Amateur Quail Championship. The dog was a mainstay bitch of Trevor's Gunsmoke line, grandsired by the legendary Smokepole himself. It was a lucky buy: Fred Cheep, the man Craig hired to handle the dog, called her the smoothest-running little bitch he'd ever seen.

Craig went around to trials with Cheep and the dog and got to know some of the ritzy folk who held them on the quaily, lespedeza-planted acres of their plantations, in places like Union Springs, Alabama; Camilla, Georgia; Kingstree, South Carolina. They were a sporty, thirsty crew of people who wore French-made coursing jackets and sat their horses well, and Craig enjoyed their company. He began reading books on breeding and canine nutrition. He ordered kennel trailers, latigo whistle cords and electrical collars.

By Thanksgiving he had bought three more dogs, another pointer and two setters. He had part of his barn converted into a kennel and he refenced the garden as a dog yard.

Throughout the fall he thought less and less frequently of Joe Santo. For a week after the night of the Mr. Southeast Contest he had been frantic to get in touch with him but couldn't: Santo had no phone, Craig had never known exactly where he lived, and Foss, who had moved in for the week to take wren-like care of him, discouraged it. When he got back from his trips in September there was a gnomic postcard from Santo with no return address, postmarked Tucson, Arizona. The card showed a romantically painted Navajo Indian squatting by an arroyo between two buttes. On the back Santo informed him that, " 'I keep as delicate around the bowels as around the head and heart. Copulation is no more rank to me than death is.' Hope you are the same. Stay hungry. Love, Santo."

Craig had not heard from him since, and was fairly sure by now that he didn't want to. Life was not tiring any more; there were too many things he didn't have any idea how to say to Santo.

About Mary Tate he couldn't think at all.

One sunny morning in December as he was having a third cup of coffee and reading the newspaper, suited for business in the orange-juice brightness of the breakfast room, he came on a picture of an impressively mangled Chevrolet, crushed like a wad of paper and lying on its roof just off the Montgomery highway. The article beneath the picture said the car had been going over a hundred miles an hour when it went through a guard rail and turned over. The army recruiting officer who was driving had been killed on the spot. His only passenger, one Franklin Coates, had suffered a severely damaged back and was presently in poor condition in St. Mary's Hospital. Craig folded the paper and gazed out the window at the dazzling day, his breakfast ruined. "Sonofabitch," he said to the entering maid.

That afternoon he thought of sending Franklin flowers but was stopped by doubts as to whether Franklin would want them. He did call the hospital and was told that Mr. Coates' condition was the same, and he could not have visitors. Craig settled for sending Franklin a brief, formal telegram, wishing him well. Then he tried to forget him.

But the idea of Franklin lying snapped in half in a hospital bed haunted him. He took it with him to bed, to work, everywhere. He thought of Franklin's mother, the dietician, seeing her as a plump, thick-ankled woman in institutional white wringing her coarse hands by Franklin's bed. He thought of Franklin's skinny calves, of his freckles; of globes of atrophying muscle. After a week he called the hospital again and learned that Franklin had undergone surgery and that his condition had improved to fair.

He slept better that night and in the following weeks he had much more luck in trying to forget about Franklin.

He was reminded of him again accidentally one Friday afternoon while lost in the northern reaches of the city. He was on his way to a field trial at a plantation called "Morning-Glory Acres" outside Winchester, Tennessee. Craig had met its owner and the owner's daughter, a willowy hard-riding thing who drooled over guns, horses and dogs, in south Alabama. The girl had asked him up for the trial and for "a few shots behind a bird in some really first-rate cuva." He had been following Cheep who, with three of Craig's dogs in his covered pickup, sped and short-cutted ahead of him through north Birmingham—knowing this part of town was as unfamiliar to Craig as the Serengcti Plains and pleased, Craig imagined, when he lost him. The world was full of Fred Cheeps.

Poking ignorantly eastward toward the highway, down blocks strewn with dirty tenements and body shops, he was suddenly confronted with a long, doleful, slate-gray building bordered by a scruffy yard. This was St. Mary's Hospital.

He paused; considered. It had been over a month since Franklin's accident—he might not even be there any more. And if he was, Craig wondered what he would say to him. On the other hand, he was in no particular hurry and it would be good for Cheep to worry about being an hour or so ahead. He parked the car and went in.

Squeaking down the waxed floors to the desk he realized that a big part of what had compelled him in here was the abstract fascination of seeing Franklin incapacitated, suddenly and totally harmless, like a knife with the blade broken off. He realized at the

258

same time with some surprise that he'd always been afraid of Franklin.

Franklin was located in a region called "third floor west" that took Craig ten minutes to find. He had a minuscule private room. His window overlooked an alley and the room smelled loudly of garbage and disinfectant.

"Whausay man," Franklin said apathetically. He was flat on his wounded back in a hospital gown reading Spiderman and chewing gum. On the table by his bed was a tall stack of muscle magazines and comic books.

"How you doing?" asked Craig, his hand still on the doorknob like a visiting intern's, rooted by the smell of the room and the sight of Franklin.

Franklin chewed his gum silently for a minute, studying the comic. "I'm awright. Come on in."

Craig sat gingerly on the edge of the bed (the only chair in the room had a torn, infected-looking cover) and looked at his hands. "You look pretty good. You feeling all right?"

Again Franklin didn't answer for a long moment. He lifted up his right arm and made a muscle over his head. The arm was still sinewy but so thin now that it looked like maybe the leg of a skinned animal.

"I been working out—do chins on this," He pointed to a monkey bar above his bed. "Look under the bed." There were two thirty-five-pound dumbbells down there. "Do some stuff with them."

"Good, good," said Craig inanely. "I've been meaning to come by but I've been really busy. I was sorry as hell to read about your uh, the accident . . . God, I mean what can you say?"

"You shoulda saw the other guy," said Franklin. "Hey, you want to see something?" He was looking hard into Craig's face. He picked the sheet away that had covered him to his chest. The gown was pulled up above his waist. Franklin's bare lower body rested on a pad of something that looked like lamb's wool. His hips, always small, were now narrow as a rabbit's; at the top of each innominate bone was a large moist hole, a gruesomely ulcerated eye that seemed to go down forever into Franklin.

"They call 'em decubitae. Bedsores. I got 'em on both sides."

Not until then did it occur to Craig, looking at the hips and shrunken thighs, now almost as skinny as the calves, that Franklin couldn't walk.

"You can't walk."

"Notchet. I can move 'em though." The legs bounced twice by Craig. "I had uh, some shit, blood and bone and stuff pushing on the nerve. When they operated they took it out. I'm gon be able to walk in a few weeks." There was a scientific joy in Franklin's voice, an academic-sounding interest in his own condition that upset Craig even more than the staring hips.

"What they do is," Franklin went on, "they turn me over every couple of hours. This thing I'm on—see this thing I'm on?" He lifted the lamb's wool pad, showing a thin cushioned board. "Called a Bradford frame. What they do is put another one on top of me, strap 'em together and turn me over real fast. Then they take the old one off the top."

Craig saw a jigsaw puzzle being flipped over between two card tables, saw a sandwich being made of Franklin, sores and all, every two hours, and decided he had no more time for this.

"I'm glad you're going to be all right, horse," he said cheerfully. "Look, I've got to run—I'm on my way up to Tennessee. Is there anything I can get you?"

Franklin stared at him. There was a strong slant of late sun falling through the window. It lay across his head and shoulders like a board. "Joe comes in every day," he said quietly.

"Santo? I thought he was out west someplace."

"Was for a little bit. But Thor got hit with a big term and Joe come back to try to *hep* him. Can you believe that?"

"I heard about Thor. How is he? Santo I mean."

"Fine. Having a ball like always and big as a house. He don't train heavy any more though, just keeps in shape. They held the Southeast over in Memphis while Joe was ridin the range and he wouldn't even come back to get in it. Let that scumbag Stewart win."

"What kind of work is he doing?"

"Washing new cars for Long Leavis Ford over in Bessemer. Says he loves it." Franklin straightened out his left arm above him and rubbed his right hand over it. The hand moved tentatively, as if curious where the rest of the arm had gone.

He yawned. "He comes up every evening all the way from Bessemer and we just shoot the shit. Like y'all used to do, I reckon."

He held the arm, eying it, and his face began to work strangely in a burst of little twitches. Then he threw his head sideways as a dog will and looked out the window.

Craig wondered if he needed a nurse.

"Joe knows a lot. He says I had all this coming. Says anybody drives in the passing lane all the time like me's gotta know he might get hit . . . says thas what you pay for passin people. For the fun of being out there."

"I thought the army guy was driving."

Franklin snorted. "That ain't what he meant. I thought you was smart."

He went on talking, head turned, with a distinct new quality in his voice—hostility or bitterness, Craig wasn't sure which but he stood up anyway. Franklin's face worked away like a hand kneading dough. The winter sunlight fell across him heavy as an ax.

". . . You know he coulda won it all? Every fucking one. And I'm talking about the *big* ones, Bru. Joe Santo was the best there was."

Franklin flopped his head over suddenly and glared at Craig, eyes shining, face popping.

"Why don't you get on outta here now, shithead?"

"What?"

"I said get on outta here." Franklin was *crying*. "He would of maaied her too, you prick."

Craig edged toward the door, horrified by this transformation, imagining Franklin's shuffle. "I'm sorry," he said. "I didn't mean . . ."

"Hey." Franklin stopped him at the door. "You *look* at me, buddyro." His voice was calm now and dry. Craig looked. "I don't look like much now. But when I get out I'm gon come around to see you. And I'm might gonna clean your greens."

Craig pulled at the door and it closed behind him with a nasty, sucking sound. He walked down three corridors, not looking into open rooms, trying to carry himself properly. He took the elevator down to the ground floor and smiled at the woman behind the admitting desk who did not smile back. Then he walked through the lobby and out of the hospital into the late afternoon.

His car was a block away in a small lot surrounded by old oak trees. Craig got in and sat perfectly still for a moment staring at the dashboard, feeling rendered: clarified as lard. He started the car. The sun was low now, practically gone over Ensley and the steel mills, but as he backed out, what was left of it dropped wild and sudden through the trees into his eyes. He had to stop and steady his hands on the wheel. Then, looking out of the sun to the pavement, he finished turning around and drove out of the lot, remembering peevishly that he was lost.

Stay Hungry
Charles Gaines

This is an extraordinary, exuberant story of two men and two worlds which meet and finally collide. At the center of the roller-coaster action is a weight-lifter named Santo, a body builder, a joyful, sensuous man whose comprehension of life and total commitment to it are both enriched and strengthened by the neon lighting of his bizarre existence.

His integrity is thrown into vivid contrast by an aimless aristocrat whose desperate craving for new experiences and mingling with "Authentics" drives him into an attempt to share Santo's world, good times, workouts and even his woman.

Pitting strength against weakness and integrity against fragmentation, Charles Gaines captures the essence of raw reality in a novel that is loud, funny, colorful and essentially serious; stay hungry and you'll taste life.